BACK FROM
THE DEAD

DARK. BIZARRE. DANGEROUS
AS HELL. WELCOME TO
NECROMUNDA!

UNDERHIVE WATCHMAN ERIK Bane is a marked man.
As a former hive city Enforcer he has made a lot of
enemies, many of whom have followed him into the
lawless underhive to extract their revenge in the most
brutal way possible.

But when a deadly plague breaks out leaving the
living dead in its wake, Bane must put the past
behind him and seek help from the criminals he
once swore an oath to stop!

NECROMUNDA

BACK FROM
THE DEAD

NICK KYME

For dad, never forgotten, forever missed.

A BLACK LIBRARY PUBLICATION

First published in Great Britain in 2006 by
BL Publishing,
Games Workshop Ltd.,
Willow Road, Nottingham,
NG7 2WS, UK.

10 9 8 7 6 5 4 3 2 1

Cover illustration by Clint Langley.

A CIP record for this book is available from the British Library.

ISBN 13: 978 1 84416 376 2
ISBN 10: 1 84416 376 8

Distributed in the US by Simon & Schuster
1230 Avenue of the Americas, New York, NY 10020, US.

Printed and bound in Great Britain by
Bookmarque, Surrey, UK.

See the Black Library on the Internet at
www.blacklibrary.com

Find out more about Games Workshop
www.games-workshop.com

In order to even begin to understand the blasted world of Necromunda you must first understand the hive cities. These man-made mountains of plasteel, ceramite and rockrete have accreted over centuries to protect their inhabitants from a hostile environment, so very much like the termite mounds they resemble. The Necromundan hive cities have populations in the billions and are intensely industrialised, each one commanding the manufacturing potential of an entire planet or colony system compacted into a few hundred square kilometres.

The internal stratification of the hive cities is also illuminating to observe. The entire hive structure replicates the social status of its inhabitants in a vertical plane. At the top are the nobility, below them are the workers, and below the workers are the dregs of society, the outcasts. Hive Primus, seat of the planetary governor Lord Helmawr of Necromunda, illustrates this in the starkest terms. The nobles – Houses Helmawr, Catallus, Ty, Ulanti, Greim, Ran Lo and Ko'Iron – live in the 'Spire', and seldom set foot below the 'Wall' that exists between themselves and the great forges and hab zones of the hive city proper.

Below the hive city is the 'Underhive', foundation layers of habitation domes, industrial zones and tunnels which have been abandoned in prior generations, only to be reoccupied by those with nowhere else to go.

But... humans are not insects. They do not hive together well. Necessity may force it, but the hive cities of Necromunda remain internally divided to the point of brutalisation, outright violence being an everyday fact of life. The Underhive, meanwhile, is a thoroughly lawless place, beset by gangs and renegades, where only the strongest or the most cunning survive. The Goliaths, who believe firmly that might is right; the matriarchal, man-hating Escher; the industrial Orlocks;

the technologically-minded Van Saar; the Delaque whose very existence depends on their espionage network; the fiery zealots of the Cawdor. All strive for the advantage that will elevate them, no matter how briefly, above the other houses and gangs of the Underhive.

Most fascinating of all is when individuals attempt to cross the monumental physical and social divides of the hive to start new lives. Given social conditions, ascension through the hive is nigh on impossible, but descent is an altogether easier, albeit less appealing, possibility.

excerpted from Xonariarius the Younger's
*Nobilite Pax Imperator – the Triumph
of Aristocracy over Democracy.*

CHAPTER: ONE

THE HOODED FIGURE dogged his thoughts – slashes of colour through a narrow vision slit. Then Bane's world exploded into white fury as the gaoler exercised his brutality.

Erik Bane drew a ragged breath. With waking came pain. His head hurt so badly that he thought the pipe they had hit him with must have bent on impact. A tooth had been dislodged and the copper tang of blood filled his mouth. Tenderised and raw, he felt like he had been pounded on a meat-vendor's block.

His arms were a dead weight and Bane was vaguely aware they were suspended above him. Rubber hose bit into his wrists, binding them. The floor was cold against his bare feet. Numb, they were tucked beneath his legs. He was kneeling, his head slumped forward and his eyes closed in an ironic parody of a penitent man.

Though he could not open his eyes, Bane knew he was being held in a small utility chamber. The close confines of his cell exacerbated the stink of stale sweat and stagnant water. Directly above, a ruined moisture condenser dripped languidly. The deposits from the broken unit ran onto the ridges of his face and chilled his naked torso. A drop landed in Bane's eye. He blinked. Light flared, bright and angry. He shut his eyes, waiting for the painful afterimage to subside. It was a halogen lamp; he could hear the faint buzz of its power cell. Outside was a wall of silence. His captors usually taunted, promising beatings and blood-duels; they were never silent. Something was wrong.

'Hey!' His voice was a choked rasp. 'Hey!' Louder this time, echoing off the metal cell interior. 'Bastards, get this lamp out of my face. I'm awake.'

Silence answered. The sporadic drip of the moisture condenser seemed abruptly louder, almost maddening.

'Are you scavving listening?'

Bane paused. He made out a dull machine noise, far off and muted by plascrete. His unease grew. The room became unbearable and he panicked. Struggling to his feet, he kicked at the door, thrusting his head forward.

'Let me out,' he cried, straining at his bonds. 'You bastards,' he screamed, his false bravado disintegrating. 'Answer me.'

He thrashed back and forth until his head struck the halogen lamp and he sank to the ground, his hysteria exhausted. The lamp hit the floor and went out.

Outside, the persistent drone of the distant machinery mocked him.

In the darkness, he gasped foetid air. Opening his eyes, he saw a faint half-light issuing through the door slit. More light spilled through the gap where a hinge had been shot out. A large dent in the bottom left corner had not been there before. It was as if something big had been driven hard into it, almost forcing off the other hinge. Bane could kick it open. Free of his bonds, he could get out! Heart pumping, Bane arched his neck, ignoring the stiffness and pain. Eyes adjusting to the darkness, he saw the hose binding his wrists. A single length held them both, wound around a thick metal bolt jutting out of the wall. The dripping water had perished it slightly. Bane listened again for any sign of disturbance.

Nothing.

Bracing himself against the cold metal wall with his feet, Bane pushed. A sharp creak of rubber as the hose stretched, but it did not give. Torsion slammed him back into the wall. Head pounding from the effort, he breathed in and tried again. Mustering all his strength, Bane heaved until his face touched the vision slit. With the sound of rubber slapping metal, the hose split and snapped. Bane slumped forward and blacked out.

BLOOD SEEPING BACK into his arms woke him. They tingled and then burned, as sensation slowly returned. He tested his grip; weak, but it would do. Crawling back up onto his knees, Bane wondered how long he had been out.

Silence still endured.

Head heavy against a rusting side wall, more of Bane's memory started to return. Fragments at first, slices of sibilant non-sequiter punctuated by the ominous din of a slamming metal door – the sound that heralded another beating. He saw a girl's face. She was about sixteen. Almond shaped eyes seemed to pierce his soul, and the olive skin on her arms were marred by gang tats. One on her left cheek looked like a cattle brand.

'Alicia,' he gasped, and was abruptly alert. It was his botched rescue attempt that had got him here. But she had escaped. His last memory was of her running for the gate that he had opened with bolt cróppers. If she'd made it to Former Glory, perhaps there was still a chance. The Razors had beaten him night and day for that information, it was the only reason they had kept him alive. They wanted her back real bad. He had held out though, bent but not broken. He had given them nothing. Now he had to find her.

Bane willed his body up. Using the shaft of light spilling through the door as a guide, he kicked the hinge. A spike of agony shot up his leg. He bit the exposed flesh of his arm to stop from crying out. Another kick. The

same pain but this time the door shifted. Lathered in a
veneer of sweat, he booted with the other leg and the
door gave at last, rusted hinges cracking. A clang echoed
through the darkened corridor as the door hit plascrete.

Exhausted, pain kept him moving. That and the desire
to find Alicia. She needed him.

Damn it! Where had he told her to go? He was so
hung-over he could not think. The Salvation, that was it.

'Get to The Salvation, it's a bar in Former Glory,' he had
said. 'I'll find you.'

Had Bane faith, he would have prayed. Yet it was
redemption he was looking for. As it was, he wished he
had a drink to steel his courage. He could not lose Alicia.
Not again.

He limped from his cell and was faced with a long, narrow corridor stretching out in front of him. Thick pipes
ran its length on either side, corroded by moisture and
age. Bloody marks stained the floor, left by his dragging
feet after the blood-duels; brutal one-on-one, to the
death battles between prisoners. He had killed six men
down here. Six innocent men.

Overhead, raw halogen lamps hung at intervals from a
networked cable array. Caked in filth they shed little light,
but through the gloom he discerned two bodies.

The first was a few feet from the cell. Bane almost
tripped over it. Head caved in, it looked like it had been
used as a human battering ram, though he faced away
from the door as if he had crawled on his belly. The
bloody crevice in his skull was the fatal wound. Close-
range, blunt force trauma with a pick or axe. It spoiled a
thick green mohican, jutting from an otherwise glabrous
skull. He wore a torn leather jacket, sleeves ripped off at
the shoulders. Gang tats covered his arms. The symbol of
a black skull with a blade lodged in the forehead was
most prominent.

It was the motif of the Razorheads, a house Goliath
gang, the frikkers who had subjected Bane to who knows

how many days and nights of torture in this hole. Other than that, he wore grey factory-issue fatigues and black steel-toed boots – nutcrackers.

Halfway down the corridor, its back against the wall, was another Razorhead corpse. Feet sticking out at impossible angles, his legs were obviously broken. Head shaved, a chain ran from his left nostril to his ear and into the back of his skull. He was similarly attired but only a thick chain crossed his otherwise naked torso, which was riddled by long, knotted scars. A stomach wound had killed him; something big, high calibre and close. It looked like the blast had tossed him into the wall, away from the exit ahead. Most of his chest was gone, leaving a gaping crimson void in its wake. Both bodies reeked of decay; they had been dead a while.

Bane stubbed his toe against something on the ground. It was a crowbar, probably dropped by one of the now-dead Goliaths. Bane picked it up and carried on. Bullet holes pockmarked the walls further down the corridor, shell casings and chipped plascrete crunched underfoot. No guns lying around though. With a gun he would need to be careful. Without one, if he met a live ganger, he was screwed.

Ahead the corridor branched to the right. A steel ladder ran up the wall on his left. It led to a hatch that could open onto the roof. He was not ready for a climb. Besides, up on the roof he would be completely exposed, so he pressed on down the right branch. Walking became easier with each step. The movement in his muscles, however painful, was returning.

Another few feet of corridor, and he found a half open door. An upturned oil drum and some plastek packing crates made for a poor barricade. Blood stained the walls and floor. An impact spatter on the left side looked like it was from a head shot. Bane examined it. The blood was congealed, like whoever had been shot was already dead. No bodies though. Something had happened while he had been unconscious. A hit from a rival gang? Bane dismissed it instantly. The Razorheads had enemies for sure, but they were the most powerful gang in this part of the Underhive. No one could touch them. No, this was something else. Gripping the crowbar, Bane used it to rake a plastek crate aside. Then, as quietly as he could, he edged through the door.

Bane stood in a large square room. The sheer size made him feel small and vulnerable. The machine noise was louder in here. An overturned wooden table had spilled a deck of cards onto the lino flooring. Two stools lay nearby, one with its legs broken as if it had been used as a weapon. A bent mattress was crammed against the far wall, stained with sweat and blood. It faced a large holo-pict viewer, a downmarket 2D variant that spat white noise into the room.

Wan light crept in from the right, where an anteroom led off away from the wretched gloom. Opposite was another room, wreathed in darkness. In front was a closed door. Bane made for the right anteroom.

A sickly yellow glare from a single naked bulb threw shadows from where it hung in the ceiling. It revealed a wooden bench. Clamped to it were a rotary saw and a grinding block, a workshop of some sort. An empty tool chest spilled its guts in the dark beneath the bench: a few rusty spanners, some nails, bolts and a bent screwdriver were all that remained. A cracked mirror was bolted roughly to the facing wall. Bane looked into it. A thin, dishevelled wretch looked back, eyes red-ringed and bloodshot, chin covered with white stubble. Ugly bruises, shallow cuts and red-raw burns ravaged his body. A roughly shaved head reflected the light. Burst capillaries were visible beneath the skin where it had been pinched by clamps, manifesting as dark, crimson wheals.

Averting his gaze, Bane noticed a stool in the corner. A white muscle-vest lay over the top and it propped up a shotgun. He pulled on the vest. With his skinny frame it was a good fit. Bane checked the shotgun, but it was empty and the barrel ruined. It had been left for fixing. There was nothing else of any use here, so he crossed the main room to the second antechamber.

He saw a small burning lamp on a scorched metal table. It was a narco-lab. It had been days since his last stimm and he felt the sudden craving like a hammer-blow. Hands trembling, throat like ash, he licked his lips and searched the table. He found a scalpel, foil dishes, paper gauze and flare goggles. Raking them aside, he went through a set of drawers beneath with growing fervour. One was empty, barring some stub rounds – no good for the shot gun, so Bane ignored them. The second drawer was locked. With frantic abandon, he smashed it with the crowbar. There were plans inside, dome maps. He slumped against the table despairingly. He needed a fix, badly. He tried to focus, to think about Alicia. He got up and staggered back out, trying to pull himself together.

With regained composure came renewed fear. Where the hell was everyone? Bane opened the last door slowly and wished dearly he had a gun.

A vast work-yard, stretched out before him. As he entered, the machine noise grew louder and he realised this was where the noise was coming from. Two industrial-sized fans droned and whirred in eerie unison, kicking up a decaying stench in their blast drafts. Bane held his breath against the foetid air pumping into the room.

Only one half of the yard was visible, a faulty overhead strip light providing a flickering vista that hinted at more beyond the light's reach. A large gang motif was revealed by the stuttering light, daubed in red paint – the skull with the razor in its forehead. It covered most of the floor area. Fresh handprints overlaid it, darker than the paint.

Huge stone slabs delineated a body-building area. House Goliath valued brawn over brains, and the Razors were adherents to that tenet. The raw, muscle-temple of hulking weight benches, lift bars and punch sacks was a testament to that. A massive metal tri-frame dominated the space, bolted into the stone slabs. A sturdy pulley system was set at its apex and monstrous plascrete blocks were attached via steam-bolted chains. Whoever was capable of lifting it would be capable of crushing a man like he was styrene. Drawing closer, Bane saw a clutch of dumb bells at the foot of the tri-frame; one was coated in a veneer of gore and matter. He suppressed the urge to flee. He had to find a way out and the only way to do that was to stay calm.

Dismantled weapons were everywhere, lined up on ranks of tables. Racks of lasguns, stubbers and autoguns were in abundance. Those that were assembled were locked in metal cages. Belt-fed ammunition, solid rounds and power packs, grenades and other munitions sat in piles. Moving closer, Bane saw large metal packing crates containing heavier weapons: rotary cannons, stubb-killers and other high-calibre arms. The Razors had been planning something big. They had enough firepower to lay siege to a city.

Bane tried to open one of the cages but the lock would not yield. It was high end security and a crowbar was not going to prevail. He doubted he could remember how to reassemble a lasgun or autogun. Even if he could, his trembling hands made that task impossible. He was wasting time. He had to get out.

He eyed the darkness warily, unwilling to stray into it. Closer to the edge, the stench grew stronger. Then he saw the power array. Fixed into a wall its sputtering wires cast tiny iridescent sparks into the darkness that fizzled and died as they struck the floor. Bane was no technician but he had seen enough to know a good, hard whack often got results. He struck the power array with the crowbar. With stuttering reluctance, a vast bank of strip lights lining the length of the work-yard came to life. As they did so, they revealed what the darkness had hidden. The entire Razor-head gang was here, all of them dead.

The scene was of a grisly massacre. At least fifty bodies stretched the width of the room. Two were slumped head first in a raised water sill that looked like it provided for the whole complex. Three more lay in the open, raked by bullet wounds, clutching knives and rusted cleavers in cadaverous fingers. Bane wandered tentatively into the carnage. Body piled on body greeted him as he moved slowly across the yard. Ahead were the outer walls of the Razorheads' lair, thick plascrete drilled by bullet holes and seared by las-burns. A chain-link gate bisected the wall in the middle, crowned by coiling razor wire. Another body was entangled in it. It looked like he had been trying to climb over. Overlooking it was a makeshift watch tower. Whatever had killed these bastards would do for him too if it found him here. If the Razors could not kill it, he doubted a stimm-addict with a crowbar could. He ran quickly to check the gate, covering his nose and mouth against the stink of death.

Locked.

He shook it hard but the chain was strong and looked new. What he would not give for some bolt-croppers. One of the corpses might have the key. He approached the nearest body. A gaping neck wound hung open like a second mouth, caused by what looked like a bite, with teeth marks that looked human. Bane forced the thought out of his mind and worked quickly. Patting the body down, he found nothing.

He moved to another. As he got nearer, he recognised him. Nagorn, the Razorheads' leader. They had met a long time ago. Thin strips of metal embedded in his forehead spelt his name. There were no obvious signs of his demise, but he was definitely dead. Lividity around the eyes and dilated pupils told their own story. The stench was overpowering. Bane retched before he could examine him. His heart leapt when he saw the key chain around Nagorn's neck, but his attention was drawn to something else. Tucked in the ganger's belt was a pistol;

black, well-made with a gold fist insignia on the stock. It might have been a fine weapon once, but it was tarnished and in need of repair. Bane recognised it. It was an Enforcement service pistol. Only officers who gave twenty years service got one. It belonged to him. He reached over the corpse and took it, but as he pulled the weapon free he felt something twitch.

Nagorn was looking at him! Heart thundering in his chest, Bane shrank away as Nagorn sat up, reaching out to seize Bane's wrist. He tried to break free but the dead man's grip was strong. Bane aimed the pistol pointblank at Nagorn's chest, squeezing the trigger. Nothing happened. Age and neglect had rendered the weapon useless. The other corpses stirred, moaning balefully as they dragged their bodies up out of the dirt. Horrified, Bane lashed out with the crowbar as Nagorn lunged to bite him. The blow crushed the ganger's cheek, ripping off his jaw. A second blow broke his arm and, prising away the dead fingers, Bane hurried to his feet. Nagorn did not stay down, he lumbered upright unsteadily on twisted limbs, reaching out for Bane with dirt-encrusted claws.

Bane backed away, disbelieving. Another zombie got close, eyes wide, jaw slack. The flesh on its face had rotted away, revealing bone. Bane struck it with the crowbar, smashing the thing to its knees. A third was in front of him, its skull caved in. Bane battered it. Then another moved up, a gaping torso wound exposing black, putrefied innards. He cracked its skull with an overhand swipe and there was an audible crunch. Bane was tiring. His arms burned and he could not breathe in the miasma of decay. All the while the living dead shuffled closer, regarding him from around the work yard with malicious, hungry eyes.

Adrenaline fuelling his body, Bane ran urgently for the entry door. Those things blocked the gate and filled the yard – he had to go back.

Bane smashed the door aside as he bolted through it. The zombies converged on him, the promise of fresh meat driving them. Inside the large room, Bane dragged the mattress over to block the door he had come through. Moments after he had rammed the mattress into place, a heavy impact made the door shudder. It popped open a few inches. Dead fingers reached around the crack. Bane kicked it shut, severing them. The holo-pict viewer hissed at him. Wrenching it from the wall, wires spitting sparks, he heaved it across the door.

Backing out of the room, Bane watched the door give. From the gloom beyond, the zombies pressed through the opening, two and three at a time; the mattress clawed aside, the holo-pict viewer crushed underfoot. Growing in vigour, they almost reached the next door before Bane could slam it.

He was back in the corridor. He kicked over drums and crates, launching one behind him in a vain effort to impede his pursuers. He barrelled around the corner, hearing the second door smash open. A wailing chorus of deep and terrifying groans came with it. In the long corridor he saw the ladder to the roof. He ran to it, limping. As he grabbed the first rung his leg was yanked back. The shaven-headed Razor he had left there snarled as it crawled toward him on its belly, tearing at his ankle. A bone crunching kick snapped the creature's neck and it lay still, releasing its grip. But the rest of the horde was almost upon him. Panting for breath, Bane pulled himself up the ladder, rung by painful rung. All the while, the corpse by the cell door lay dormant. Unable and unwilling to think on it further, Bane climbed madly, smashing the ceiling grill open with the crowbar. Heaving himself onto the roof, he took one last look below before shutting the hatch. Faces, deathly grey with rotten flesh and sunken eyes, glared back. They clawed at the air, snarling and moaning.

There was a freight elevator on the roof. Former Glory was ten kilometres away. He only hoped it reached that far.

As Bane hobbled over to it, the roof hatch was thrown open. The zombies came crawling forth, shambling towards him with even greater vigour.

Staggering inside the elevator, Bane raked the concertina door shut. He fell back as the first of the zombies hurtled into it, hissing curses and clawing through the slits in the gate. Then another came, and another, reaching, snarling. At this rate they would pound the gate down with sheer weight of numbers.

Beside him, a control panel hung down from a thick cable. There were only three operation symbols. Bane pressed the one to make the elevator go up. With a shriek of protesting servos and rusted gears, the elevator car began its grinding ascent. At first the creatures held on, the deathly pallor of their misshapen visages staring wildly. But as the car increased its speed they fell away, eerily silent, into the void below.

As the elevator rose, Bane tried to stop his heart hammering so loudly in his chest. He slid down the corrugated metal siding, fingers slipping off the controls as he sank to the floor. Foetid air washed over him, faster and faster as the car picked up speed. Operational warning lamps were a hazy amber blur. They cast intermittent slashes across Bane's face. The steady *thwump* of the rising elevator car filled his senses. On his back the twinkling lights of uphive were like dying stars.

Exhausted, he drifted into unconsciousness.

CHAPTER: TWO

The vapour from the massive precipitators fell like rain, wetting Alicia's hair and clothes. She looked up but could not see the huge machines. Many levels above, at the lowest point of Hive City, they gathered moisture from the air. Stored in vast wells, it was made chemically safe and farmed out by the Hydro-X guilders to those with creds to pay for it.

It was known as 'Fresh', though it was anything but. Yet it drew a high price and many guildsmen had grown fat on its profits. There were no such luxuries in Alicia's life. Born on the streets of lower hive, she had to take what she needed to survive. Petty theft led to worse, until she ran with a very bad crowd: Underhivers, the Razorheads. She had wanted out and she had got out. At least for now…

Alicia had been running madly, through claustrophobic access pipes and tunnels as black as sump tar. Her lungs burned. It had been five days since she had escaped. Five days sleeping half-awake in shadowed corners. Five days bunking under plas-sheeting when the precipitators vented and the turbine fans blew hard and cold through the skeleton of the Underhive, circulating stagnant air.

A morose wind from the turbine fans whipped through the underpass beneath where Alicia sheltered to avoid the rain. She hugged her storm cloak tighter around her body, flicking her hair out of her eyes. Ahead, dark structures soared into a false firmament of winking lights. It was not how he had described it. She was lost.

'Hey baby,' a lascivious male voice said from behind her. She turned towards it, heart thumping. A male juve, his bandana too big for him, stood a few feet away, legs slightly apart. She had not seen him crouching quietly in the shadows. He walked towards her, into the flickering glare of a halogen lamp. He was Alicia's height and wore black fatigues. A battered crimson jacket hung on his wiry frame. A longing glint in his eyes held with it the promise of something dark as he appreciated her pretty, young face. When he pulled out the combat knife from behind his back, Alicia realised what that was.

'C'mon sweetheart,' he said, bringing up the blade so she could see. 'Let's have some fun.'

Alicia straightened up, opening her legs to adopt a more promiscuous stance.

'You man enough for that?' she purred, swishing one half of the storm cloak aside, revealing a long and supple leg. For added effect she put one hand on her hip.

Juve-boy was a little taken aback by her brashness and he faltered.

'Well, are you?' She leaned towards him, pursing her lips as she said it, her voice little more than a whisper.

Juve-boy recovered his composure, smiling as he advanced.

When he was almost next to her, Alicia threw open the storm cloak. Underneath, all she wore was a pair of skin-tight booty pants and a leather top that hugged her breasts and left her midriff exposed. The juve's eyes widened. When Alicia pulled the stub pistol from a leather garter, they widened further.

'Oh sh–'

Alicia smacked the knife from the dumbstruck ganger's hand with the pistol butt. It clattered uselessly to the floor as she pressed the business end of the stub gun into his face.

'Listen, you little twip,' she breathed, voice low and menacing. 'See that?' She turned her left cheek, brandishing the tattoo on it like a badge. 'You know that mark, right?'

Juve-boy nodded.

'And you know what they do to little twips like you?' He nodded again, tears welling.

'Well it's nothing compared to what I'll do if you don't leave me the frik alone.' She grabbed his crotch with her free hand and squeezed hard. Juve-boy stifled a yelp.

She fixed him her best 'don't frikk with me' glance, sniffed derisively and cracked the pistol butt over the back of his head. He sank like a sump rat, hitting the floor hard, and stayed down.

Dropping to her knees, Alicia checked the Juve. He was out cold. She searched his pockets, tucking an errant strand of pink hair behind her ear as she did so. She found three stimm-sticks, a knife sheath and an igniter. She took all of it, dumping the stimm-sticks and the igniter in a pouch inside her storm cloak. She strapped the sheath to her leg. Stooping over his body, she stowed the knife and tucked the stub pistol back into her garter. Glancing round quickly, she made sure there was no one else lurking. Then, she wrapped herself in the storm cloak, tugging the hood on, and fled out into the rain.

ALICIA STOPPED RUNNING when she reached the settlement. She saw a rusted, weather-beaten sign. It creaked on chains hung from a steel arch.

Former Glory – population 10,065.

The number on the sign had been slashed through recently with black paint and modified to 10,049 in an untidy scrawl.

Her heart leapt. This was it.

Large tenement blocks rose up around her. They housed the multitudes that lived here and, she supposed, must teem with people.

It was late, and a vendor whose premises were opposite one of the tenements drew a heavy steel security curtain over a grimy-window. It looked like some kind of eatery; fusion dried cuisine and mystery meat were the big sellers.

'Hey,' Alicia called out, shivering as she ran over to him. The vendor took one glance at her bloodied, dishevelled appearance and gang tat and stepped back into the eatery, shutting a second gate down behind him.

'Hey,' she said. 'I just want some food. I have creds.'

She pushed her breasts against the security bars, hoping for a reaction.

'Closed,' was the dour response. The door to the eatery slammed shut.

'At least tell me where I can find the Salvation bar,' she hollered.

No answer.

'Frik-head,' Alicia spat, kicking the gate, making it shudder.

She was about to turn when she saw her reflection in the filthy glass of the eatery window. It was the first time she had seen it in five days.

She looked drawn and thin. Grime smeared her face. Her make-up was ruined, long streaks of pink merged with blue. There was dirt under her fingernails and blood from several small cuts had dried hard and black on her face. Lank from the precipitant rain, she tucked her pink hair back under the storm cloak's hood and shrugged. She had looked worse.

The promise of food had made Alicia hungry. Her stomach growled as she trudged away. She needed to find that bar. She needed to find Erik.

Alicia ran the narrow strip between the vendor and the tenement habs. Hammering on doors, she tried to rouse people but was met with the sound of sliding bolts. She moved on, heading down an alley. She was tired, but had to keep going. No way was she going to get caught again. She tugged her hood down further over her eyes to ward off the worst of the rain. Head down, she ploughed through the alley. In her urgency, she failed to notice a tramp huddled among some packing crates and plas-sheeting. She ran straight into him and fell. The storm cloak parted, revealing her glistening legs.

The tramp gazed at her as he picked himself up, his expression hungry. Alicia quickly covered up but it was too late. The tramp struggled out of the trash and staggered towards her, hands outstretched, fingers twitching. A wretched, filthy sack barely covered his body, and he had plas-sheeting tied around his feet with wire for makeshift boots. Alicia backed away on her hands and knees, until she felt the alley wall at her back.

'Back off, skank,' she snarled. If he touched her, she would bust him up good.

He ignored her and was almost upon her when she yanked the stub gun out from her garter.

'Don't!' she cried. Closing her eyes, she fired three times. The first shot ricocheted harmlessly off the wall but the second two caught him in the shoulder and chest. He was spun off his feet and lay still. Alicia thought he was dead. She had never killed anyone before.

She got up and walked over to him tentatively. Some plas-sheeting covered his face. She had to move it aside. Hand outstretched she took hold of it and pulled it back slowly.

The tramp jerked his hand towards her, snarling as he tried to take a bite out of her hand.

Alicia screamed, recoiling. He lurched up and she kicked hard. His head snapped back, but he was up again in seconds. Alicia ran, the tramp groaning balefully in her wake.

A stairway leading to the overhead walkway loomed ahead. She took it, scaling the stairs two at a time.

'That frekker should be dead,' she whispered to herself. 'He should be dead.'

She ran hard, the metal gantry clanked loudly. Bolting around a corner, she barrelled smack into a bunch of disused cables hanging from an upper level and nearly lost her footing. No way down, so she drove at them, trying to work them aside with her arms. They were thick and she got entangled and slipped on the slick metal, tearing down a thick wad of cables as she struggled for purchase. Her hands slid off the rest and she fell.

A vendor's awning broke her fall. She ripped through it and struck the ground. Fire surged through her leg as she landed badly, breaking a boot heel. Gasping for breath, running on adrenaline, she tried to get up. Her leg buckled and she went down. Her vision blurred, tiny dark spots emerging at the periphery. She was blacking out. She fought it, trying to focus, to stay calm. It passed.

Her leg was broken and she was stranded in the back alleys of nowhere. Alicia cast a fearful glance in both directions but there was no sign of anyone. Shouting for help would probably be a mistake. She checked the load in the stub pistol. Only two rounds. She crawled up against the wall, biting her lip against the pain, trying to figure out what to do.

A shadow fell across her. She looked up, gripping the stubber. It was a man. He was wearing long, tan leather robes. The top half of his face was hidden by shadow. Religious symbols hung from a cord of rope around his waist and he wore sandals on his feet.

'Are you lost, my child?' he asked benevolently, voice low and languid. He bent down as he said it, into the lamplight. As he spoke, his perfect teeth flashed and Alicia saw that the darkness hid an actual mask, the dull gold glinting. It was strangely hypnotic. Her grip on the stubber loosened but not of her own volition.

Her mouth felt numb. All she could manage was, 'I'm looking for salvation.'

The man smiled, extending a hand to her with long, claw-like manicured nails. 'You have found it.'

CHAPTER: THREE

BANE DRIFTED IN and out of consciousness. Tunnels, vents and cable conduits flicked by in a myriad of colour and sound. The hardness of the floor was the only constant as he lay prone on the elevator deck. Former Glory was miles up and traversing the old Underhive freight channels would take time. Arching his head to one side, his vision darkened. Old memories gnawed at him. He was slipping back. Powerless, he went under and remembered. Three years ago, another place, another life…

DUST DRIFTED DOWN from uphive in swathes, thick and grey, dislodged by heavy machine activity above. Matt-black smocks repelled the worst of it, keeping the fine particles out of their weapons and equipment. Beneath the smocks was a solid mass of carapace armour, shoulder-slung combat shotguns and hip-holstered bolt pistols. Each man was a towering sentinel of honed musculature and violent potential. With their heads encased in combat helmets, visors down and respirators active, they were faceless. Intimidating, powerful, silver precinct shields gleaming, they were the ultimate custodians of Necromundan law. They were Bane's men, his enforcers.

Bane waited silently as the dust fell. Upright, strong and determined, he was the very model of Enforcer machismo.

You could have slapped a slogan beneath his clean-shaven, chiselled stone jaw that read, 'Join up now!' and the Enforcer ranks would have swelled. He was the original poster child. The ideal.

On Bane's left was Proctor Vaughn. A capable officer, Vaughn had sped up the ranks with gusto. Next to him was Dugan, a heavy auto-loading stubber cradled lovingly in his immense grasp. Vincent and Lorimir stood alongside him. Both were big men, but they were dwarfed by Dugan. On Bane's right stood Zan, a weapons specialist, favouring a grenade launcher tonight. Choke gas and lethal rounds filled a belt around his waist. Heske, Rannon and Keller were alert beside him. The nine men stood in a semi-circle in front of a large disused warehouse, waiting.

Out of the darkness a tenth enforcer emerged, Nabedde, a tech-adept. He held a pair of high-intensity magnoculars in one hand.

'Thermal imaging confirmed, sir,' he said.

Bane nodded. 'How many?' His tone was deep and resonant through the respirator.

'Six, plus our target.'

If Bane felt anything, he did not show it. 'Our target is on your internal display, Miss Alcana Ran-Lo.'

A tiny screen inside Bane's visor crackled to life. An image of a young girl appeared, around sixteen, pretty and obviously Spireborn. She had to be, no way anyone but the ruling elite of Necromunda could requisition enforcers. Backed onto green-screen, the grainy image flickered – a result of the dust interfering with the Precinct House uplink.

'We are tasked with her live extraction,' Bane continued without emotion. 'Lethal force against the Razorheads has been sanctioned. That is all.'

An audible click and the voxponder link died. Commsilence from here on in.

Ahead, the massive derelict structure of Toomis Pre-fab Residential loomed high. Twin plasteel reinforced doors

barred their advance, leading to a cargo docking zone;
Enforcer mission tacticians had deemed this the best point
of entry.

Switching to signal communication, Bane motioned to
Nabedde.

The tech-adept hurried to the reinforced doors and
brought a high-end las-cutter to bear. The lock offered no
resistance to the super-heated beam, burning through in
seconds. The sound of the doors creaking open was muffled by their helmets.

Bane held up his left arm. Making a fist, he flicked out
his fore and index fingers and pointed towards the door.

Rannon and Keller hurried over to it. Nabedde stepped
aside as, edging the door wider, the two men made visual
checks. Rannon gave a thumbs-up, whilst Keller maintained a vigil at the door. Bane and the rest advanced.

Bane approached Nabedde. He held a holo-pict viewer,
flat screen, high-resolution, displaying a schematic of the
building. The location of the gangers was denoted by a
red triangular symbol. Two separate channels, divided by
a thick plascrete wedge, led to them – perfect assault posi-
tions.

Bane allowed himself a smile beneath his respirator.
The bastards wouldn't know what hit them.

Bane was first through the doors, the rest of his men
following in his wake. Nabedde brought up the rear, closing the doors. With the room sealed, Bane removed his
respirator. The rest of the patrol team did likewise.

The cargo docking zone was a reinforced plascrete
square at least a hundred metres across. Slim gantries ran
in a 'U' shape along the side and back walls, forty metres
above the docking floor. Dead-bolted trapdoors were
inset into the corrugated ceiling another forty metres
that, leading up to the roof. Numerous walkways
stretched across the gulf of space between one end of the
docking floor and the other, suspended by hefty chains.
Overhead strip lighting cast stark light onto the packing

crates, plas-tubing and cable drums scattered thickly
across the cargo zone floor. Power-haulers, servo-lifters
and mechanised arms lay dormant throughout. An exo-
loader slumped in one corner Tracked design, its
operator's harness was bent and split, both loader arms
slack and lifeless. From the torso up it was vaguely
humanoid, the tracks below crude and functional.
Covered in a layer of clogging dust it was like some
ancient mechanised soldier, forgotten and disconsolate.

Offices and caged equipment bays branched off from
the gantries. Bane doubted there was anything left in
them. The disused building had been that way for years.
Once part of a frontier district, the Underhive had risen
up and swallowed it. It had become gang territory. The
broken glass, graffiti and scorch marks left by fires were a
testament to the looting. Toomis was long dead. His
legacy, this building, was just another rotting wound in
which the disease of lawlessness could fester.

The upper levels did not concern Bane. He was certain
the Razors were down here. The sergeant turned to
Vaughn, raised a fist, splayed out his fingers and pointed
sharply to the right channel as indicated by Nabedde's
schematic.

Vaughn nodded and turned to the rest of the men, indicating Zan, Lorimir, Vincent and Keller, who followed
him as he moved quickly but cautiously down the right
channel in silence.

Bane took the left, the rest of the squad with him.

About fifteen metres down the left channel, the strip
lighting gave out with the sound of sputtering circuits. A
grey gloom covered everything and the packing crates
and disused machinery became dark shapes in it.

Bane pressed the night vision rune on his helmet's control array and a green spectrum overlaid his visor. The
men followed suit.

Another ten metres and they rounded a sharp bend.
Immediately ahead were metal packing crates, stacked

high and deep, and machine junk blocked their path.
Bane bent down to examine the drag marks still visible in
the plascrete. They were recent.

Gunfire and shouting echoed distantly ahead, emanating from the right channel.

'Oh crap, Vaughn,' Bane breathed.

They'd been set up.

The warehouse exploded with roaring gunfire and muzzle flashes. From the gantries above, silhouettes of the
Razorheads poured down hell and hot lead.

Nabedde was hit twice in the chest; another shot in the
leg put him down.

'Hug the walls,' Bane bellowed over the raucous din of
exchanged fire, strafing the left gantry with his bolt pistol.
From across the docking floor the throaty retort of Enforcer
combat shotguns erupted.

'Back to the junction. Go!' Bane cried, squeezing off a
couple of rounds. One of their shadowy assailants
screamed and fell.

Dugan withered the suspended walkway overhead with
his heavy stubber, severing suspension chains. More
screaming as three silhouettes fell into the blackness. As he
backed up the corridor, suppressing fire echoing, a batch of
wooden crates on his left burst open. The splinter storm
enveloped Dugan, taking him down.

Through the settling dust and carnage, an exo-loader
lumbered into view. A Razorhead sat in the harness. It
blocked their escape. With hissing servos and screeching
machine metal, Heske took a hit to the chest with one of
the loader's hulking pneumatic arms. Ripped off his feet by
the impact, he was smashed into a junk pile and lay still.

Bane drove at the machine, ignoring a stub round as it
ricocheted off his carapace shoulder guard, strafing the
harness with a full clip. The shots exploded in a shower of
sparks and metal debris. A head shot killed the driver
instantly. He slumped, held upright by the harness and the
machine sagged on its tracks.

Bane did not stop. He found Heske, and heaved him to his feet. He was spitting blood and screamed in agony.

Dugan got up, the bottom half of his face a patchwork of savage cuts. His cannon roared as it raked the gantries above, keeping the Razors at bay while they fled the firestorm.

On the deck, Nabedde wasn't moving.

Rannon reached the junction. Bane could see him as he dragged Heske along, the wounded enforcer protesting loudly. Dugan followed, backing off as he pummelled the gantries. The belt-feed in his stubber grew hot and shell casings cascaded.

'Nabedde?' Bane asked as they converged on the junction. They crouched at the plascrete wedge. The gantries did not reach this far so they had a brief reprise.

Dugan, the last to arrive, shook his head.

Bane swore beneath his breath and said a prayer for Nabedde. He looked to the door, acutely aware of the approaching Razors and the gunfire still echoing from the right channel.

The door had been sealed with some kind of super-heated torch.

Bane looked at Heske and then Rannon and Dugan.

'You two are with me. We weren't meant to get out of that corridor. We back up Vaughn and his team and break through to the girl.'

'What about Hes–' Dugan's words caught in his mouth. Heske stared ahead blindly. He was dead.

Bane returned his grim expression. 'We get her out and reconnoitre here.' Dugan and Rannon nodded.

Bane rammed a full clip into his bolt pistol and took Heske's shotgun before all three men headed down the right flank.

It did not take long to find Vaughn and the others.

They were bottled in and blasting at the overhead gantries. Muzzle flashes lit up the scene. Vaughn was

wounded, his left leg shot up and useless. He dragged it
after him as he tried to find cover. The rest of the
enforcers were on their feet – they had faired better than
Nabedde and Heske.

Bane ran, firing his bolt pistol. A silhouette fell with a
grunt. Dugan and Rannon bagged three more.

For a moment all was silent, gun smoke descending
like a veil.

Suddenly, shots exploded out of the gloom. Lorimar
took one in the neck, the impact ripping off his respirator. It came from the docking floor. They had moved
down; the gantries were no longer safe as they were riddled with gunfire.

'Damn it, sir,' Vaughn cried above the din. Vincent
supported him. 'We're getting crucified.'

Bane paused a moment, thinking. He knew it was
only a matter of time before the rest of the hive gangers
boxed them in.

'There's no going back,' he snarled, gritting his teeth as
a shot exploded overhead. The fire coming from the
Razorheads was fearsome.

Vaughn had to shout above it to be heard. 'And the
girl?'

Bane could not leave her. He spoke to Dugan through
the voxponder. 'Bring that cannon up.'

'Affirmative, sir,' Dugan replied.

Bane turned back to Vaughn. 'She's coming too.' The
captain focused his attention on Zan who was ripping
down more crates to improve the barricade.

'Gas that corridor,' Bane ordered. 'We're gonna rush
'em.'

Zan nodded, fixing a choke round in the chamber of
his grenade launcher.

'And stay alive,' Bane added. 'You're our exit.'

'Dugan,' Bane bellowed. 'Covering fire!'

Dugan stepped up and let rip on full auto. Vaughn
stayed with him and fired his combat shotgun.

There was a hollow *thwump*, air expelled from a thick tube, as Zan fired. Gas engulfed the Razorheads coming down the narrow cordon towards them.

Bane was first to leap over the barrier.

'Keep low and to the sides,' he growled through the voxponder.

Fire spitting over their heads, the rest of the enforcers advanced, ducking in and out of packing crates and machinery. Through their visors, they could penetrate the gas cloud and find targets. Overhead, Dugan's heavy stubber sounded like a battle cry.

The Razors were everywhere. Through the darkness and dissipating gas, Bane fired repeatedly as target after target presented itself. The room where Alcana Ran-Lo was being held was not far away. He did not know who had made it through the fusillade. Dugan's cannon still roared behind him and he thought he saw Rannon and Vincent.

He reached the end of the cargo docking zone. There was a door. He kicked it down. Two Razors loomed through the murk; they'd shattered the overhead strip light. Bane killed them both. He advanced. Vincent was a way behind him. He heard him shout Rannon's name.

His nerves were raw. He was reacting on instinct alone. From his left, another shadow darted towards him. Bane turned to it and fired.

A girl's scream echoed in his mind, clear as ice in the confusion.

Alcana Ran-Lo seemed to fall in slow motion. Bane's legs were leaden as he threw down the smoking bolt pistol and tried to reach her.

Hitting the ground where she had sprawled, Bane felt time return to normal. Blood oozed from Alcana's frail body. She was breathing rapidly and turned her head slowly to face the man who had shot her. Bane looked back as he tried desperately to staunch the bleeding.

'Stay with me. Stay alive,' he begged.

She looked up at him, her eyes cold, pleading, her gaze seemed to pierce his very soul.

'No,' he gasped. His hands were slick with her blood. The noise of the gun battle around them sounded like muted thunder.

The light in Alcana's eyes faded and she was still.

'No...'

BANE AWOKE, AWASH with sweat. A stranger loomed over him. He stank of stale body odour and urine. He started as Bane came round. A filthy coat covered his body. He wore fabric gloves, fingerless and stained and his boots were too big. Around his neck were numerous icons and symbols – too many for one person. He was a corpse tinker, a wretched skank who stole from the dead.

Bane got to his feet, even as the tinker retreated. Wasted as he was, Bane was still bigger and towered above the scrawny man.

'Your coat, boots,' he said with the raw insistence of a man with nothing left to lose. 'Hand 'em over.'

'Frik you,' spat the tinker, trying to sound confident.

The service pistol was suddenly in Bane's hand. He thrust it forward with intent. 'Hand 'em over.'

The tinker shrugged off the coat. He was naked from the waist up beneath it and as filthy as his attire. He kicked off the boots, eyes on Bane the whole time. A wag of the gun and he ran out into the darkness.

When he was long gone, Bane tucked the pistol back in his trousers, pulled on the coat and boots and tried not to hate himself. Funny really, he'd just robbed the skank with a defective gun. The poor bastard would probably freeze to death.

As Bane stepped out of the elevator, the nightmare persisted. He shook his head, trying to quash it. Alcana was dead, but Alicia lived. A second chance. His redemption.

He had to get to her. He knew the Razors were dogged, had seen enough corpses dead by their handiwork and people who had tried to elude them, but to reach out from beyond the grave... How do you kill the already killed? It did not seem possible. He suppressed a shudder at remembering the creatures and tried to crush that memory too. He really needed a drink.

The elevator had stopped abruptly, the winch's power cell exhausted. A deserted service tunnel stretched in front of him. An oil-smeared sign in front of it indicated that Former Glory was three kilometres up.

Bane gave a long sigh.

He would have to go the rest of the way on foot.

By THE TIME Bane reached Former Glory, his arms and legs burned. The long climb had toughened his muscles, but had not helped his head. It pounded relentlessly, the nagging ache gnawing at his resolve.

He had entered via the township's mining district, little better than a slum rammed with lofty tenements and saloons for the numerous ore prospectors passing through. Soup kitchens and seedy vendors were the norm here but today the streets were deserted. Stalls were overturned and trashed, habs and refineries lifeless and dark. Bane's anxiety increased.

Somewhere along the way he had lost the crowbar, so it was with tentative steps that Bane walked past the first high-rise tenements. Heading further into the settlement, he noticed that the sector lamps were down. At first he thought it was a power outage, but he was soon aware that they had been smashed. Oil drum fires littered the streets, casting the nearby buildings in sickly, flickering orange. They were beacons to skanks, strays and other lowlifes but they were deserted. Bane wandered past a saloon called Kreegan's. He knew it. They did not serve him anymore because of some trouble a few months back. It looked like Kreegan had gone out of business.

The door was boarded up. Same for the window but it had been ripped open and large splints of wood were still bolted to the plascrete like jagged teeth.

There was blood on them.

A machete lay in the dirt. It looked like it might have been used to get in the window. There was blood on it and the blade was still tacky. As he crouched to examine it, Bane had the feeling he was being watched. He looked around quickly.

There was no one there.

He listened hard. Somewhere in the darkness he heard a faint sound, scraping or shuffling – he could not be certain which.

The pistol in his pants was useless, so he wiped the machete on his coat and took it. Bane hurried quickly to the shadows, hugging the wall as he peered nervously into the dark. Salvation was only a few streets ahead.

The further he went, the more dilapidated Former Glory became. Buildings and habs were little more than burned out ruins. The town had always been a hole, no question, but this was a frikking war zone.

Above, he heard a muffled din like thunder. The precipitators were venting again. Vapour came down in sporadic droplets, hissing as it struck the drum fires. Gradually, the light shower became a barrage. Bane had no desire to be stuck out in it; he knew what chemical reactants were in the untreated run-off. A door to a tenement block hung open. Bane hurried through it.

The room of the tenement was dark, lit only by the ambient light spilling in through the open doorway. It was some kind of lobby area. Bane kicked something as he entered. It was a small halogen lamp. It refused to work, so he smacked its power cell with the palm of his hand. Three more jolts and it sparked into life. It was running virtually on empty so the lamp's glow was weak. It looked like skanks had been slumming here. Filth raked the walls and the detritus of broken glass and furniture lay underfoot. One of the walls had a blood smear going all the way up to the ceiling.

Bane gripped the machete tighter.

Swinging the lamp over into the corner, he noticed a small pack, the kind ore-prospectors used to carry rations while they dug. He opened the pack up. There were dark spots on it that might have been blood. Bane's heart leapt when he saw the contents. It still held miner's rations: thin wafer cakes and meat strips. The wafers were dry and the meat tough like leather but Bane devoured it anyway. Pity there was no liquor, and he had not met a prospector yet who was a stimm-head, so no joy there either.

Wiping his mouth as he cast the pack aside, Bane carried on further into the lobby. He had got his bearings. The lobby was long and shaped like a lozenge. Walls that might once have been white were yellowed with age and filth. Paper peeled off in places, exposing damp and hefty cracks. Three doors on either side led off into other rooms. Bane decided to take the first on the left.

Barely inches from the doorway, the lamp gave out and darkness engulfed him. Bane smacked the power cell but nothing happened. He tried again. Still nothing. He dumped the lamp with the ration pack.

Edging inside, the drumming of the precipitant rain was crushed by the sound of Bane's beating heart. He was shaking, from withdrawal or fear, he could not tell. A strange sensation came over him. His legs seemed reluctant to move and every shadow held a threat.

He clutched the machete to his chest. 'Someone in here?'

Something moved in the far corner. Swathed in darkness, Bane could not tell what it was. Maybe it was Alicia? Perhaps she had got lost and squatted here.

Bane came forward a pace. 'Alicia?'

Whatever it was shifted again. In fact, there were several of them. A low and menacing hiss emanated from the corner of the room. It was not Alicia.

Bane ran out into the lobby and tripped on the discarded ration pack. Cursing, he got up quickly and fled out of the tenement into the rain.

After a few metres, he stopped, crouching in a boarded-up vendor's doorway, while he caught his breath. Lungs burning, he looked behind him. He could not see a thing in the darkness. He waited but nothing happened. He could see the Salvation ahead. It looked quiet, almost dead.

'Where the frik is everyone?' he muttered.

In the distance he heard the same shuffling, scraping sound again but could not place its origin. He suddenly had no desire to stay there. Venturing from the doorway, he made for the bar quickly, praying that Alicia would be waiting for him.

UP-CLOSE, BANE saw that all the doors and windows to The Salvation were boarded up. He peered through a crack in one of the windows. It was totally dark inside. There was someone in there, he could hear them breathing. Whispers too. He could not tell what they were saying, but they sounded fearful, as if they knew he was out there but were too scared to reveal their presence.

Bane moved to the door. He cast another look into the darkness behind him. It seemed quiet but something nagged at his raw nerves. He needed to get off the streets, right now.

Bane hammered at the door. In the darkness behind him came the shuffling, scraping sound, only louder. He flashed a glance back. Blinking away the rain he saw something move. Bane hammered harder. 'Let me in, damn it!' He glanced back around. There was definitely something there. It was coming towards him…

The door in front of Bane was thrust open. Hands grabbed him roughly and yanked him inside. The door thudded shut in his wake and darkness surrounded him.

Bane was slammed onto his back and disarmed. A small oil lamp was thrust into his face. He tried to get up, swipe the lamp out of his face, but strong, gloved hands held him down. He made out two large men. Thick scarves covered their faces. He opened his mouth to speak but one of the men shoved a thick wad of cloth into it.

'Is he bit?' a tremulous voice hissed from the back of the room.

'Dunno. Bring the dog.' It sounded muffled; must have been one of the men holding him.

Heavy footsteps came over as a fourth man brought a snarling mastiff over. Its breath assaulted Bane's nostrils and flicked saliva felt wet on his chin and neck. The brutish beast sniffed him vigorously and then backed off. He heard the leash fall slack.

'He's clean,' said the fourth man, his voice gruff and old. Bane recognised it.

Bane felt the pressure on his arms lift as he was released. The lamp withdrew and he saw the people hiding out in the bar for the first time.

The two men holding him down wore the garb of ore prospectors, thick clothes, lots of layers with robust-looking gloves and boots. Both wore oil-smeared caps and pulled the scarves down from their faces once they realised Bane was not a threat.

A little further back, a tall, heavy-set man regarded him. He wore a brown leather apron over a pale blue shirt and dark leggings. His sleeves were rolled up, revealing brawny arms covered in thick hair. With his balding pate and handlebar moustache, he was every inch the frontier barman. The mastiff's leash was balled around his fist and in the other hand he held a shotgun pointing straight at Bane.

'Gilligan,' Bane said, smiling as he recognised the face that went with the voice. 'Is that any way to treat your best customer?'

Gilligan snorted contemptuously and lowered the shotgun.

'Gil,' Bane said, taking in the faces around the room. 'What the hell is going on?'

'Survival, that's what's going on,' he said, barely containing his disgust. 'And hell is right. Hell on the streets.'

Drama. Gilligan had a talent for it. He used to be a brawler. Underhivers paid hard creds to watch him fight in the pits. No augmetics, just brawn and balls. He whipped up the crowds with his antics. But time was inexorable and pit fighting was a young man's game, so when he won his freedom he opted for the 'easy' life and became a barman. He told that story every night, least those that Bane could recall through the alcoholic haze. Gilligan liked regaling his customers with stories, but this was no tale.

'What are you talking about?' A bottle of grain liquor sat half empty on the bar. Bane walked towards it.

'While you were gone something happened,' Gilligan began. In the frail light from the oil lamp his eyes seemed on fire. 'People got sick and died. No one knew why. But they didn't stay dead. They came back.'

Bane's stomach lurched and his heart quickened as he thought back to his ordeal in the Razorheads' lair. He reached for the bottle but Gilligan grabbed it and held it down.

'People fought,' Gilligan continued. 'They fought with everything they had. Mothers and children fought with sticks and rocks but how can you kill the already killed?'

Bane's own words echoed in his mind.

'One bite,' Gilligan said, looming closer. 'Just one, that's all it takes and you're one of them.' The barman paused, allowing it to sink in as he fixed Bane with a stern glare. 'Far as I know, we're all that's left.'

He let go of the bottle.

Bane brought it to his lips a little too quickly and supped deep. The liquor burned as it gushed down his throat.

'I see some things haven't changed,' Gilligan said accusingly, leaning back.

Bane gave him a rueful look as he wiped his mouth and set the bottle down.

'I've seen 'em too, but way down-hive. It must've spread.'

'For sure,' Gilligan's voice was edged with sarcasm. 'That's why we're hiding here. The streets ain't safe.'

'Gil,' Bane moved towards the barman as he said it, his voice urgent, 'have you seen a girl come through here. I was supposed to meet her. Young, pretty, gang tats on her arms.'

Gilligan was disgusted and recoiled, 'Damn it Bane, I knew you were low but this… What is she, a streetwalker, or another junkie like you?'

'It's not like that,' Bane protested. 'She's called Alicia, has she been here?'

Gilligan snorted in surprise. 'You went after *that* girl?'

'Have you seen her?' Bane insisted.

'No,' Gilligan shook his head. 'No, she hasn't been here.'

Bane's heart sank. He had hoped she might be in another room or that maybe she had fled when all this started and left him a message. Instead he had nothing. He was no closer to finding her than when he was a prisoner.

'Why do you care?'

'I just do,' he said curtly. He looked around the room. 'Who are these people?' Bane asked, indicating the group of survivors.

'Name's Lyle.' One of the prospectors came forward, average height but well-built. He had a scar down one side of his face, probably from a cutting tool accident.

Bane nodded to him.

'The big fella's Oheb,' said Lyle, jerking a thumb in the direction of the second prospector, a dark-skinned giant, with hands like shovels and skin that shimmered like oil.

Oheb gave an almost imperceptible nod. He looked like
the kind of guy who only moved when he had to, but
when he did it was fast and with all the force of a piston-
driven hammer.

'You know my daughter, Jarla,' Gilligan said. A timid little girl appeared from behind her father's bulk. She was
sixteen, just like Alicia. She did not have Alicia's savvy or
toughness though. Her father had cosseted her, tried to
shield her from the depravity and terror of the Underhive.
No way could he do that now.

Jarla's innocent eyes held fear enough for all of them
and she clutched Gilligan's tabard, knuckles whitening.
The big man laid a hand lovingly on his daughter's head
and she seemed to relax.

'Doctor Halem Mavro,' Gilligan indicated a small,
weedy looking man hunched in a long tan coat. He had
thinning, straggly black hair and stubble around his neck
and chin. He toyed with a razorblade, rolling it across his
knuckles and between his fingers. Behind wire frame
spectacles, his beady, vermin-like eyes narrowed and a
thin smile split across his lips as he recognised Bane.

'Mr. Bane and I are already acquainted.' His voice was
naturally insinuating.

Bane clenched his fists and tried to keep his expression
impassive.

'Who's the guy in the corner?' he asked, changing the
subject.

'Ratz. He's an outlands scavenger, far as I know,' said
Gilligan.

Ratz had the dark tan and bone totems of a Ratskin.
Bands of them roamed the outlands. Most thought of
them as savages who were not to be trusted, but Ratskins
had travelled most of the Underhive and beyond and
were excellent guides. This particular specimen did not
look in the mood to be guiding anyone. He rocked back
and forth, staring straight ahead, muttering constantly
beneath his breath.

'I found it, they took it,' he said. 'I found it and it spoke to me.' Poor bastard was raving.

'What's his problem?' Bane asked.

'Dunno. We found him like that. Couldn't just leave him out there to be eaten by those…' Gilligan stopped. There was a noise outside, like a dull thud.

'What–' Bane began but Gilligan hissed him quiet.

Lyle tossed Bane the machete and took out a large rockcrete hammer. Oheb hefted his much larger hammer and, for a big man, moved quickly to the back of the room and put his hand over Ratz's mouth, who was wide-eyed and looked like he was about to pop.

Mavro cowered in the corner, twisting his razorblade more vigorously as he squatted next to a dust-ridden synth-organ. Jarla was sent to hide behind the bar, while Gilligan primed his shotgun. The mastiff at his heel sat stock still, ears pricked up, a low growl in its gullet.

They waited in the darkness for several minutes. The silence persisted until Gilligan's shoulders slumped down again and they all relaxed.

The big barman exhaled loudly, moving behind the bar to pour a drink.

Bane noticed that the bar floor had been totally cleared. The tables and chairs now served as barricades over the doors and windows. The only entrance not barred was the one Bane had come in by, but even that was bolted and boarded. The only piece of furniture in the room that had not been moved was the synth-organ. It was bolted to the floor.

'Noise and light attracts them,' Gilligan whispered, knocking back the liquor. He grimaced as it went down. 'They hunt in packs. If they knew we were in here…' he paused, noticing the fearful look in Jarla's eyes. 'Well, you know what could happen.'

'So what's your plan? You're gonna hole up in here until what? Until help arrives?'

Gilligan was about to answer, but the words caught in his throat. He had no plan. He had only got this far out of necessity.

Bane looked beneath the shelving and through the drawers behind the bar.

'What the hell are you doing?' Gilligan asked. 'These two bottles are all the booze I've got left.'

Bane looked up at him. 'You got any more weapons in this dung-hole?

'Just the shotgun, and what you mean by dung-hole?'

Bane ignored him. 'We can't stay here. It's not safe.'

'Since when do you tell us what we can and can't do?' It was Lyle walking up to the bar with Oheb towering behind him like a slab of pure muscle.

Bane looked up and was about to answer when he felt suddenly dizzy. The liquor had gone straight to his head. He was sweating profusely as another stimm craving took hold. He gripped the edge of the bar to stop from falling over.

'Besides,' Lyle continued, not noticing Bane's discomfort. 'The Watch'll come looking for us. They'll be clearing the streets right now.'

Bane sniffed derisively and shook his head. He spoke through gritted teeth. 'I am the Watch.'

Lyle looked over to Gilligan, who, expression grim, just nodded.

'He's talking about *real* watchmen, Bane,' the barman countered. 'Ones who uphold the law.'

'No one's coming,' Bane told him, straightening up as the craving started to pass. 'This plague is spreading fast. Who knows how far it's got. By now, this whole sub-level could be overrun. Frontiers in the Underhive change all the time. If a settlement is consumed by gangers or plague or whatever, then another will crop up somewhere else. If you want to survive, we need to get off this level and we can't do that without weapons.'

'So what are you suggesting, lawman?' Gilligan's annoyance at Bane's audacity was palpable.

'We get out of this building and head for the Watch House. It's fortified, maybe those things haven't got in there yet,' he said. 'There's an armoury. We get tooled-up and head uphive.'

'We can't survive out there,' Gilligan hissed with an involuntary glance at his daughter.

All the while he and Bane spoke, Mavro continued to manipulate the razorblade. He was yet to settle down after the earlier scare and was not paying attention to the conversation. His eyes were on the doors and windows. Metal flashed in the lamp light as the blade danced faster and faster across his knuckles.

The shine caught Bane's eye and he grimaced.

'Will you frikking cut that out?' he growled.

'Huh?' Mavro looked up and then winced in pain as the blade cut him. He dropped it and it fell into the synth-organ. Without thinking, he groped into it to retrieve his obsessive-compulsive trinket but he activated the ancient device and it roared spectacularly, terribly into life.

The room filled with noise, a tinny ditty that crackled and cracked. Bright lights flared out of the organ as the tune played.

'No!' Gilligan gasped. He raced across the bar room floor, heaving aside Mavro who came up clutching the razorblade.

'It's lucky,' he blathered.

It took all of Gilligan's resolve not to strike him. He scowled, a look that promised a later reckoning. Desperately, he tried to switch the machine off but was struggling in the dark and panic.

'Turn it off, turn it off!' Jarla cried, huddled behind the bar and peering around the corner.

'They took it! They took it!' Ratz whooped, bouncing up and down.

Bane advanced, about to intervene, when there was a mighty *thunk* and the noise abruptly stopped. Oheb stood over a crackling, hissing synth-organ, a small pall of smoke gathering around him. The blow from the rockcrete hammer had destroyed the device utterly.

Silence descended again. No one moved. They barely breathed.

After a few moments, Gilligan relaxed. Then it happened.

Thick splinters of wood tore into the room as one of the boarded up windows was destroyed. Faces, skin sloughed, eyes sunken in their sockets peered back through the gap left behind. They reached in, scrabbling desperately, driven by unnatural hunger as they tried to force their way inside.

The shotgun roared. Lyle ducked to avoid its blast, and a zombie who had made it as far in as his torso exploded. Gore and blood showered them. Jarla screamed. All the while, the mastiff strained at its leash, barking loudly at the grim intruders.

'Seal it,' Gilligan bellowed. Oheb grabbed a strewn table from one of the barricades and rammed it hard against the window. Bones cracked and shattered with the impact. Heavy thuds rammed against it instantly as the creatures battered it. Oheb gritted his teeth as he fought to keep them at bay.

A second window caved in. Gilligan swung his shotgun around, fired and missed, the scatter peppering the wall. A zombie, clothes torn, skin pallid grey, lurched inside. Gilligan brought the shotgun up again as the thing lumbered towards him, hissing and snarling.

There was a click. The shotgun had jammed.

Gilligan worked at the loading mechanism, trying to clear it as the zombie came at him.

Bane ran forward, beheading the creature with a brutal swipe of his machete. Behind him, a third window was rent open and the door rattled so hard it almost came off its hinges.

'We can't stay here,' Bane told him. Lyle rushed to the window. He smashed a zombie with his hammer. 'Our only chance is to get to the Watch House.'

Gilligan licked the sweat off his top lip and nodded.

Bane looked around the room, quickly. Jarla was still crouched at the bar. Mavro had dragged Ratz to his feet and the two of them stood next to her. Lyle and Oheb were doing their best to hold the creatures off.

'Is there another way out?' Bane asked, shouting to be heard.

Gilligan paused, trying not to look at the things fighting to get in.

'Come on,' Bane urged.

'The cellar,' Gilligan gasped. 'It leads out into the street. It's around the other side of the bar. It might be clear.'

'Good enough. Get them out, we'll follow,' Bane ordered, pointing at Mavro, Ratz and Jarla.

Gilligan nodded. He whispering a few words to his daughter as he lovingly cradled her cheek.

The cellar was located behind the bar where an iron trapdoor led into a tunnel. A couple of metres across and it opened up into a delivery bay that led to the street. Gilligan yanked open the trapdoor with one hand. Hefting Jarla onto his shoulder, leash and shotgun in his free hand, he descended into it, the others following closely behind.

In the bar room, Lyle cried out. The window was breached, he could not hold them off and they were getting inside. The back door too was almost torn open; a horde of terrible faces regarded them through the widening crack.

'We move, now!' Bane bellowed, rushing forward to cut down a zombie that was tearing at the door.

Lyle backed away. He swung wildly, but there were too many getting through. Bane grabbed the scruff of his collar and heaved him back as the growing horde within the room slowly advanced. They fell back to the bar, calling to Oheb to do the same.

BACK FROM THE DEAD

The giant looked behind him at the zombies shuffling forward. He was cut off. Roaring, he whirled round, allowing the table he was using to block the window to fall. He dived into the horde, rockcrete hammer swinging to the stomach-churning chorus of crushing bones.

'Get out,' he yelled. 'I'll follow.' His deep voice was like a clap of thunder, but it lacked conviction.

As Bane backed away, dragging Lyle who was screaming for his friend, he crushed feelings of remorse. Oheb was doomed. From behind him, more of the zombies surged. They hooked onto his back with filthy talons and gored him with their teeth. The first he shrugged off, heaving it into the wall with his mighty shoulders but then came a second and a third. They swarmed over him, front and back. He bellowed defiantly, the sound muffled by the press of bodies assailing him.

Averting his gaze, Bane heaved the trapdoor to the cellar shut. The last thing he heard was the dull thud of Oheb's rockcrete hammer falling to the floor. Above the shuffling and scraping overhead, he could hear other sounds – tearing and sucking. Oheb was a big man with lots of meat on the bone. Eating him would take time, hopefully enough to get to the street before the horde came looking for them. Bane shut off his mind to the imagined horror above and together with Lyle, headed down the cellar tunnel to find the others.

CHAPTER: FOUR

It was dark in the tunnel and Bane was glad of it. It smothered his thoughts, made it so none of what he had just witnessed was real. Lyle's hard breathing alongside him was a reminder though. Still, at least he didn't have to make eye contact. Bane thought of Alicia and he crushed the memory quickly.

Gilligan had kept the light off deliberately. A shaft of light emanating from the chinks in the metal exit door that led to the street would attract the creatures. There was a chill too; Bane felt it on his bare skin. The stink of stale alcohol pricked his nostrils. A few bottles of grain liquor would go down well, right about now. Dense metal racking was aligned either side so he used it to find his way.

After a few minutes of charged silence, he saw figures ahead.

'That you, Bane?' Gilligan whispered.

Bane let his heartbeat steady before he answered.

'It's me.'

They clustered together like sump cattle. Gilligan was at the centre, shotgun in hand, one big arm wrapped protectively around his daughter. Mavro skulked nearby. He held Ratz by the scruff of the neck and the ratskin muttered quietly into the darkness.

They hovered at the foot of a rockcrete exit ramp, beneath the twin metal doors that led to the street. Light, grey and weak, filtered in from above, casting them in monochrome. Bane and Lyle stepped into it.

'Where's Oheb?' asked Gilligan.

Lyle looked down. Bane gave the faintest shake of his head and Gilligan's face fell. Bane walked past the huddled group, up the ramp.

'Dead?' Mavro muttered. 'He's frikking dead. They killed him? He was a giant.' Mavro released Ratz's collar and stalked up the ramp after Bane. 'What chance do the rest of us have?' he said. He was right in his face.

Bane ignored him, instead he listened outside.

'I'm talking to you,' Mavro said. 'You drag us out of the Salvation, where we were safe and anonymous. Now we're on the run, without protection.'

Bane blocked his voice out.

Incensed, Mavro put a hand on him. It was a mistake.

Bane lashed out, faster than a man exhausted and hungover should have been able to, and clamped his hand around the scrawny doctor's neck.

'Be quiet,' Bane snarled between gritted teeth. He nodded surreptitiously towards Jarla, cowering at her father's side. 'You're scaring her.'

Bane leaned closer, this was just for Mavro. 'And if you force me to touch you again,' he said, voice low and menacing, 'I'll break you.'

Bane let off and Mavro slumped to his knees, choking.

'You finished?' Gilligan asked.

Bane returned his dark expression.

'Whatever's between you, keep it that way,' Gilligan warned him. 'Don't forget, to me you're still just a damn drunk.'

Bane sniffed. 'Just help me lift this.'

Bane pushed at one of the metal overhead doors. Gilligan heaved with him. Lyle joined them, peering through the small gap that had been made onto the street beyond.

'It's clear,' he whispered. Whatever remorse he felt for Oheb he held in check. The desire for survival overrode it.

Bane nodded, breathing hard from the effort. His voice was strained. 'Ok, push.'

THE CELLAR TUNNEL opened up on the other side of the Salvation. They scurried from the hatch quickly, into the shadow cast by a neighbouring building. Gilligan looked back across the gloom at his bar. He knew his livelihood was gone.

There were signs of movement within. Shadowy forms lurked around the periphery. Their hunger briefly sated, the plague zombies milled about in groups. As more of the creatures joined them, crawling out of the gaping windows, sloping awkwardly through the broken door-way, Bane realised they were not wandering about in some random fashion. They were waiting for the others.

'Did you see that?' Bane muttered.

'See what?' Gilligan's reply was caustic. 'What the hell you talking about Bane? Let's just get to the damn Watch House.'

Bane looked back. The others were already on the move, hugging the walls as they went. Most of them had lived in Former Glory for years, eking what meagre exis-tence they could, whilst all around them gangbangers fought tooth and nail. Frontiers fell, territories were swept away, engulfed by fire and violence, yet they had endured. It was a way of life. It was the Necromundan way.

Lyle glanced over his shoulder at Bane. His expression turned to horror and he pointed.

Bane turned back around to where they had come.

'Oh shit,' he breathed.

They had been seen. Or rather *sensed*.

'Run,' Bane bellowed.

Packed together like foetid deck rats on a sewer cruiser, the zombie horde came at them, slow and shambling at first. Then it was as if a light had been switched on in their dim and primal consciousness, and they ran.

Ratz stumbled, half-crazed, half-comatose. Gilligan hoisted Jarla onto his back, the snarling mutt straining at the leash in his other hand. Lyle urged on the doctor, who kept glancing back. It slowed them down and gave Bane a chance to catch up. It also meant the creatures were gaining.

'There,' Bane said, pointing to an alley.

The alleyway was narrow; a tight cordon might slow the zombies down. Rain dripped from a slick metal gantry and further down, thick cables obscured it. Some were torn and littered the street below as if they had been ripped loose.

Ahead, a clutter of packing crates and plas-sheeting debris impeded them. Lyle was first to it, the prospector leaving Mavro behind. He kicked away a packing crate. As he heaved away another, something dark that had been hiding flew out of the sheeting at him.

Lyle was pitched over by the sudden attack. On his back in the grime and filth of the alley, he wrestled with his assailant.

'Get this frikker off me,' he cried.

Hunkered over him, the wretched thing snarled and clawed, trying to bite the prospector. It was clad in rags of factory-grade sacking. Bane noticed the serial numbers etched into it before he kicked the dreg in the face.

Lyle scurried back on his elbows, kicking with his legs for purchase. When he was far enough away, he got to his feet. So did the dreg.

Bane's kick was good. He heard bone crunch. The dreg's jaw hung loose. It lolled up and down as it snarled and hissed, like a marionette with half its strings cut.

'It's one of them,' Lyle shouted.

The thing came back at him, claws outstretched, teeth bared, broken jaw distended. Bane stood in front of the prospector and swung the machete. It caught the creature's arm, digging deep into withered flesh. But it felt no pain and drove on, this time at Bane.

'They're coming,' Jarla cried.

Bane gripped the machete, struggling against the creature's swinging arm. Lyle held the other hand back, head turned away as spittle and blood flicked out of the creature's mouth.

Bane risked a look back as he fought. The horde had found the alley. They were right behind them.

'Gilligan–' he began, but was cut off by the booming report of the shotgun. Bane felt shot, sharp and hot, graze his ear. He heard Lyle scream in pain, turning away instinctively as the creature's head exploded.

Ears buzzing, Bane felt a strong hand lift him to his feet.

'Get up,' Gilligan urged, his voice sounded smothered as if he were speaking to him underwater.

Senses returning, Bane was running again. Lyle was next to him. The prospector's right side was covered in blood; a long gash ran down it where the shot had nicked him. Powder burns raked his neck. It looked like he had got the worst of it.

They burst out of the alley and down Vendor's Row, a seedy district of lofty tenements, subsistence emporiums and soup kitchens. Former Glory had three entrances and exits, and this was one of them. A huge metal sign swung over the gate. A low-riser access tunnel from this main thoroughfare would take them to the Former Glory's epicentre and the Watch House.

They were nearly there.

That's when Bane saw the doors to the tenement buildings open. Zombies rushed out in a flood of pallid flesh and snarling voices, but without the same purpose as the others.

Merely a few metres away, the sudden attack startled Gilligan. The leash slipped from his grasp. Already straining hard, the mastiff raced off towards the nearest creatures, barking wildly.

'Boy,' he cried. 'Boy!' He put Jarla down. In their flight, the group of survivors had become separated and ranged

along both sides of the street. Mavro, Ratz, Gilligan and
Jarla hugged the tenements, Bane, Lyle and the vendors on
the other side. When Gilligan turned, it was the doctor
who was closest.

'Take this,' he urged, thrusting the shotgun into his
hands. 'Get her away. I've got to get my dog.'

'Gilligan, no,' Bane said. He tried to cross the street, to
get to him. The mutt had reached the zombies coming
from the tenement, barking and snarling. One of the
creatures held a thick lead pipe. Bane closed his eyes
when he heard the poor thing yelp.

Mavro backed away. Surrounded by the glaring faces of
the undead filled with malignant and cannibalistic
intent, he was paralysed. The shotgun felt awkward in his
hands. He held it up, retreating steadily. No way was he
going back for the girl. She was forgotten the moment he
saw those things emerge.

Gilligan bellowed in anguish, pausing momentarily as
he saw the mastiff felled. The lead pipe rising and falling,
slick with dark red matter, was permanently etched on his
memory. Gilligan had rage in his heart and a desire for
vengeance. He drove on at the creatures. Bane realised he
was not going to stop.

Gilligan reached the first zombie which had shambled
ahead of the group. He gripped it hard around the waist.
Heaving it up above his head, he smashed the creature
down across his knee. The spine crunched.

He floored a second with a heavy punch to the jaw,
breaking its neck but the numbers around him were
growing and he was fighting blindly, tears in his eyes.

'Shoot, Mavro,' Bane shouted, as the zombies started to
encircle the barman.

The doctor started at the order. He twitched and the
gun went off in his hands, severing a link in the chained
sign that rocked above him.

There was a crack and then the sound of lurching metal
as the sign swung free, hoisted by what was left of the

chain on the other side and driven by the impetus of its own weight. Bane reached Mavro and threw himself at him, bringing him down as the massive sign swung overhead. He watched as it continued across the street, ploughing deep into the dirt, the stink of wet metal wafting in its wake, a sudden rush of air passing his ear. It was headed straight for Gilligan.

'Gil,' Bane cried.

The barman turned. The rage in his eyes turned to shock and then panic as the hefty sign smashed into him. It was only a glancing blow, but it was enough to take him off his feet. Mercifully, the impact threw him clear of the hordes, out into the street where he lay still.

Lying on his stomach, Bane heard Jarla scream before he saw the sign mash into the tenement, sending chunks of plascrete and debris flying. A moment passed. Then there was a harsh cracking, splitting noise and the throaty rumble of shifting stone as the building started to collapse. Chunks of masonry fell from the highest apartments above. Two zombies were crushed as they wandered into its path. A pillar split and toppled, and then the entire tenement collapsed. It buried the zombies beneath as the roof fell straight down, the supporting walls, reinforced steel rods bending under the immense pressure, cascading outwards. The tenements were some of the highest buildings in Former Glory, built without safety in mind, only the need to pack in as many bodies as possible. It came crashing down like a felled tower of cards. It was a fitting, if ironic, tomb for the living dead.

Huge clouds of dust kicked up by the fall gushed into the air, covering everything nearby. The demolition closed off most of the street, the rubble so high it granted them a reprieve. The shambling horde would have to scramble over the debris to get to them.

Bane spat out a mouthful of dust-clogged air as he dragged himself to his feet. He ran over to Gilligan. Jarla was already there, kneeling at her father's side.

Incredibly, the barman was conscious.

'Thought you were dead,' Bane said.

'Get me up,' Gilligan spat. His face was pale, smeared with blood from a cut across his forehead and half-coated in dust. The cut was a flesh wound, the real damage was inside and to his leg; Bane could see the impact marks where the sign had hit him. It had torn his clothes, even gone through the leather apron he wore. A purple bruise blossomed beneath. It was bad. If the sign had hit him full, he would probably be dead.

'Can you walk?' Bane asked, vaguely aware of Jarla's faint sobbing next to him. Despite everything, she was holding together.

Gilligan heaved himself up with a massive effort, so he was close to Bane's ear. 'Just get me up,' he snarled. 'I'll do the rest.'

'Lyle,' Bane called the prospector over. 'We need to get him moving,' Bane said, flashing a glance at the dust settling over the rubble. 'I don't know how much time we've got.'

Gilligan cried out when they lifted him and they nearly fell. Though not as big as Oheb, the barman was still bulky and at first he could not take his own weight. Bane was exhausted and Lyle injured and the two of them struggled to hold him upright, although the thought of the zombie horde leant strength to their muscles.

Gilligan swallowed the pain, remembering back to those last few fights in the pits, when he knew his body could not take it anymore. It was screaming at him now to stop, to rest, even to give in but he was defiant and with gritted teeth he hobbled onwards.

'Where's Jarla?' he breathed. She was ahead, scavenging in the wreckage of another dilapidated building. Finding what she was looking for, she ran across to him.

'Father,' she said, appearing meekly at his side. She clutched a bent steel rod in her hand and was wrapping a wad of thick cloth around the l-shaped end. 'Take this.'

Bane helped Gilligan put the makeshift crutch under his arm to support the broken leg. It was a good fit.

'Nothing, my little girl can't fix,' he said lovingly, stroking her cheek with his free hand. The pain from the effort made him wince and Jarla's face became knotted with concern.

Bane picked up the shotgun from where Mavro had dropped it. Looking up, he noticed shapes emerging through the dust. On bent, misshapen limbs, the zombies clambered across fallen stone, shattered piping and the pitiful belongings once owned by the now plague-addled occupants.

'Get moving,' he ordered. 'Into the access tunnel.'

They reached it before any of the zombies made it into the street. A rusty, wire-link fence barred their advance at the mouth of the tunnel. The fence had a gate, a crude padlock held it shut, a thick chain wreathed through it.

Bane hammered the lock free with two blows from the shotgun's stock. The broken lock fell to the ground. Bane dragged the chain free and yanked open the fence. Once they were all on the other side, he shut it again, wrapping the chain back around.

'Lyle, your hammer,' he said. Lyle left Gilligan propping himself up with the makeshift crutch. The barman had got used to walking with it and could do so unassisted.

Bane took the hammer and wrapped each end of the chain around the two ends of the long haft. The heavy hammer made it hard work. Once he was satisfied that the chain was attached, he began winding it clockwise. The chain dragged in with each successive rotation. Lyle saw Bane's plan and gripped one end of the hammer. The two men then proceeded to wind the hammer end over end, the chain tightening gradually as they did so. Once it was taut they gave it a few more, laboured turns, heaving hard to make the gate secure.

Bane leant his back against it, the wire rattling against his weight. Gasping for breath, he looked up into the gloom. Overhead, an electrical storm raged, massive power conduits shorting and thick energy cables sparking with life, filling the sky with iridescent amethyst and azure. High above, hive technicians would be working frantically to stabilize the power fluctuations, to the Underhivers far below it was the closest thing to nature's wrath they would ever see.

The sporadic energy bursts hinted at the vast skeleton of superstructure above, the foundations of higher levels built on top of those below. It lit up great gouts of cloud and noxious gas lingering in the false stratosphere. Huge atmosphere compressors and suction vents in Hive City many miles above pumped them downwards into the Underhive. Banks of filtration units raised high on the stalks of lofty metal towers were meant to dissipate the gas, but were prone to malfunction. Particularly bad malfunctions would result in a dense fog. It was called 'creeper', on account of it clinging to the ground due to the gaseous combination's density. Warning clarions would be sounded, signalling people to get indoors, to put on re-breathers if they had them. It looked like a creeper fog was imminent, but there was no one to sound the alarm. The living dead roamed the Underhive, and no breath passed through their lungs, nor was there compassion in their still hearts or jealously of the privileged masses above. Only hunger drove them. They were less than beasts.

Bane looked down at the bedraggled band of survivors. They were looking at him too, for guidance, for leadership. It was an alien feeling.

Why am I doing this, he thought as he regarded their faces? I don't need them. I can find Alicia by myself. They're slowing me down. He could leave them once they got to the Watch House. It wouldn't be hard, just hunker down for the night and fortify the building. He could tool up and slip out unnoticed. They couldn't follow. Gilligan could barely walk and Lyle's wound slowed him too. Of the able bodied, Jarla was a sixteen year-old girl who wouldn't leave her father and Mavro was a spineless bastard who'd be dead in a heartbeat without them. As for Ratz, he was just frikking crazy. It would be easy. But then he thought of Alicia. She was why he was here. She was his chance at redemption. But it wasn't just her, maybe this was part of it too.

'Come on,' Bane said at last, 'they can't be far behind. The Watch House isn't much farther.' He checked the ammo in the shotgun. There were three rounds. 'We can all rest there.'

As he walked past, Gilligan gripped his shoulder. Bane turned to find him looking him in the eye. He found sincerity there.

'I misjudged you. I'm sorry.'

It was a big thing for him to say. He had never known Gilligan to apologise. This man had always regarded him as a drunken skank. It made Bane's answer all the harder.

'No, you didn't.'

CHAPTER: FIVE

THE WATCH HOUSE was deserted. Outer walls circumventing the main building provided a plascrete perimeter. Razorwire crested it like some sharp and deadly crown. A steel gate with a viewing hatch led through to the Watch House itself. It was wide open, bent and twisted as if it had been pulled. There were blood stains on it.

Bane approached the gate. His head spun. His body burned. Whilst they had been fleeing for their lives, he had forgotten about the stimm-cravings and crushed them to almost nothing. Now they were back and he was feeling it; withdrawal was tough.

The blood on the gate was dry, possibly a few days old, judging by the colour. Bane looked back at the group, a few metres away, scared yet hopeful. There was no way they could see how shitty he looked from here. If this was going to work, if they were going to get out of Former Glory alive, he would need their confidence. He wiped the sweat from his face and neck with his jacket sleeve. He realised abruptly that he stank. Satisfied he looked fairly together, Bane hurried back to the group, keeping his head low.

'There's blood on the gate,' he admitted, aware of the sudden panic welling amongst the survivors. 'I think it's old, a few days maybe.'

'Lyle,' he said, 'you and I are going to check it out.'

The prospector nodded.

'You got another weapon?' Bane asked him, unhitching his machete.

Lyle took out a small pick from his belt and swung it ably in one hand.

Bane turned to Mavro. 'You take this,' he told him, offering the shotgun.

Mavro folded his arms and backed away. 'I won't touch it,' he rasped, flashing a dark glance at Gilligan. 'Besides, won't you need it?'

'No,' Bane was emphatic. 'If we find anything in there we'll be running, not fighting. You'll be covering our escape and protecting yourselves if those frikkers make it through the tunnel.'

'I won't touch it.' Mavro repeated, shaking his head.

Bane advanced, clenching a fist.

'Give it to me,' Gilligan said.

Bane looked over to him. 'You sure?'

'I can handle it.'

Bane cocked it and gave him the shotgun. 'Three rounds left,' he warned.

'I understand.'

With that, Bane nodded to Lyle and the two of them scurried over to the gate.

The Watch House's exterior was a steel and plascrete composite. Thick buttresses supported three walls, and a tower with search light and heavy stubber emplacement rose twenty metres or so above them all. It was well fortified, although nothing like the Enforcer precincts uphive, but a bastion nonetheless, especially when compared with the diminutive habs and low-grade refineries that surrounded it. The zone was largely industrial. Gantries criss-crossed high overhead, pipes and access ladders ran up the steel walls of disused silos and gas vented sporadically from vent grills, relieving the pressure from heat conductors and cooling electrical relays that provided the area with power. At the centre of the area was the Watch House; the cold, beating heart of the area.

A short run of steps led up to the main doors. On either side were large meshed windows. No light emanated from them. The main door was open.

Bane held up his hand, falling back on his signal code. He proceeded through the door, edging it open further with the tip of the machete blade. Darkness prevailed inside, a greyish haze invading through the mesh windows and a skylight overhead. Strips of amber emergency lighting winked intermittently on the floor, doing little to alleviate the gloom. Going further, Bane noticed more old blood smears on the floor. A desk was upturned. Two metal data-file cabinets lay on top of it at angles forming a barricade. Papers and holo-plates were littered underfoot; Bane cracked one as he stepped on it.

He froze, listening hard. His beating heart mocked him. A metal gun rack hung in ruins from a single bolt on a flanking wall. It was empty. Some shell casings were scattered around it, as if whoever had been loading the weapons was in a hurry and had dropped them. Bane moved to the back of the office. Tentatively, he edged down a narrow corridor. A smashed halogen strip lamp above him, shattered plastek on the floor beneath. Two anterooms led off. They flanked each other in a kind of cross-junction. A bunk, latrine, a globe-lamp and a desk adorned with random junk, were in each. Other than that, they were empty. The corridor went on for a few more metres. At the end was a thick metal trapdoor. The automated lock pict-display read in hazy crimson, 'SECURE'.

Bane sighed in relief. He moved quickly back through the room to the doorway where Lyle was waiting anxiously.

'Wave 'em in. It's clear.'

THE WATCH HOUSE door closed with a dull thud. For a moment they waited in the darkness. They had all been like that for so long that it seemed unnatural to do anything else. A chorus of exhaling breath, exhaustion tinged with relief, accompanied the silence.

Bane wrinkled his nose at the stagnant air. It smelled like death. The creatures had been here. Some kind of battle had taken place. Moving over to a plastek unit on the wall, he flicked a switch. There was a shallow hum as atmospheric purifiers in the ceiling went to work.

'Get the blinds.' Bane's voice was deep and low.

Lyle and Mavro, standing near the two windows, obliged. Blinds engaged, Bane threw the main power switch. Flickering, stuttering halogen strip lights – those that had not been shattered – came to life. It was a dull light, Bane had made the necessary adjustments to ensure it, but at least they could see.

'Rest,' he told them. 'We're safe, at least for now.'

Gilligan slumped in a nearby chair. He looked pale and drawn, the chase had taken a lot out of him. Jarla crouched alongside her father as the others all found places to crash.

Bane called her over. He was going through a desk drawer. He found what he was looking for. Placing the medi-kit on the desk, he looked up at Jarla. She returned his look with silent resolve. Maybe she was not so coddled after all.

'You know how to use this?' Bane spoke softly, indicating the medi-kit.

Jarla nodded.

'Good. Lyle has cuts that need patching up and burns that require ointment.'

'I understand,' she said, taking the box over to Lyle who resisted at first, claiming he was ok. At Jarla's quiet insistence he relented.

Meanwhile, Bane went through the second drawer. A bottle of grain liquor lay nestled beneath some old paperwork. He licked his lips and reached for it. He stopped, a fingertip away, hand shaking. He glanced up at Gilligan, who had his eyes closed and was leaning back. The old

man was breathing hard and heavy. Nothing in the kit
could do anything for him. The barman's words, his
vouch of confidence in the tunnel came back to him. He
shut the drawer slowly and swallowed.

'Tempted?' Mavro's voice was insinuating. Bane had
not even heard him slink over to him. He returned
Bane's initial shocked expression with one of quiet confidence and veiled malice. The razorblade was back in
his hands and he flicked it back and forth, absent-mind-
edly.

Bane ignored him, turning back to look in the third
drawer. There was a stub gun inside. He cradled it in his
palm and checked the ammo – a full clip. That was good.

Then he smelled Mavro's breath, sweet and sickly, and
felt it on his cheek as the doctor got close. 'Because if that
liquor's not enough, I've got something that'll ease your
pain.'

Bane turned to him again. He knew what Mavro was
talking about. The craving came back, forceful and insistent. It gnawed at him. He felt it in his gut.

'The pain you feel for that little girl,' the doctor continued. 'The reason you're even here,' he spat beneath his
breath, angry this time, eye-to-eye.

'Back off,' Bane warned, a little uncertainly. He jabbed
the stub gun surreptitiously into Mavro's stomach to
emphasise the point.

The doctor looked down and almost gasped. The razor
in his hand stopped abruptly but he clawed back his
resolve. He backed away slowly. 'You'll be back,' he
mouthed, before retreating into the corner.

Bane watched him go. He tucked the stub gun into the
back of his trousers. It nestled next to his service pistol,
which he had kept for some reason. Bane considered
leaving it behind in the drawer but thought better of it
and cast his jacket behind him again, covering both
weapons. Kneeling down, he started to sift through the
papers and holo-picts on the floor. Most of the picts

were shattered and the papers revealed little, just arrest records and administrative data.

'What are you looking for?' It was Lyle. Jarla had done a good job. She had mopped up the blood and stitched the cut, sealing it with adhesive gel. The burn on the prospector's neck still looked raw but at least it was clean; a thin gauze dressing overlaid the worst of it. Bane suspected she had used what was left of the roll.

'Something about what the hell is happening,' Bane answered. 'Watch Houses are the first and only link between Underhive settlements and the Enforcement Precinct houses uphive. If this neurone plague is as bad as I think it is, then they would issue an alert or there'd be clues, an upturn in cannibalistic crimes. But there's no record, just something about increased raids on guilder caravans.'

'Wouldn't you already know?' Lyle asked, 'As the Watchman, I mean.'

'I was held captive for three months before all this started. My deputy, MacDaur, should've dealt with any communication from the precincts.'

'Your deputy? Where is he?'

Shuffling through some scattered papers, Bane saw another large blood smear ingrained in the floor.

'I don't know.'

Lyle went quiet when he saw the blood smear and realised what it implied. He quickly changed the subject.

'Perhaps Doc Mavro should take a look at the barman,' he suggested.

Bane looked over at Gilligan. He looked like he was asleep, chest rising erratically.

'No point,' he said, averting his gaze to Mavro who was listening to them. 'He's not that kind of doctor.'

Bane got up and walked away before Lyle could question him further. End of conversation.

Bane went into one of the anterooms. Crouching down, he looked beneath the bunk and found a shallow, large metal chest. There was a clenched fist insignia rendered in gold-replica on the lid; the symbol of the Enforcement.

Bane unclasped the lid and slowly opened it. Within, transparent plas-sheeting covered a black jacket and trousers. Bane took them out and placed them reverently on top of the bunk. Beneath the attire was a pair of black boots, similarly preserved and polished. These too he put on the bunk.

Standing, he shrugged off the filthy, stinking corpse tinker's coat he had stolen and removed the worn boots and pants, setting both guns he had tucked there on the desk next to the globe-lamp. Both packages were wax sealed with the same insignia on the chest stamped onto them. Bane broke both seals carefully. He pulled out the jacket first, holding it up in the wan light cast by the globe. It was his service uniform. He had worn it only once before, when he hadreceived his long service medal, the one that came with the pistol. The silver clasps that ran down the left breast still shone. The lapels bore his rank in gold threaded filigree. A plain belt finished the ensemble, the clenched-fist insignia rendered in silver for a buckle. The rubric beneath read in tiny engraved script *Firmitas ex Justitia* – Strength from Justice.

It had been a long time since he had thought about those words.

Bane put it on and then the trousers that were adorned with diagonal slashes of gold thread down the outer seam. Donning the boots, he stood and clasped the jacket belt shut. There was no weapons harness, so both pistols went into the back of the trousers like before. It felt good, not just because he had shed the wretched garments of the tinker. It felt as if he had made a choice – the first in many years.

Bane was about to re-join the group when a resonant clang, dull and distant, echoed beneath him. He stopped and listened. It happened again, coming from the trap-door. Bane was out in the corridor. Lyle joined him,

Mavro loitering a way behind. Neither could conceal their reaction to Bane's attire. He ignored it.

'What's down there?' Lyle asked, realising it had come from the trapdoor.

'The cells and armoury, but it's secure I checked it.' Bane waited. The noise came again.

'Go get the shotgun,' he said, pulling out the stubber.

Lyle was back quickly, shotgun in hand. Mavro stayed back, Ratz had wandered over with him. 'They took it,' he mumbled. 'It spoke to me and they took it.'

'Get him out of here and stay with Gilligan and his daughter,' Bane ordered. Mavro was too afraid to argue or backtalk this time. Instead, he grasped Ratz by the collar and hauled him away.

Once they were gone, Bane turned to Lyle. Both of them were crouching next to the trapdoor.

'I assume you're accustomed to tight spaces,' he said.

The prospector snorted his amusement. 'Home from home,' he replied, gripping the shotgun tightly.

Bane turned back to the trapdoor. A keypad operated the locking mechanism. It had had been a while and a whole lot of liquor since he had last opened it.

The first attempt failed. He could feel the tension rising. He tried again. Another clank from below, but still nothing. Wiping sweat from his brow, he tried a third time. There was a faint clunk and the crimson display script changed to green.

Pneumatic wedges punctuated the trapdoor's bare metal surface at intervals. As Bane released each one there was a shallow hiss as the pressure was released. All four wedges disengaged and Bane slid the hatch open. A short stairway and a low sloping tunnel led down about three metres, from there the darkness beckoned them.

'Ready,' he mouthed.

Lyle nodded and they entered. They reached the slope quickly. It was a narrow tunnel but Bane had enough room to hug the left wall, giving Lyle space to bring the shotgun to bear if needed. Bane kept his stub pistol outstretched in a two-handed grip. He hoped in the gloom that Lyle did not see his hands shaking.

After about ten metres the slope flattened out and plastek cracked and crunched underfoot from broken overhead strip lighting, the sound was becoming a regular motif.

'Slowly,' Bane hissed, as loud as he dared, as they passed through the cells. Bane checked left and right, moving into the middle of the tunnel, searching the darkness for movement, listening intently. The clanking, which now sounded more like hammering, continued in sporadic bursts.

They passed ten cells, five either side, all empty. There was a door ahead. Bane raised his fist when they were almost upon it. Lyle knew enough to realise it meant stop. Then Bane raised his index finger on the same hand and circled it clockwise. Lyle understood and moved around to stand on Bane's right. The tunnel had branched out slightly into a wider cordon and the two of them could stand on either side of the door.

Bane crouched and listened at the door jam. Voices, faint, whispering. Two, maybe three men. One grunted as he struck something hard, metal on metal – that was the hammering sound they had heard.

The door was slightly ajar. Bane eased it open further, very slowly. He peered inside.

Three shadowy figures stood in a small anteroom, crowding around a fortified door that led off from the armoury. An access hatch led out from the back of the room. It was locked too. The vehicle yard lay beyond. One of the shadows, huge, almost as big as Oheb, worked at the fortified door with a long metal spike. It looked like a railing he had ripped straight out of the ground. Sparks flew with each massive blow aimed at the locking mechanism. Another shadow stood next to him, shorter but well-built, judging by the width of his shoulders. He carried a portable halo-lantern on low power, its faint blue radiance was just enough for the giant to see what he was doing. The feeble light cast them into silhouette. The third was tall and had a different bearing to the rest. He stood back, observing.

Bane glanced up at the ceiling. The halogen strip unit was still intact. The room was sealed, no reason why they could not use it, probably force of habit. Light attracts them – it had become part of Bane's survival dogma.

Three against two, he did not like those odds. Then he saw something that would tip them in his favour.

ONCE HE WAS certain that Lyle was ready, Bane wrenched open the door and activated the strip light. Stark light blazed angrily into the room, exacerbated by the white wash interior. Bane opened his eyes and bellowed.

'Don't move!' He was in a crouched position, Lyle stood over him, shotgun covering all three. Wearing sleeveless, black jackets replete with iron shoulder plates, white waist sashes and bandanas discoloured at the slag face, they were every inch House Orlock.

They cowered against the sudden burst of light. Only one, the ganger who stood back from the other two, had drawn autopistols, one in each hand.

'Hold your arms,' Bane warned, finger on the trigger, heart thrashing in his chest.

In the light, he had a chance to examine them more closely. The big guy at the back had arms like girders. Smelting scars ravaged them, overlaying numerous tattoos beneath. His face was similarly adorned; a bird of prey, possibly a spire-hawk, dominated the entire left side like war paint. On the right a curved sword rendered in black, small, just under the eye. Thick, iron-shod boots covered his feet and a heavy bolter rig that could only be his lay on the floor a few feet away. The belt-feed was almost expended.

The second ganger, the one with the halo-lantern, had a knife at his belt but no other visible weapons. A shock of grey spiked hair jutted from his head where he wore a crown of iron. His nose was flat, as if it had been broken. It looked like the crown was bolted into his skull, bandana wrapped around it. Fewer scars and gang tatts this one but with hairy arms.

The last was the leader. Slightly built but still muscular, something about the coldness in his ice blue eyes gave Bane pause. His hair was cut down to small jutting spikes and two, evenly spaced furrows shaved into it revealed bare skin. A long, sleeveless leather coat hung down to the floor. The twin autopistols never wavered in his grasp which was light and poised. Both weapons were trademark, not out of the weapon shops of House Orlock, possibly Van Saar tech with some personal customisation. Each stock was steel tipped and shaped into a skull. A gunfighter. All three wore factory-grade work pants, grey and coarse. Each bore the blade tattoo beneath their right eye. The leader had one on his shoulder too. Bane recognised it.

'So what now officer?' the leader asked. 'We wait like this until we grow weary or until you twitch and I shoot you both.'

Lyle re-adjusted his grip, anxious.

'Easy Lyle,' Bane assured him. 'If they were going to shoot, they would've done it by now.'

'Is that right?' the leader purred. He had an accent, an ethnic hive settlement lilt that Bane could not place. Well spoken too, it suggested Hive City education at the very least. There was something about him. Bane had seen his face before.

'I know you,' he said.

'And I've definitely heard of you,' the Orlock returned. The calm of his demeanour was unnerving.

Bane sniffed dismissively. 'I don't doubt it. You're Grakken Nark.'

'Who?'

'Leader of the Sabres, militant gang faction of House Orlock, an overlord, cold-blooded killer, gun fighter and wanted outlaw, and if you had any ammunition in those pistols we'd probably be dead already.'

'Looks like I had you all wrong. I heard Sergeant Erik Bane, disgraced *ex*-enforcer, was a drunk and a stimm-freak, sump fodder for the lash worms. Yet here you are, decked in parade finest pulling your guns on me,' Nark replied. 'Of course, some of your information is erroneous.'

Bane's heart skipped a beat and he kept his eyes fixed on Nark's trigger fingers. 'What would that be?'

'I don't kill in cold blood,' he said smiling, returning both pistols, smoothly, expertly into a twin hip holster. His mood grew suddenly more serious. 'Every man and woman I ever killed had a gun in their hand.' Nark waited a moment. He let the silence grow; let it gnaw at the nerves. 'So, I repeat,' he said finally, smiling again. 'What's it to be?'

Bane thought a moment. His arm ached from holding out the stub pistol, knees too from being crouched. 'Keep that shotgun on them, Lyle.'

The prospector nodded, mustering his courage.

Bane got to his feet, tucking the pistol back behind him.

'Would I be right in thinking that pistol didn't come with the formal attire?' Nark gibed.

Bane ignored him, instead he said.

'You've seen what's happening outside on the streets. The plague, I mean.'

'I've seen it,' Nark's response was dark. 'We fought them three levels down. Got separated from the rest of my crew. Reached this dump and the ammo ran dry. Only places that have still got any guns left are those that are locked tight. A Watch House seemed a good choice.'

'I should arrest you,' Bane told him. 'You're a wanted criminal and it's my duty to uphold–'

Nark cut him off. 'You're upholding nothing right now, friend. Did you find peace in that last bottle? I've got to tell you that uniform is fooling no one.' Serious again. It was difficult to gauge his mood.

'I assume this chipper is the best you've got,' the gang lord continued, looking at Lyle, 'which means you got nothing.' Nark came forward, utterly fearless considering a loaded shotgun was pointed at him. He got close. 'You need us. We need you.'

Bane opened his mouth to reply when a heavy thud came from beyond the door that the gangers were trying to wrench open.

All of them turned. Lyle swung the shotgun instinctively but dragged it back quick when he realised he was not covering the gangers. Bane had drawn his stubber. Nark too had both autopistols in his hands, even though they were empty – a conditioned reflex.

The big Sabre backed away from the door, holding the metal spike at his waist like a spear. The other one downed the halo-lantern and took out his knife.

More thuds.

'You want a truce?' asked Bane, pistol trained on the door, heart pumping. 'You've got one.'

'Good,' Nark replied. 'The brute's called Skudd,' he added – the spear-wielding Orlock nodded – 'and that hairy bastard is Zeke the Wulf.' Zeke responded with a wink.

'You know me. That's Lyle,' Bane said, indicating the prospector. 'There are others upstairs, survivors.'

'Now we're all acquainted, you think we can open that damn door?' Nark's voice betrayed his fear, buried as it was beneath his cold bravado.

'The code is "Elysium",' said Bane. 'Input that into the panel. I assume you can read Necromundan-Gothic.'

Nark nodded at Skudd, the brute set the spike down and worked the keypad according to Bane's instruction. A shallow hiss emanated from the locking mechanism and then came the scraping metal retort of retracting dead-bolts.' Open it,' Bane demanded, moving opposite the door.

Skudd looked to his leader, who nodded his approval. The big Orlock took hold of the inset handle and pulled.

The door lurched open, screeching loudly. Bane was about to move forward when a shot rang out from inside. He threw himself prone and rolled to the side, the shot narrowly missing as it imbedded harmlessly into the plascrete wall behind him. Nark had already moved to the blind side of the opening, like Skudd, using the door as cover.

Another shot came from the dark within.

'Cease fire!' Bane cried, 'Cease fire.'

A voice came out of the shadows at him. 'Bane, is that you?'

Bane heaved a sigh of relief and let his head sag. Holstering the stubber, he got to his feet and approached the armoury door. A figure stepped out from the gloom brandishing a halogen strip lamp, re-breather hanging around his neck, autogun in his hand.

'Stand down,' he said to Lyle and his new allies. 'It's my deputy, MacDaur.'

MacDaur was young, barely mid-twenties with a thin rash of stubble around his chin and neck, and dark brown hair cropped short but not shaved. A long Watchman's coat hung from broad shoulders, beneath it a worn, charcoal body glove. Leather, fingerless gloves covered both hands and a red neckerchief sat snug under his chin. The re-breather overlaid it. A belt of ammunition around his waist was barely touched. A small black tome was hanging by gold brocade at his hip, a clenched fist, etched in silver adorned the cover. It was a law codex – the legal bible for all Watchmen that cared to read it. Most did not bother.

His expression was one of surprise and relief. 'Bane, I thought you were dead.' It quickly turned to shock and belligerence. 'What the hell are you doing with gangers?'

A scream, muffled by layers of plascrete and steel, prevented Bane from answering. 'They must be inside,' he rasped. 'Upstairs, now.'

MacDaur led the way, the Sabres followed at Bane's insistence. They didn't even have time to arm themselves. Skudd toted his metal spike and Zeke wielded a knife.

'Here,' Bane cried, tossing the machete to Nark who caught it effortlessly. Lyle, shotgun at the ready brought up the rear with Bane.

When Bane emerged from the trapdoor, MacDaur's autogun was barking loudly. Skudd was at one of the windows, heaving a data-file cabinet to hold up the battered mesh. Beyond it, the zombies clawed and snarled. The second window was already broken through, the mesh lay crushed and crumpled beneath it, torn blinds and shattered glass entangled with it.

MacDaur raked the gaping window. Plascrete chips flew and gore spattered the immediate area around it as hordes of the foul creatures poured in. Gilligan was on his back, wrestling with a zombie. Jarla fought it too but it was impossible to see if they were winning. Nark and Zeke, back-to-back, cut a bloody swathe through the creatures surging into the room. Mavro cowered behind the upturned desk, holding Ratz down. The outlander screamed and wailed as if he was pumped with too much spook.

Clumsy and slow, the zombies were ineffective fighters, but there were so many. One bite and it was over. They needed space to keep clear of their undead assailants, something that inside the confines of the upper office of the Watch House was gradually diminishing.

'Help me get to Gilligan and Jarla,' Bane bellowed at Lyle, who was just coming up from the trapdoor.

Bane ran. The thunderous retort of the shotgun erupted behind him and a zombie in front of him lost an arm and part of its head. The thing slumped to the ground in a smoking ruin. A second lunged at him, arms outstretched, snarling to reveal blackened nubs for teeth. Another explosion. Bane felt fire at his cheek, and the creature was tossed into the air like a macabre doll. A third felled another zombie, destroying its legs and abdomen. Three shots. The shotgun was empty. He was on his own.

Bane approached the zombie torso which had heaved itself up onto its belly and was crawling. Two sharp shots from the stub pistol and it lay still. He reached Gilligan and Jarla and kicked off the first zombie which was trying to take a chunk out of Gilligan's arm. Jarla held a second zombie at bay with the makeshift crutch. Bane shot it. Crouching down, he hooked an arm underneath Gilligan's shoulder and pulled. The barman cried out in pain. He was heavy and Bane could not get him to his feet. Jarla screamed. Another zombie came at them but one of its arms was broken, and it held the other out toward them. Bane fired twice and got it in the neck and eye, right before the stubber clicked empty.

They had to get out. No way could they fight them off, even with the extra muscle from the Sabres.

'Skudd,' Bane roared over the chaos. The big Orlock turned; he had since dropped the spike. Both arms were braced against the data-file cabinet he was using to block the first window. He understood instantly. He pushed into the cabinet, mashing it through the bent mesh of the window, crushing the zombies outside as it landed on them. He moved, quickly and certainly, picking up Gilligan in his stride but grimaced with the effort.

'Back to the armoury,' Bane said. 'Everyone.'

MacDaur covered the retreat, cutting into the vile press of living corpses swelling inside the room with his autogun. He and Bane were the last out. The trapdoor slammed shut and darkness engulfed them.

'Where's Lyle?' Bane asked urgently. He had not seen him get inside.

'He didn't make it,' an impassive voice came from the blackness. It was Nark. The gang lord's eyes glinted. 'They dragged him down, easy meat. That's all any of us are now.'

'I didn't even see him,' Bane breathed. Above there was the *thunk* of flesh on metal as the zombies tried in vain to pound their way inside.

Bane ignored it and slumped against the cold wall of the tunnel, closed his eyes hard and clenched a fist. He breathed deep, thought about Alicia and found strength. Standing, he realised he was alone but still needed weapons. The armoury was ahead.

The Sabres were already tooling up. Skudd draped two belts of heavy bolter shells over each shoulder like the vestments of some violent priest. Zeke carried a lasgun; two stub pistols were tucked in a weapons belt across his torso. He rammed power packs and clips into a large ammo pouch, throwing Nark two full clips for his autopistol; four more went in with the other spare munitions.

Bane's instincts told him it was a mistake to let them raid the armoury, but what choice did he have? Lyle was dead which left just him and MacDaur. It was not enough. He entered the fortified room and found it nearly stripped bare. A bolt pistol lay on a metal small arms rack. He took it, along with three clips and some spare ammo for the stubber. MacDaur holstered another pistol, a snub-nosed las, and hoisted a shotgun onto his back.

A glass case at the back of the room got Bane's attention. Using the butt of the bolt pistol he smashed it open. Reaching inside, he took out a combat shotgun, shaking off the broken glass. Short stock, half barrel, complete with a black leather shoulder harness – a quick-loader. It bore the Enforcement insignia. No trigger guard meant

quicker reaction time. A box of shells lay on red velvet
next to it. Donning a Watchman's coat, dangling on a
nearby hook, Bane emptied the shells into one of the
pockets. Each tip was engraved with a tiny skull – Executioner rounds.

'Beyond that hatch is a sub-basement, the Watch House
vehicle yard,' Bane's voice invaded the feverish activity as
he nodded towards the exit at the back of the room. It got
their attention. Securing his weapons, he turned to Mac-
Daur. 'We still got the *Bull*?'

MacDaur nodded.

'Good.'

THE SUB-BASEMENT was about thirty feet in all directions,
with reinforced plas-steel walls. A key-pad was bolted to
one of them, providing the only illumination in the pitch
black. Bane threw an unseen switch. A hanging light array
thudded into life above them. It revealed a stocky vehicle,
armour-plated on all sides with thick mesh over the forward arc vision slits and three meaty-looking, chain-tread
reinforced wheels on either flank. A heavy, iron v-shield
at its snout gave it its name, a prison transport – the *Bull*.

'The upper level will be swarming with those things,'
Bane warned them. 'We'll never make it on foot. This is
our best chance at getting out of Former Glory.'

'Getting out to where, Bane?' Nark asked.

Bane's face grew dark. 'There's an Enforcer Precinct
House a few levels up. They'll have troops and weapons.
We head for that.' He fixed the gang lord with a stony
gaze, shaking his head. 'I can't let you go, Nark.'

Nark's eyes narrowed, his face unreadable. 'Sure, sure.'
He headed over to the transport.

Gilligan lay on his back. They had put him in the prisoner bay in the main body of the vehicle. Jarla was with
him, sitting on a metal bunk, clutching the makeshift
crutch for security. She pulled at the sleeves of her jacket,
anxious about her father's condition. Loose restraints

hung above her on a long chain. The back section of the bay was cordoned off by thick bars, a mobile holding cell for particularly recalcitrant law breakers. Ratz and Mavro sat opposite the barman and his daughter. Skudd too, there was no room for him or his cannon up front in the cab. Mavro was dissatisfied about being thrown in with the 'sick, insane and dangerous' – his words, hissed at Bane. Skudd overheard him and was doing his best to freak out the scrawny doctor, intimidating him with his sheer bulk and violent potential.

'I have big hands,' he said, his tenor voice made deeper and more resonant by the metal confines. 'How big is your head friend?' he asked, clenching a mighty fist meaningfully as he stared over at Mavro.

The doctor shrank away but found he had nowhere to go.

A menacing grin split Skudd's tattooed features. 'Think I could fit it in my hand?'

Bane, MacDaur, Nark and Zeke sat up front in the cab. It was a tight squeeze, but there was little in the way of tech to crowd things further: elliptical steering unit, drive lever and three metal foot pedals. Coarse leather seats did little to cushion the bare metal of the cab. A diode read-out displayed fuel, speed and engine temp in dull, green neon. It was stark, cold, heavily industrialised and of House Orlock manufacture. MacDaur had the wheel.

'Sorry I shot at you, Bane,' he said. He knew it might be his last opportunity to say it.

Bane put a hand on his shoulder. 'Next time you're hiding in an armoured room, I'll knock. How long were you in there?'

'Soon as I heard the trapdoor opening, I got inside.'

'I saw blood smears,' Bane said.

'Not mine. I abandoned the upper level after the first sightings. Easier to stay fortified below.'

Bane thought about it for a moment, nodded and stood up, yanking open a metal hatch above him.

'Hold on,' he called below, tapping activation runes on the nearby wall panel. The light array gradually extinguished, powering down with an audible hum that decreased rapidly in pitch. Overhead, the dull whirr of mechanised servos ripped through the dark. The pressurised hiss of activated pneumatics followed. There was a hollow *clank* as four thick chains set at right angles to each other went suddenly taut. Resting on a rectangle of metal, chains steam-bolted securely to each corner, the *Bull* was rising. Four harness-winches, grinding and groaning against its weight, dragged the behemoth up.

Bane left the hatch open and a thin sliver of grey light appeared above him, growing steadily wider with each second; a shrieking protest of age-old gears accompanied every inch. It was thirty feet from floor to ceiling. Their ascent was short-lived. As the *Bull* edged slowly into the light, Bane shut the hatch.

Looking through the forward viewing slit, his vista cut into small sections by the mesh, he saw the horde. The Watch House teemed with the creatures, surging through the gate and past the perimeter walls, roaming outside in hungry packs. The vehicle lift had brought them outside the perimeter wall. The drone of the winch array and the activation of the outer doors had alerted the zombies. They were coming.

'Start her up.' Bane's voice held a hint of urgency.

MacDaur gunned the ignition. The engine juddered, emitted a wailing protest and died. There was a loud thud as a zombie threw itself against the armoured hull.

'Again!' Bane bellowed. The zombie snarled at the vision slit, biting and clawing at the mesh.

The engine juddered and died. Another corpse hit the *Bull*. Then another and another. They hammered at the outer hull, wielding pipes, crowbars and pieces of crudely torn metal.

'MacDaur, get us moving,' Bane urged. Something crawled on the roof. The front arc mesh bent and twisted as the zombies heaved at it.

'I'm trying.' He was sweating and wiped a swathe of it off his forehead. 'Come on, come on!' he cried and punched the starter hard with his fist.

Amidst screeching protests, the engine roared into life. The throaty rumble filled the cab and the massive rear exhausts rattled hard against the metal hull as they belched thick, acrid smoke into the atmosphere.

'Go,' Bane cried. 'Give it everything.'

MacDaur slammed it into drive and smashed the fuel pedal. Tyres squealing, the stench of friction-burned rubber in their nostrils, they surged off the ramp and out into the street. The clinging zombies were thrown free by the sudden lurching movement, some crushed beneath the wheels, others thrown back into the mob surrounding them.

Rotting bodies were smashed aside as MacDaur ploughed through them to a chorus of crushing bone and squashed matter.

After a few minutes, once they were clear, Bane re-opened the ceiling hatch and looked out behind them. MacDaur was heading outwards at full speed, towards the exit tunnels that would lead them up. In the blackening distance the horde was still visible. Hundreds, too numerous to distinguish individually; a single, undead mass bent on consuming all the living they came across.

MacDaur pumped the throttle as they ground up a sluice ramp once used as a sewer tributary. Rising higher, Bane saw that all of Former Glory had been consumed. Vendor's Row, the longest strip in the entire settlement was overrun, a swarm engulfed the industrial sector and the low-riser tenements and even the slums were infected. Flames rose up randomly, surging from the smoke smothered structures. Bane could smell it on the turbine induced breeze, as the air whipped past his face.

The smoke billowed high and dark, coiling black tendrils reaching up. The foul stink of burning, decaying flesh came with it. No one could survive in that. Glory was lost. He only hoped that Alicia was not lost with it.

He came back down into the cab, shutting the hatch and listened to the monotonous engine drone, a slave to his own thoughts.

IT FELT LIKE *they'd been driving for hours. The drone of the engine was strangely soothing, like the dulcet tones of some slumbering, nameless beast. Nearly everyone was asleep and those who were awake were quiet and fixated on their own thoughts. It was worth risking a glance.*

The bite looked bad, worse than before. No one had seen it happen – it had been chaos in the Watchhouse – they'd have been killed by now if anyone had. The half-congealed blood wasn't clotting, the wound a sticky mass of gore and torn skin. They fought the temptation to lick it, taste a piece of flesh.

Someone stirred. They covered up quickly. Closing their eyes they feigned sleep. No one must know. No one must ever find out.

CHAPTER: SIX

'So the plague has infected the badzones too,' Bane said, rattling around in the cab of the *Bull*. He was driving as MacDaur slept next to him. The deputy looked pale and sickly. Lack of sleep and nourishment will do that to you, Bane thought.

'So it seems,' Nark replied, staring out through a vision slit at the harsh grey light of the Underhive. He dug around in the top pocket of his gunslingers' coat and pulled out a dark stick of organic matter. From another pocket he produced a silver igniter with the Sabre motif.

'Kalma-root,' he said, wetting his lips and placing the root between them. A snap of the igniter and the root was lit. Nark took a deep drag, held it for a few seconds and blew a long, thin plume of purple smoke through the mesh. A grin cracked one side of his mouth while the other held the root in place.

'Mellow, yet flavoursome. Want a taste?' he asked.

Zeke who sat next to his leader chuckled under his breath. He was working the ends of stubber rounds with a small, flat-edged file, turning them into dum-dum bullets that were less reliable, but had more stopping power. He pushed each round back into its clip. Once a clip was full he dumped it back into the pouch resting between his legs. He scratched absently at the strip of iron on his head. Bane realised it harboured a skull chip.

He made out scar tissue in the hazy light filtering into the cab.

'Keep it,' Bane said, eyes front. It was tempting. The cravings had diminished to a nagging ache at the back of his head and his throat was dry like grit. He needed to stay focused so he changed the subject. 'What about the rest of your gang? Last count, I heard you were pushing fifty.'

'Try eighty, split right across the Underhive.'

Bane turned to the gang lord in disbelief.

'The Sabres, Ironhammers and Jack-ratchets were all mine,' Nark continued. 'I've got territories the length and breadth, believe me. Before all this Spire-damned shit happened we were in the middle of a turf war. The White Ghosts, whore-son Delaques, raided the Fire Stacks and Ironwater, my territories. We were returning the favour when the corpses showed up. You know the rest.' Nark took another long drag and leaned back in his seat.

'What about the Razorheads, ever get any trouble from them?' Bane's mind flicked back to their lair and his first encounter with the plague zombies. Maybe that was where it all started? The hooded figure rushed back into his thoughts.

'Not for a while. They're downhive, a kilometre or so above the sump, give or take. Rumour was they were connected.'

'Connected?' Bane's interest was piqued.

'Someone with influence or with the means to extort it,' Nark explained.

Bane nodded. He suddenly remembered the plans he had found in the Razors' narco-lab, but he could not recall any details.

A sudden jolt ripped through the *Bull*. A steady thud came from the left side as the vehicle lurched over. Screeching metal resonated within the interior as it started to slew out of control, the cab shaking violently. Bane jerked the steering wheel hard, trying to pull into the skid, but something had snagged them underneath and it would not budge. MacDaur was jarred awake. Nark lost his Kalma-root and it ended up in his lap. He batted frantically at the smouldering tip, perilously close to his crotch, as it rolled back and forth.

Bane felt his head smash into the low roof. White fire blazed for a split second, becoming a hot line of pain as something warm trickled down his face: blood.

'Hold on,' he screamed above the rising din and jammed on the brakes.

Smoke filled the cab through the mesh vents and there was more screeching as the brake blocks ground down to nothing. Eventually the *Bull* skidded to a stop, trawling over a mass of rusted girders and other industrial debris, kicked up into the vision slits as they ploughed through it.

Bane coughed the smoke out of his lungs, wafting it ineffectively out of his eyes and unhitched the ceiling hatch. Nark and Zeke kicked through the mesh of the forward vision slits, unlatching the outer hatches from the inside. MacDaur crawled past the gangers as they heaved themselves out and yanked open the right side access panel. Bane dragged himself up and out of the roof hatch.

'Damn it,' he muttered. The two wheels on the left side were bent inwards and issuing smoke. Steam hissed from the engine block through the gaps in the riveted armour plates. Brake fluid, boiled almost to vapour, spurted from ruptured piping, exposed as the undercarriage plating was torn away.

'Everybody out.'

'THE DRIVE SHAFT is all twisted and the undercarriage is tangled with razorwire.' Jarla's voice was muffled underneath the *Bull*. Skudd pulled her out, Gilligan watching all the time – she was the only one small enough to get under the wrecked transport to take a look. She also knew her way around vehicles.

'Found this embedded in one of the tyres,' she added, getting to her feet, wiping a streak of oil and grime from her face. She brandished a crude-looking iron spike in her hand .

'Stinger.' Nark's voice, nonchalant and confident, emanated from the gloom. 'It's designed to waylay for an ambush.' He was leaning back against the outer hull of the *Bull*, smoking Kalma-root.

Bane regarded their surroundings. They had stopped in a low-tunnel, wide enough to get through with room to spare. But it was dark and crammed with machine junk on either side, creating a predetermined route for a vehicle. In retrospect, the ideal place for an ambush.

'A remnant then,' Bane said. 'Whoever's trap this was is either dead or long gone.'

'Evidently,' Mavro breathed. It was the first time he had spoken since they had been joined by the Sabres.

Bane pretended not to notice. He walked over to Gilligan and spoke softly. 'We'll have to go the rest of the way on foot, Gil.' Bane's eyes held a question.

Ashen faced and bathed in sweat, the barman rasped through gritted teeth. 'I can make it.'

The knuckles on the hand that clutched his make-shift crutch had turned white.

'You don't look so good,' Bane said. He was suddenly aware of the others listening, and swore he could feel Nark's eyes burning into his back.

'I can make it,' he repeated earnestly.

Bane paused for a moment, searching Gilligan's eyes and then nodded. 'Ok.' He turned to address the rest of the group.

'The precinct house is about a kilometre up in that direction,' he said, pointing towards the right fork at the end of the tunnel. 'If we don't stop we can reach it in two, maybe three hours.' Bane turned, about to lead the way when Nark's voice stopped him.

'Sorry lawman but no, we're not going to that precinct house,' he stated calmly.

Bane looked back at him suspiciously. His hand strayed near the bolt pistol. 'What?'

'I've no desire to head into an Enforcer facility where I'll probably be interrogated, incarcerated and possibly executed,' Nark continued, stepping towards Bane. 'No. We take the opposite fork to Traitor's Nest, Sabre territory. Most of my gang should already be there. We need reinforcements and I've also got to make sure no one has moved in on my turf.'

'Nark, if we don't work together there'll be no turf left to fight over,' Bane urged. He couldn't believe what he was hearing. 'We're fighting a war here. Survival, our survival, is the thing at stake.'

'All the same,' Nark replied, 'we *are* going to Traitor's Nest.' There was a shallow *clank* as Skudd cranked a round into his heavy bolter trained on Bane.

MacDaur reached for the pistol in his belt. When he felt the bite of Zeke's lasgun in his back, he put up his arms.

'You can't make it without us, Bane,' Nark informed him. Two sharp clicks and he primed the twin autopistols that had suddenly appeared in his grasp.

Bane clenched a fist. He looked across to Gilligan, struggling to stand. Jarla, at his side, was faltering too. Mavro shrank back into the shadows, barely daring to look, whilst Ratz sat hunched against the tunnel wall, rocking back and forth, and muttering to himself. Even MacDaur looked ragged. Bane fixed Nark with a dark and meaningful glare and reluctantly withdrew his hand from the pistol.

The gang lord nodded his approval. 'Wise choice,' he said. 'Now, hand over your weapons, nice and slow.'

NARK'S ROUTE TO Traitor's Nest took them downhive into the creeping dark of Necromunda's badzones. Hot, stagnant air wafted up through narrow tunnels and blackened crawl spaces, as well as fumes exuded by tar lakes and drift fires. The gang motifs of the Sabres, rendered in black, were daubed onto the dank, curved walls. Further vents and tunnels branching off in all directions, punctuating the vast, vacuous space in which they made their descent, sealed by rusted grates and disused blast doors. There was no sign of the other Sabres though.

They walked in a tight column. Bane took the lead, carrying a halo-lantern. He kept the light weak and shone it at the floor. In the darkness of the Underhive, dead falls and sudden drops were rife and it paid to be careful. Even if the fall did not kill you, the creatures that dwell in the long-forgotten tunnels would. MacDaur walked behind him. Skudd watched them both with his heavy bolter, a few paces back. A pack strapped to his back contained their guns. Then came Gilligan, Mavro supporting him, grimacing with every step. Jarla and Ratz lingered nearby. Nark was at the back, watching the bedraggled survivors.

A dark figure appeared ahead. Bane held up the halo-lantern, risking a little more light. It was Zeke. The ganger rushed past, almost silently, to Nark.

'The watch towers?' asked Nark as Zeke approached.

'Empty and stripped,' Zeke returned darkly.

Nark thought for a moment and nodded for Zeke to go back. As the ganger disappeared into the gloom, he checked both his autopistols for the third time in the last half hour, and gave the order to move on.

THE TUNNEL OPENED onto a large, flat plaza. The first sign of Traitor's Nest were the watch towers. They were set at either flank to the opening; ramshackle structures held aloft by crude iron girders, a box of steel sheeting set on top of each, welded crudely and enclosed by a roof of bent metal. Further in was a building wrought from steel bulkheads, sturdy and wide, that looked like a disused ore-processing plant. Three stacks rose up from it into a high shaft that was a crosshatch of broad gantries, interlinking pipes, thick industrial chains and half broken girders. Two of the stacks had collapsed, sprouting into the air like rotten teeth. A third remained, the metal rungs of an access ladder barely visible. Bane noticed it went as far as an exit hatch set into one of the conjoining pipes above.

Zeke was waiting for them in the shadows, crouched behind a stack of industrial debris, as they reached the outer threshold of the plant.

'Any sign?' Nark asked him, letting Skudd corral the others.

'Nothing,' Zeke replied, 'but this is as far as I got.'

'I don't like it,' he muttered. 'We should've seen someone by now.'

'Maybe they moved on?' Zeke suggested.

'Yeah, but why? I don't see any walking corpses.'

Zeke fell silent.

Nark turned to the group and looked at Bane and Mac-Daur.

'You two first.'

Bane stepped forward and then stopped.

'I'm not going in there without a gun, Nark,' he said.

Nark thought about it for a moment. 'Skudd,' he said. The big Orlock nodded, reaching into his pack. He threw the stubber and MacDaur's laspistol at the men's feet.

As Bane stooped to pick the weapon up, he felt the cold metal of Nark's autopistol at the back of his neck.

'Now I know you won't shoot me in the back, Bane, it's not your style,' he said, 'but don't expect the same courtesy from me.'

Bane arched his head up deliberately so the pistol muzzle pressed harder into his neck and spoke through gritted teeth. 'I thought you never killed in cold blood.'

'True. They all had a gun in their hands, but I never said we were face-to-face.' Nark straightened back up, letting the pistol drop to his side. 'Now get up.'

Bane got to his feet and headed towards the complex, MacDaur right behind him, laspistol in hand.

'And remember,' Nark said. 'Skudd's got your back.'

Bane did not need to turn to know that the heavy bolter was levelled at them both.

A WALL OF steel confronted them, bulkhead plates steam-riveted together. An immense concertina door granted access into the plant itself. Bane noticed a filthy security panel inset into one of the wall plates. He hammered the activation rune. The door retracted with agonising slowness, servos whining and finally clanking noisily into a holding position above.

Darkness beckoned within. Bane was reminded of Toomis Pre-fab Residential. He crushed the memory instantly, reaching for the heavy crank to activate the lights.

'Leave it,' Nark hissed. The gangers were right behind them.

Across a long stretch of bare plascrete, strewn with mechanical debris, rusted piping and other detritus, lay six low-rise smelting vats, visible in the ambient light cast through the open door. The shadows of the survivors were long, crude slashes in it. They shrank and eventually diminished as, with clunking monotony, the concertina unfurled downwards, shutting them all inside. Darkness prevailed and the sound of breathing and uncertain steps was exacerbated.

At Nark's urging, Bane went first, approaching the nearest smelting vat, drawn by a yellow diode winking in its activation slate. MacDaur ranged wide. Skudd followed, covering the angles with his heavy bolter, swinging it back and forth in slow, wide arcs. Nark was three steps behind Bane, eyes narrowed, searching the alcoves and crawl spaces afforded by the flanking walls. Zeke waited with the settlers at the gate.

Reaching the vat, Bane examined the activation slate. He waited for Nark to reach him and pointed at the glowing, yellow diode. It was active, reading low temperature.

Not enough for the smelter to function at production capacity, but enough to generate significant heat to stay warm.

'We're not alone,' Bane breathed.

In the sickly yellow light, Nark's expression was grim.

They moved on and got as far as the second vat when they saw something slumped against the access ramp that led to the observation gantry circumventing the vat itself. Getting close, Nark recognised the body.

'One of mine,' he rasped, reaching over to touch it. 'Lukas.'

'Careful,' Bane warned, readying the stubber.

'Bite marks,' said Nark, tilting up the head to reveal the jugular.

Bane shifted back. He had seen this before.

'Bullet hole to the head,' Nark added.

Bane relaxed, crouching down next to Nark to examine the corpse.

'Rigor has set in,' he began. He pulled at the ganger's shirt, 'See that mark?' the light from the diode illuminated a dark patch of skin, 'It's livid. He died here.' Bane examined further. 'Something else too.'

'What is it?' Nark asked. Skudd and MacDaur congregated around the vat.

Bane turned to Nark.

'He's been stripped of all his weapons and ammo. Recently, I think.'

The gang lord looked at Bane, searching for any hint of deception. When he spoke, he held his gaze without wavering.

'Remember Bane, there's a gun pointed at those settlers,' he said.

'I remember.'

Nark held Bane's gaze for another second, still thinking.

'Skudd,' he said at last, 'give them back their guns.'

* * *

THEY MOVED SLOWLY across the rest of the work yard, inspecting all of the vats in turn but found no more bodies. They even risked the halo-lantern on its lowest setting to be sure. Zeke remained at the gate with the rest of the survivors and only Bane, Nark, Skudd and MacDaur advanced.

At the back of the work yard was another door, a huge sliding blast plate set into the right flanking wall. Nark crouched next to it, listening hard.

Nothing.

'Skudd,' he rasped. Skudd carefully unhitched his heavy bolter, belt-feed and all, and set it down quietly against the wall. In two meaty hands, he gripped the blast plate's entry bar. A glance at Nark to check they were ready. The halo-lantern was extinguished.

Nark nodded and Skudd heaved. The blast door shrieked open. Beyond, bleached white faces, eyes covered by thick black rubber goggles, stared at them in shock and disbelief.

'White Ghosts,' Nark spat maliciously, as if the words left a bitter taste.

'Stinkin' Sabres,' snarled one of them by way of riposte.

Silence descended. It shattered a split-second later into a bout of frantic weapon priming as a mutual threat was realised by both parties. Then the screaming started.

'Don't you frikkin' move!' bawled a Ghost, autopistol quivering in his grasp.

'I'll shoot you, I'll shoot you,' MacDaur raved, thrusting the muzzle of his autogun towards the strangers threateningly.

'You bastards opened the wrong frikkin' door,' another Ghost shouted.

'Down, frikkers, put your weapons down,' screamed Nark. 'You killed Lukas, you bastards!'

'We didn't kill nobody. That fool was already dead,' the pistol toting Ghost protested.

'You killed him and took his gun and ammo.'

'We killed no one in here.'

Bane said nothing, just kept his gun up. There were three guns pointed at them. Skudd was unarmed, screaming with the rest and MacDaur looked about ready to snap. One was a skinny wretch with his teethed gritted. He was young and scared and might pull the trigger out of fear. If that happened... Bane had to do something.

'Stop,' he yelled. 'Stop.' He slowly set down his gun. 'You know about the plague?' he asked the middle Ghost, the trench coat he wore made him a Delaque. It was of a finer quality than the others which made him the leader.

'We've seen it,' he replied, face knotted with belligerence.

'And you're hiding out in here?'

'Yeah, that's right.' Calmer this time, that was better.

'There are a lot of those things out there,' Bane told him, mastering his breathing. 'Could be the entire Underhive is infected.'

'What's your point?' A question. That was good. It meant he was listening.

'Seven guns are better than three, am I right?'

The Ghost licked his lips. Bane could not see whether he was looking at him through the goggles, but he felt his gaze all the time. His trigger finger started to relax.

'All right,' Bane said, gesturing for them to lower their weapons. MacDaur obeyed instantly, setting his autogun down slow and easy, palm raised.

'We've got another guy at the gate,' Bane added. The Ghost leader flinched, yanking the gun back up. Bane showed his palms. 'I'm telling you so you know I'm giving you the truth. There's wounded too, just settlers, they need rest just like you.'

The tension persisted. At first neither side was willing to break the stalemate. Vitriol between the gangs ran deep, that was obvious but there was a mutual goal here: survival. Scores could be settled later. The charged silence continued for a moment more.

Breathing hard, face-to-face, the gangers slowly lowered their weapons.

THEY SEALED THE room, blast doors yanked shut on either side. An uneasy silence descended, fuelled by fear, exhaustion or enmity, or all three at once. They were holed up in the chamber that housed the central blast furnace for the plant, the only functioning blast furnace left in the dilapidated ruin. The fire stack, as it was known, rose into the air, a plascrete sentinel with a heart of burning iron. It was used to melt down ore surplus. A conveyer array once used to facilitate this purpose was dismantled and lay rusting about the chamber, junk like the rest of downhive. A gantry circumvented the stack and from that a ladder bolted to it provided access to higher levels. They had since rotted away to nothing and only a small plateau of rusted metal remained, drenched in a patina of dark soot, seared by burns. Beyond that, a second ladder led to a wide exit pipe in the ceiling.

The stack was the only significant feature in the room, which was vast. Plascrete columns, reinforced by riveted iron plates, stretched down from the ceiling, supporting the roof. A dense network of twisting coolant pipes gave shape to the outer perimeter and surrounded the massive furnace floor, creating hidden alcoves that harboured shadows. Signs, replete with warnings and industrial rubrics hung down from chains attached to the ceiling. These trappings of order and habitation were disquieting.

Bane sat alone in the darkness. They had set up drum fires throughout the massive room, but he preferred to shun the light. His thoughts were dominated by Alicia. He believed she was dead and half expected to find her wielding a rusty pipe and shuffling toward him for a taste of his flesh. Maybe he would let her. Embrace the sweet, painless oblivion. Despair was a heavy weight to bear and Bane felt it rest about his shoulders like a rusted chain. He looked around, trying to wrest himself free of his dark thoughts.

Huddled near the glow of the stack furnace, Gilligan slumbered fitfully on scavenged sacking. Skudd sat cross-legged on the bare plascrete, his heavy bolter dismantled in front of him. He cleaned it meticulously, piece by piece with oil and grease. Zeke stood nearby, back against one of the support columns, lasgun cradled in his hands like a security blanket. His eyes were closed, as if he was sleeping but he seemed oddly alert. MacDaur had crashed out near one of the drum fires. In the flickering light, he looked pale and cold, hugging his legs close to his chest.

The Delaques sat together, away from the rest, around a drum fire. The bright angry light shone off their bald pates.

House Delaque dealt in information and secrets as much as raw, tangible material. Bane hoped to question them once things had settled down some more. They might know something about the spread of the epidemic, or even its cause. Their leader, who called himself Malik, faced him. Black goggle lenses blazed with the reflected glow of the flames and he smiled, exposing cracked, mis-shapen teeth. Next to him another Ghost, Kepke, picked at his nails with a broad, combat knife. The last of them, Spectre, was long-limbed and gaunt; he looked like he was made from bent wire wearing a trench coat too small for him, he shrugged it back over his bare wrists constantly, only for his pointed shoulders to eke it back. He mum-bled, counting off rounds in an autogun clip. Once he finished, he started anew, recounting the whole clip over again. It seemed like a maddening ritual, although some-times that is all you have to keep you sane when the gunfire stops, the smokes clears and the real deamons make themselves known.

In the darkness beyond, sitting alone like Bane, was Nark. A stick of Kalma-root smouldered between his lips, its ephemeral glare revealing Nark's narrow eyes intent on the Delaques. As Bane watched, the root burned to nothing. It must have seared Nark's fingers but he didn't acknowledge it, just took out another root and fired up, all the while his gaze fixed.

'Mr. Bane,' a faint voice came out of the darkness.

It was Jarla.

'Shouldn't you be with your father?' Bane returned. He did not want company.

'He's sleeping.'

'I see.'

'That girl you're looking for, the one you mentioned at The Salvation, is she your daughter?' Jarla asked, sitting down next to him.

Bane did not have the energy to protest, so answered. 'No, she isn't.'

'So why are you looking for her?'

Bane licked his lips, thinking. What the hell, he thought.

'She came to me, to the Watch House, just over three months ago needing help,' Bane explained, 'She wanted protection from an Underhive gang. She wanted out but they didn't want to give her up. Back then I was lost, a drunk and a wretch, just like your father said. In some ways, I still am.'

Jarla kept her expression impassive. Bane continued.

'She reminded me of someone I failed to save a long time ago. It gave me hope of a second chance, brought me back but the gang found her again and took her prisoner. I tracked them to their lair and tried to get her out,' he said. 'She got away, but I was caught.' Bane told her of his incarceration at the hands of the Razorheads, leaving out the grim details of the beatings and the blood-duels of his escape, the plague zombies and his eventual return to Former Glory.

Jarla listened quietly and intently throughout. 'Do you think she's still alive?' she asked.

Bane paused for a second, looking into the flickering flames of a drum fire. 'I don't know,' he said.

'I hope you find her,' Jarla said, getting to her feet.

'So do I,' Bane muttered as she walked away.

Malik was looking her up and down, lasciviously. She did not see him. When the ganger noticed Bane's stern expression he blew him a mocking kiss. Bane's fists clenched and he gritted his teeth. He turned away, raked some sacking across the floor towards him and lay down, eyes wide, looking into the darkness. He shifted uncomfortably and tried to lie on his side. It was no good, so he switched. Still no good. He returned to his back, exhaling his annoyance.

'Trouble sleeping?' Mavro asked.

'How long you been standing there?'

The doctor emerged out of the shadows cast by one of the drum fires.

'What do you dream, Bane?' he asked, ignoring his question. Bane looked at him and then followed his gaze.

Ratz was curled up next to the furnace, on the opposite side to Gilligan, gathering warmth. Even in sleep he mumbled, his body afflicted by a rash of nervous affectations. Bane wondered what he was dreaming, whether it was any different to the Ratskin's waking hours.

'I've treated those who've ventured to the Abyss.' Mavro's voice interrupted Bane's thoughts. 'None of them ever survive; the horrors witnessed kill the mind you see.'

'You discover that before or after you were thrown out of Hive City?' Bane gibed.

Mavro ignored him and slunk down next to him, getting close.

'All you can do is ease their pain,' he breathed. 'You know about that, don't you Bane?'

Bane opened his mouth to speak and then clamped it shut. The cravings came back, hard and insistent.

'I've got something to help you sleep,' Mavro said, goading. 'We both know what you dream about.'

Bane looked at him. Mavro opened his long coat. Inside was a flat metal rack adorned with vials. Sealed packets and thin blades that gave off faint iridescent hues in the weak light hung off the rack by slim hooks. He delved inside, produced a small glass bottle with a cork stopper, secured with wire. Within was what looked like a thick mould, ground up into a fine blue powder.

'You can owe me,' he said insidiously. 'It'll blow your mind.'

Bane reached out, hand quivering. Mavro's grinning visage was an unfocused blur in the background as the bottle came into stark resolution. His heart was pumping, body yearning.

He closed his hand into a fist and dropped his head.

'Get away from me,' Bane breathed.

'What?' Mavro was incredulous. 'Bane, don't deny your desires.'

Bane looked up. He held the stubber, finger on the trigger. 'I'll kill you if you don't.'

Mavro's eyes grew wide when he saw the gun. It was the second time Bane had pulled it on him. This time was different. Bane's hand was shaking, desperation and fury in his expression. Mavro stood up quickly, secreted the powdered stimms back into his coat and shrank away into the darkness.

Bane slumped down onto his back, gasping for breath, swallowing hard to lubricate a tongue that felt like chewed rat hide. He closed his eyes, clutched the gun to his chest and begged for sleep.

Curled up on the floor, he started to think about Alicia and the first time they had met.

A LOUD HAMMERING woke him. His head pounded with it, a deep and insistent throb that made him want to vomit. It was dark. Bane rolled out of the bed that was on the floor beneath his desk, and fumbled over to the Watch House door.

Where the hell's MacDaur? Then he remembered that his deputy was out on patrol. It couldn't be him hammering, he had a key.

Wearily, Bane pulled the door open – it could have been anyone out there, but he was so wasted he did not even have his gun. Bleary-eyed, he regarded the silhouette in front of him.

'What the hell is it?' he snarled, liquor-breath misting the cold night air.

That was when she stepped into the light.

'Please, help me,' she said.

When he saw her – pink hair, gang tats and all – Bane gasped, she had a more sobering effect than any caffeine.

He let her in, took a belt of grain whiskey and listened to her story.

'So why do you want to leave them?' Bane asked the girl after she had finished. She had said her name was Alicia, which could not just be coincidence. 'Most gangers don't want out, they want leadership, status, a better gun.'

'It was different in the beginning,' Alicia told him, eyes far away as she seemed to look past the Watchman.

'How so?'

'I was starving, trying to scrape an existence just above Hive bottom. That was when Woden found me,' she explained, tucking a piece of errant hair behind her ear. She adopted a nervous posture, legs tight together but splayed out at the knees. She clasped her hands and lowered her head, looking up at Bane through tangled strands of pink, eye lashes flicking.

'Woden?' Bane asked.

'The Razorheads' old leader,' said Alicia. 'He was a bastard, like all the rest, but not to me. He looked after me. He'd had a daughter, but she'd died of sump pox. Maybe that's how he saw me,' she added. 'Not as meat, like the others.'

Bane stared at her.

'But he died. Nagorn put a blade in him and killed him; bled him 'til there was nothing left.' Alicia's expression darkened, she looked at the floor. 'Things changed. Nagorn didn't see me as his daughter.' Alicia looked back up, into

Bane's eyes. 'He gave me this,' she said, brushing away the hair from her face, revealing the mark of a branding iron on her cheek. 'And this,' she pointed to her stomach.

Bane looked down, but could not see anything remarkable.

'I'm fending for two, now,' she said.

Bane understood and looked back up.

'I need your help.' Her eyes pleaded.

Bane rubbed his stubbly chin. He looked at her again and the resemblance was uncanny.

'Why are you looking at me like that?' Alicia's tone was wary. She balled her fists.

Bane showed his palms. 'Not for that,' he said. 'You just remind me of someone, that's all.'

Alicia relaxed and Bane got to his feet. He walked over to the window and peeked through the blinds. 'You can stay in the Watch House tonight,' he said to the darkness outside and then turned to Alicia again. 'There's a cot out back. The room has a door and you can lock it from inside. You won't be disturbed.'

Alicia's face lit up instantly and she gave him a long look.

'The girl I remind you of,' she said, so slight in Bane's eyes, 'was she your daughter?'

'No… No she wasn't.'

MAVRO FLED, THE image of the gun still in his mind.

That frikker's gonna crack, he thought. Like that deputy of his. That bastard looks more strung-out with each passing hour.

He had seen it many times during his medical tenure in Hive City, before he had realised he could scam more creds pedalling illicit substances to stimm-heads, spur-fiends and spook-jackers. It was Bane who had brought him down. Ironic, that after his fall from grace their paths had crossed again, in entirely different, more lucrative circumstances.

Mavro allowed himself a smile at that and decided to have a walk around. He was bored, and had no desire to speak to any of them. He was lamenting his current predicament, thrown in, as he was, with such pitiable wretches, when a strange stench assailed his nostrils.

A rotted coolant pipe, contents trickling on the floor beneath in a morass of silver-grey matter, exuded the stench. Mavro crouched next to it. The coolant mixture in the pipes must be gas permeable; air was travelling through it, wafting down the stench. Mavro followed the pipe, determined to find the source, all thoughts of fear and anxiety vanishing as he sought the truth. It was an old feeling, one of the reasons he had become a doctor. He had forgotten what it was like.

The pipe stretched far into the distance. As Mavro traced its path, he lost sight of the others. He did not notice as he delved into the labyrinth of twisting metal. Venturing deeper, he found valves punctuating the pipes at random intervals, expelling the coolant mixture as gas and vapour, venting pressure. The sporadic bursts of super-freezing chemicals forced Mavro to duck and weave between them. After about fifteen minutes of frantically tracing the pipe's origin, he found the source of the stench: a busted vent, beneath a rack of pipes. The grate securing it had slipped, making an opening wide enough for someone to crawl through. The Delaques had checked the entire chamber and said it was sealed.

Drawing close, Mavro recognised the stench. Cloying and pungent, he gagged on it. It was decay, rancid decomposition in its earliest stages when organs blackened and liquefied, and skin became as parchment, soaked in the body's juices. Putrefaction. He saw marks on the floor, palm and knee prints, described in drying blood.

'Oh no,' Mavro breathed.

CHAPTER: SEVEN

HE WAS RUNNING, fast and hard. Shadows loomed like dae-mons, eyes ablaze in the darkness. The bolt pistol cracked and bucked, as Bane fired in panic at his assailants, muzzle flare blaring like white noise. Smoke coiled about him, ten-drils of it reaching out like claws. The dense pall obscured high towers of stacked metal crates and dust-clogged machinery that fell away in a blur of motion as Bane raced past.

He knew this place. He had been here before: Toomis Pre-fab Residential, their warehouse.

Gunfire burst suddenly into his senses, loud and threat-ening. Ahead was a door. It seemed like it was miles away, yet barely a second passed and he was upon it. The door swung open all by itself. Darkness beckoned. Gunfire noise crushed instantly by the deafening thump of a beating heart. It took a moment for Bane to realise it was his. Through the door, a hellish silence pervaded. Another shadow came from the dark, coalescing in front of him. Bane raised his gun. It was massive in his grasp, cold and heavy like a tombstone. It came up with agonising slowness, an ear-shattering crunch as he chambered another round. Squeezing the trigger a fraction at a time, there was a belt of sound like breaking thunder as the round discharged.

The figure became Alcana Ran-Lo. Her scream shook the foundations of the warehouse and she fell, slow and heavy.

Bane was on his knees, surrounded by a welling pool of blood. Sobbing, he brushed away the hair covering her face. But it was Alicia that stared back at him with dead eyes as her blood soaked hair was swept aside.

Bane turned his hands over; his palms were drenched with blood. Tilting back his head, he screamed.

SCREAMING FILLED THE factory. Bane awoke and for a moment he thought he was still dreaming. No. He was back in the furnace chamber. The drum fires had died to nothing. It was dark. Only a faint glow came from the fire stack. There was no sign of Gilligan or the rest.

There was shouting, voices indistinct and urgent. Three shots exploded. Then silence. Bane got to his feet, bolt pistol clutched in his grasp, and ran towards the commotion.

The Delaques lay in a far off quarter of the chamber. Jarla was crawling away from them, Gilligan hobbling to her with painful steps. The others encircled the scene. Only Nark and Mavro were missing.

A weak shaft of light came down from the roof. Bane had not noticed it before. It fell on them in a washed-out haze. A grate above cut it into grainy squares where it touched the floor.

A small point of smouldering amber came out of the darkness beyond. Kalma-root flared in his mouth as Nark emerged from the gloom, smoking auto-pistols in both hands.

Kepke and Spectre were dead, shot in the head. Malik took one in the back. Bane walked over to them – a dark glance at Nark – still unsure what had happened. The White Ghosts' leader was still moving. Blood oozed from the wound. He did not have long. Kneeling down next to the ganger, Bane heaved him over while all the others watched.

Malik was too numb to feel pain. His pistol fell out of his grasp. His goggles were smashed from the fall. He looked out through the shattered lenses and for the first time Bane saw his eyes. They were narrow and thin like slits. They looked hard at him, possessed of silent urging as they tried to convey a message. Malik's mouth opened and closed. His lungs were filling with fluid and all that came out was a deep gurgle. A bubble of blood burst on his lip, his head slumped back and he was still.

Bane looked up at Nark, anger etched on his face.

'They were going to harm the girl,' Nark said, holstering the pistols expertly. 'You know it,' he added. 'You saw them looking at her. So did I.'

Bane ignored him and turned to Jarla instead. She shrank away, averting her gaze from the bodies and nestled into her father's chest.

'What happened, Jarla?' Bane asked her. She looked sideways at him, as if scared to speak. She tugged on her jacket sleeves and pulled her hair down between her fingers – just a little girl again.

'It's all right,' Bane assured her softly, moving over to sit with her and Gilligan.

'I don't know,' she whispered. 'I couldn't sleep and I saw the light from the roof. I thought I saw something. It frightened me.'

Gilligan smoothed her hair, trying to reassure her. He looked bad, white and sickly.

'When I looked back down I saw something moving towards me. I backed away and fell. That's when I screamed. Then I heard the shots,' she added.

'He has a pistol in his hands, Bane, the frikker meant business,' Nark said, waiting in the gloom, taking a long drag on the kalma-root.

'Just like everyone you ever killed eh, Nark?' Bane didn't look at him, keeping his eyes down as he thought.

'I don't know what happened here,' he said after a second, 'but I know you didn't cap those poor frikkers because of Jarla.' Bane fixed the gang lord with a meaningful glare. 'You saw your opportunity to kill your

enemies and you took it. You've been watching them all
night, waiting for a chance.'

'Yeah,' Nark said, tossing the root down and crushing it
underfoot, 'and I've been listening too,' he added, his tone
accusatory.

'What do you mean by that?'

'Still trying to be the detective Bane? Using us to find
that damn girl so you can ease your frikking conscience,'
Nark snarled. 'Then you can be the big important lawmaker again. I know your story. I've heard it a thousand
times. And I know you killed that spire-born girl wearing
your Enforcer badge too, no booze or drugs to hide
behind.' Nark stepped up, got into Bane's face and tried to
goad him.

Bane stood still, fists clenched. He wanted to crush Nark,
crush him to death with his bare hands and with him the
memories of that night in the warehouse. 'Besides,' Nark
hissed, a snide smile on his lips. 'If I wanted to kill my enemies, why wouldn't I shoot you, too?'

That was it. Bane snapped. He flung himself at the gang
lord, seized his neck with both hands and squeezed. Nark
choked and spluttered. A low punch, hard and fast in
Bane's ribs made him let go. A kick to the stomach doubled him over. Nark booted him again, hard on the
shoulder and put Bane on his back. Bane breathed hard.
Nark was lean and wiry, his strength born from years of
hardship surviving in the Underhive. He pounced on Bane,
pinning his arms with his legs and pressed an elbow into
his gullet.

'Nothing to say?' he spat through gritted teeth.

MacDaur moved forward, about to intervene. He felt the
cold muzzle of a lasgun in his back. He turned. Zeke
smiled back at him, wagging his finger.

Gasping, Bane crushed his knee into Nark's groin. The
gang lord squealed and released the elbow. Bane shoved
him off. He rolled on his side, coughing and spluttering as
he fought to drag air back into his lungs.

BACK FROM THE DEAD

Skudd advanced, shouldering his way into the light, a hulking mass of muscle and bone. He could kill Bane with one punch. Without Nark to restrain him, he was like a beast unleashed. He reached down towards Bane's head with a meaty hand.

'They're here,' a voice cried from the darkness. It made Skudd pause. 'Get out, they're here!' the voice said again.

Bane and Nark staggered to their feet. Mavro was running towards them, terrified.

'Get out, get out now,' he screamed.

'What the–' Zeke was cut short when he felt cold fingers dig into his neck. He whirled round, wincing in pain as the nails broke flesh, and was face-to-face with a zombie. It had once been a Delaque ganger, maybe one of the White Ghosts. The thing was desiccated, with sunken cheeks pinned up by pointed bones, flesh pulled over them like sagging leather. The creature snarled, revealing three teeth in a tar black mouth and lunged forward.

'Crap!' Zeke stumbled back, fired two shots, burning the zombie's arm and neck. MacDaur turned too, blasting it at short-range with an autogun burst. The thing's head exploded in a shower of gore and matter. Both men were covered in it.

Out of the darkness came the rest, a shambling horde of the undead that had been in the blast furnace chamber all the time, sleeping silently, awoken by gunfire and commotion.

'They're in the walls,' Mavro bellowed, reaching the group. More zombies shuffled behind him.

Bane looked around. They were everywhere, looming steadily out of the shadows. He saw one that looked like an Escher ganger, female with a ragged mop of blood-matted hair tied around a spike. It scuttled towards him with a bloody grin on its lips, baring rotten teeth. A saw-toothed blade, dark and black with dried blood, was in her hand. Another, an Orlock, veins black in his forehead, carried a gore spattered bolt gun. There were more, many more, hundreds.

'They're armed,' said Bane, backing away and unhitching his shotgun.

'So are we,' Nark returned. Fire flared in his hands as he let rip with the autopistols. The Escher exploded in a red mist and the Orlock was torn down before he could even raise another twisted limb. More zombies filled the void.

Bane fired into them, shotgun booming.

'Get behind me,' he cried to Gilligan and Jarla. Bane ushered the civilians behind him. 'MacDaur!'

'I've got him,' the deputy returned. He had Ratz by the scruff of the neck and the outlander wriggled and whooped insanely, fighting his grip, but MacDaur held on. Mavro scurried behind him, wedged between the deputy and Zeke, who had one hand on his bloodied neck wound, the other firing the las from the hip into the zombies.

In the distance, a heavy-set Goliath ganger loomed. Clad in thick armour plates, dented and split, he hefted a heavy stubber in one hand, the bulk of the weapon chained to his torso and arm. Trigger finger twitching, the gun exploded in sporadic bursts. It took the head and shoulders off a corpse straying too close to its firing arc. Another was felled where it stood as the bullets shattered both kneecaps. Strafing wildly, old instincts driving it, the Goliath stitched a line of crimson down Zeke's chest. The lasgun squeezed off two more rounds and went silent. MacDaur backed away, returning fire as Zeke hit the ground.

The horde fell upon him like starving sump rats, tearing at flesh and bone. MacDaur looked away, firing with his eyes closed. The survivors huddled into the grainy patch of light, forming a protective circle.

The *crump* of Skudd's heavy bolter joined the gunfire chorus. Almost like a drill, it bore a wide hole into the undead tide. Amongst others, the stubber-toting Goliath went down in a red ruin. The massive Orlock swept the weapon around, forging a big enough gap with the bolter's punishing staccato fury, for them to slip through.

Bane saw it and yelled over the noise.

'Head for the stack. It's the only way out.' Bane hefted Gilligan onto his left shoulder. He slung the shotgun over his back and yanked out the bolt pistol. Away from the light, in the fiery blaze of the pistol's violent retorts, the zombies became stark silhouettes, shambling and lurching like grotesque marionettes. The zombies' numbers thinned as Bane made for the fire stack. Skudd was in front of him, scything through the creatures, belt-feed screaming. MacDaur followed, keeping Ratz, Jarla and Mavro close, putting himself between them and the horde.

Nark came last. Every shot was a kill, every kill a bullet to the head. He raced through clips with calm expedience. He fired left and right, running as he did so, aim never wavering.

They shot their way back to the fire stack. Bane heaved Gilligan as far as the low gantry. Setting him down, he gripped the weary bar-tender's shoulder hard enough to pinch; he had to be sure Gil was paying attention and understood.

'Gilligan, can you climb?' he asked urgently.

Gil was breathing hard, he looked up at the metal ladder rungs, worn and rusted. There was a slight movement which may have been a nod.

Bane gripped his shoulders tighter, the staccato frenzy of Skudd's heavy bolter ringing in his ears. 'Can you make it?'

'Yes,' Gil spat. 'Just get me on that frikking ladder.'

Bane nodded and called to his deputy. MacDaur backed up, autogun blazing in his hands. He stopped firing when he reached Bane.

'You first,' Bane said, indicating the ladder. 'Watch him,' he warned. Then quieter, the next part just for MacDaur, he said, 'If he falls, we all go.'

MacDaur nodded his understanding and got to the ladder. Between them, Bane and MacDaur got Gilligan up to the first rung.

'Use your good leg and both arms, Gil,' he said.

Gil responded with a grimace and began his painful ascent. Below, the zombies were closing in. Bane fired from the gantry, keeping the flanks clear. The sheer bulk of the fire stack kept them safe from the rear but the creatures were growing in number and they could not keep them at bay forever. They had to make the climb.

Bane looked up. Gilligan was about halfway up. Bane held out a hand to Jarla and pulled her up to the gantry. Then came Ratz, urged on by Mavro who followed. That left Bane, Nark and Skudd.

The gang lord joined Bane on the gantry, muzzle flashes white hot as he burned through clips with alarming frequency. 'Up you go, lawman, Skudd and I are right behind you. It's a promise,' he shouted.

Bane glanced at him, blasted a creature looming in from the left side and then got onto the ladder and started climbing. Mercifully, Gilligan was just reaching the dilapidated platform above and MacDaur was helping him up and over.

Skudd stood at the foot of the gantry, washing the horde in a swathe of explosive bolter shells.

'Come on,' he cried, lost in defiant fury.

'We're leaving, Skudd,' shouted Nark, holstering his pistols, a few feet behind Bane as he took to the ladder.

Skudd backed off, one foot at a time up to the gantry, footsteps resonating off the metal with his immense bulk. Continuing to roar a challenge at the creatures, Skudd got both feet on the gantry and the heavy bolter jammed. The loading mechanism whined in protest and smoke came off the barrel with the big Orlock's insistent, desperate efforts. One of the zombies reached him so he swatted it with a massive fist and broke its neck. He threw the heavy bolter at another, crushing it. A third loomed before him. He didn't see the fourth and fifth on the left, the sixth and seventh on the right, or the dozens more closing in around them.

He smashed the zombie in front of him with a two-handed hammer blow and tried to lift his arm up to fight off another. It was weighed down by two of the creatures. He bellowed in pain as they bit into his flesh. His other arm got pinned. Now he was screaming.

Bane watched from the platform as Skudd was dragged down into the snarling throng. He was transfixed as Skudd fought and thrashed but was slowly devoured. There was the sound of wrenching metal. Bane tore his eyes away from the horrific scene as the bolts that fixed the ladder to the plascrete stack came loose. Dust and fragments of it fell away into the massing horde below, swarming about the gantry like fevered ants.

Nark was only halfway up. He had stopped to shoot at the creatures, crying Skudd's name as the big Orlock was torn down.

'Nark,' Bane cried. Lurching metal screeched against his voice.

The gang lord looked up, saw the ladder bolts ping out from their holdings in the plascrete tower and watched in horror as the metal started to bend downward, creaking and inexorable, its tensile resistance losing against Nark's weight. The ladder came down sharply; Nark dropped a metre and lost his grip on an autopistol, watching it tumble into a terrible mosaic of decaying faces beneath him. He climbed quickly, swinging up three rungs on his other arm, using his body's momentum as leverage. He managed to get his footing when the ladder gave way completely. Nark leapt and found purchase on the edge of the platform as the metal ladder clanged into the darkness below. He looked down and a sea of grasping claws reached up hungrily, baying and snarling.

Bane leant over, offering his hand.

'Grab it,' he said.

Nark looked up at him and for the first time Bane saw
fear in his eyes. He did not want to die. Not that way, not
eaten alive, like that poor bastard, Skudd.

Nark swung his other arm up and gripped Bane
around the wrist. He was about to pull him up, muscles
burning from the strain, when he looked into Nark's eyes
and hesitated.

'What's to stop you killing me, killing all of us?' he
demanded, having to shout above the horrible moaning
of a thousand damned voices.

Nark reached down with his other arm, beyond Bane's
sight. The fear in his eyes vanished, hidden away behind
a mask of dark confidence.

'Nothing,' he shouted back, bringing up his other
autopistol and pointing it at Bane's head. 'But those people won't survive without you. Pull me up now or I'll
shoot and we both die.'

Bane thought about it for a second, thought about
sending Nark to his doom below, but he was right. They
needed him. He needed them. Reluctantly, he heaved
Nark up.

Nark rolled onto the platform. As he did his guard was
lowered momentarily and he was unable to keep his gun
trained. Bane saw his chance and punched him hard in
the stomach. He took the pistol from Nark's grasp and
threw it away, spiralling it across the wasted metal. He
pulled out his own gun and pressed the heavy muzzle of
the bolt pistol against the ganger's forehead, pushing
Nark down to his knees as he got to his feet. He stood
over him, execution-style, and pulled the trigger.

Bane angled the pistol at the last second and the bullet
missed. Nark winced as it scorched his ear, a smoking
hole left in the metal platform. He brought the pistol
back to Nark's forehead and crunched another round
into the chamber, still thinking about it. He felt his finger
squeeze the trigger again.

'No,' Nark said. 'Wait.'

Bane pressed the muzzle harder, there would be no warning shot this time.

'Wait,' Nark hissed loud and urgently. 'The girl you're looking for. I know where she is.'

'What?' Bane kept the pressure on. He was vaguely aware of the others watching him. He ignored them. This was between him and Nark.

'You're lying,' he snarled and pushed harder, squeezing another fraction. This close, the hammer pulling back would've been audible.

'I'm not. I swear it,' Nark urged. 'She's alive, least she was last I heard. Kill me and you'll never find her,' he told him, an earnest, desperate look in his eyes.

Bane looked at him hard, licking his lips as he considered the gang lord's words. If there was even a chance…

Bane's finger eased off the trigger. He lowered the gun, but still kept it trained on the Orlock.

'Take us to her,' he demanded.

CHAPTER: EIGHT

THE TUNNEL WAS DARK. *Dripping water from the venting precipitators was the only sound. It eked through the tunnel's seam in places where it was eroded, pooling beneath the largest cracks. The survivors hunkered down in the gloom, resting. The smelting plant was far below, just another dark memory. The infected was wide-awake. They heard the others close by; most were asleep or lost in thought. Some ate the scraps of food they had scavenged. Alone, it did not want for food though it took it, but secreted it away so no one would know. Another hunger gripped them. The infected risked a glance at the wound. It was black around the edges and there was a smell too. A feeling was growing inside, nascent and festering. It became hard to remember the things that made them human, something else was smothering it, something deep and primal. They covered up the wound, and looked into the gloom, trying to suppress the dark, instinctive urges boiling steadily to the surface.*

IF BANE FELT any guilt about leading them off course, he didn't show it. He had gone back into the Underhive to find Alicia and rescue her. To drag something out of the stinking mess that was his life. She needed him. If there was even a chance she had survived, he had to try. No one argued. They were either too tired to care or unwilling to challenge his single-minded determination. Even Doc

Mavro's recalcitrant streak had ebbed. Mind-numbing terror will do that to a man, even a hard-edged bastard like him but maybe it was something else.

There was a moment when Bane had Nark on his knees, finger on the trigger, when he would have killed him, and everyone knew it. He hoped then that his actions had not engendered a culture of fear within the group. That he had become the one thing he had, up to a point, fought against his entire life.

NARK WALKED SLOWLY at the head of the group, Bane's shotgun levelled at his back. He had been stripped of his weapons but his hands were unbound. Bane figured even he was not quick enough to dodge an Executioner shell. With his gangers dead, the balance of power had shifted away from the gang lord. Now he was a prisoner, and one Bane fully intended to bring to justice if they survived.

Any remorse Nark may have harboured for Skudd and Zeke was hidden. Leading them onward, he was as cold and unreadable as ever.

'How far is it?' Bane growled.

'Not far,' Nark replied, 'another level, at most.'

He led them to a large door of latticed metal. Wrenching it aside with both hands, the door collapsed on itself into a thick grey line revealing a commercial elevator. There was room enough for them all.

Once inside, Bane read the worn destinations written in Necromundan-Gothic, noticing the activation key glowing dully next to the first. The other five denoted higher levels and were extinguished.

'Used to go as far as Hive City,' Nark said as Bane shut the gate, hammering the lit rune. Lurching metal filled the vast car and the elevator ground upwards.

THEIR ASCENT LASTED only a few minutes, coming to an abrupt stop after only one level. Nark raked open the door and stepped outside.

'This is it,' he said.

The elevator opened out into what looked like a clerical district. Numerous small buildings, domes and shelters were packed tightly together. Ravaged by age and vandalism, the area was a ruin, little better than a shanty slum.

Bane noticed a derelict hall, an overhanging arch at its face supported by six baroque columns. Two of the columns had collapsed and the foundations were uprooted and split, doubtless by hive quakes. Part of the roof set on top of the arch had fallen in with them. A faded rubric still clung defiantly above the shattered entrance. Bane made out the words *Regium Bilbliotechas.* It was some kind of knowledge repository. Scrolls, broken data slates and ancient books fluttered weakly outside it, disturbed by a faint turbine breeze wafting through the sector.

Other buildings bore all the hallmarks of notary's offices, and other ex-municipal quarters. The whole area seemed incongruous amidst the cold industrial harshness of the lower levels. They must be close to the border with Hive City. This place had obviously once been a spike of it, jutting into the belly of the Underhive. Another of the frontier zones swallowed up in the struggle for territory, abandoned by those that once dwelled and worked there.

'It's up ahead,' Nark said, pointing to a looming structure in the distance.

It rose above the rest, more grandiose in both stature and design. There was something ancient about it. It was the only building not in a state of utter ruination.

As they got closer, Bane realised it was some kind of chapel, with religious iconography etched on the pale, age-stained walls. Stone effigies of saints, priests and martyrs were set into shallow alcoves at the entrance, barred by a single, stout wooden door. Some of the statues had been beheaded, others less pleasantly mutilated. One stood out from all the rest. It looked clean, as if it had been recently carved. Rendered in immaculate detail, the figure was that of a man, dressed in long, flowing robes. He looked larger than the rest, more austere. In his left hand he held a book and he was open-mouthed as if preaching. Part of his face was covered by a mask. Beneath, upon a hexagonal plinth was an inscription. 'Varlan Smite, father, leader, saviour.'

'What is this place, Nark?' Bane asked, starting to feel uneasy.

'A chapel,' Nark returned, 'I heard people were coming here for sanctuary. A group was seen canvassing the settlements, doomsaying and preaching any shit so as people would listen. They come like lambs to the slaughter.' Nark paused and turned to look at Bane. 'I heard your girl, the one with the Razorhead tattoos, was one of them,' he muttered darkly.

Bane met his gaze, trying to read the gang lord's intentions. 'Lead on,' he said.

They reached the threshold of the chapel. Nark pushed against the wooden door that creaked open slowly on worn hinges. It was dark inside. A building this old would have no power and no link to the hive grid. Nark hesitated.

'I don't like this,' Mavro hissed, skulking behind Bane.

'Neither do I,' Bane agreed, but beckoned Nark onwards anyway. If Alicia was here, he had no other choice.

Once inside the chapel, Bane noticed the faintest light issuing like haze through an upper window. The window was set high into the facing wall and far off. Its light pushed away the dingy gloom smothering the room. There was the silhouette of what looked like a raised pulpit.

'Close the door,' Bane said quietly. 'I don't want anything else coming in behind us.'

As the door swung shut, darkness closed in. An eerie silence descended, the merest scuffling of feet the only sound.

'MacDaur,' Bane said. 'See if you can find a lamp or torch or something, but stay near the door and keep the others together.'

The deputy kept his voice low. 'What are you going to do?'

'Nark and I are going for a walk.' He shoved the shotgun in the gang lord's back.

Bane and Nark moved slowly and carefully down a long, narrow aisle. What looked like the edges of pews were just visible on either side. Bane used them to guide him, as he and Nark got closer to the pulpit. In the blackness, the chapel seemed profoundly empty.

'Nark, if you're lying to me,' Bane warned, watching the gang lord. A sickening feeling was building in his gut.

'I've found something,' hissed MacDaur from the back of the chapel. 'Feels like... chains.' he said.

Bane was about to talk to MacDaur, but stumbled as his feet got caught up in something on the floor. He looked down instinctively but then noticed a flash of movement ahead.

It was Nark, darting off into the pews, swallowed abruptly by darkness.

'Nark,' Bane cried, veering off after him. He cranked a round into the shotgun. It was a moot gesture; Bane had made a mistake and he realised the gang lord was gone. Bane hurried forward, stumbled again and fell to his knees.

'Nark, you bastard,' he spat.

The floor was cold and hard between the pews. Bane's fingers closed around something. It was charred and brittle. The scent of oil overlaid the stink of burned flesh. Bane realised suddenly what he had in his hand and all thoughts of Nark evaporated.

'Get out of here!' he cried. It was bone he held in his hands, the charred remains of human bones. 'It's not safe,' he said. 'MacDaur, get them out before–'

Light blazed into the chapel, it hurt Bane's eyes but he saw at least twenty figures stood around him. They were wearing metal masks, each etched out of shining brass, untarnished and grotesque. From behind the twisted features wrought upon them – exaggerated noses, pointed ears and eye slits – cold, human eyes regarded him. Dressed in long brown, simple robes and draped with ammo belts, shoulder slung guns and hip-holstered pistols, there could be no mistaking what they were: Redemptionists.

The grim feeling manifesting in Bane's gut deepened. Without speaking, he put his shotgun down and raised both hands, beckoning to MacDaur to do the same. Bane saw Nark a few feet in front him. He must have felt the autogun in his chest before he saw it. His hands were up.

The Redemptionists surrounded them. They had been hiding in the shallow alcoves in the walls, knowing that any intruders would overlook them as they made for the light cast upon the pulpit.

The stench of oil came from two things. Huge lamps set around twelve supporting columns, six each to the left and right flanks of the pews, blazed with the stuff. It was exacerbated by a secondary fuel stench. It came from the flamers that many of the Redemptors were toting. Burners at the snout of each weapon, raged with blue flame. The merest spray of the liquid and a gout of super-heated mixture would strip the very flesh off the bones of a potential enemy, the fate of the poor bastards who were nothing but blackened bones at Bane's feet.

'Seek ye a benediction, weary travellers?' a benevolent, yet sinister voice asked.

Bane turned to face the pulpit, where the voice had come from. A figure stood there. It took a moment for Bane to recognise him as Varlan Smite, the subject of the statue outside. As Bane looked at him, he could swear the preacher's eyes brightened. Even behind the mask, the unfettered glee was perceptible.

'We're lost,' Bane said, carefully. Right now, the Redemptionists could kill them as easily as a gore-lizard devours a child. The fact that they had not, meant there was a still a chance to negotiate. The preacher was clearly the leader, so it was his attention and favour that Bane needed to curry.

'As are all wayward travellers,' said Smite, gesturing to the bones at Bane's feet.

Bane tried not to look again and spoke quickly.

'We came here seeking someone whom we heard had come to you for sanctuary,' he said.

Smite smiled, the lower part of his face visible beneath his mask – a dark parody of an angelic visage, rendered in gold.

'Plague has ravaged the dark belly of the hive,' he muttered.

Bane was not sure whether he was still addressing him or had begun a monologue to himself.

'The unclean are shown for what they are,' he continued. 'Damned.'

'You know of the outbreak?' Bane ventured, keen to wrest Smite from the dark mood he was falling into.

Smite looked up, eyes alert. 'Of course,' he said, smiling again as if it were a needless question to ask. 'This,' he said, lifting up a leather-bound book, from the pulpit, 'tells me all I need to know.'

Bane noticed the other silent Redemptors, in his peripheral vision, nod towards the tome. It was obviously an artefact they held in high regard, worn and scorched as if it had endured through ages. Smite got up off the pulpit and walked towards where Bane was standing.

Now Bane could see him fully. He was adorned with long, brown robes like the others, but with no weapons, just various religious symbols hanging down from a cord tied around his waist.

'I saw your approach,' he whispered into Bane's ear, once they were opposite each other. 'Your coming is foretold, it heralds our crusade into the dark belly of our world,' he continued. 'Your part is crucial, as is the part of the others in our care.'

'Others?,' asked Bane, interrupting. 'What others?' He was aware of a faint, hissing noise but, in his urgency to learn of Alicia's fate, he dismissed it.

Smite raised a finger, fixing Bane with his mesmerizing gaze. 'Look,' he breathed, opening the book. The pages were like thick, rough parchment. Curled up at the edges, they bore a familiar stench. As Smite turned the pages with slow deliberation, Bane realised it was not parchment at all, it was human skin. Despite his shock, it could not prepare him for what he saw next. Smite opened the book fully and pointed with a thin finger, claw-like, manicured nails making a light tapping sound as he rapped the page.

Scribed in a thick, dark ink was an image. It was of seven figures, all clustered together, arms raised plaintively. He recognised all of them. The likenesses were unmistakable, the posing eerily uncanny. It was them, Bane, Nark and the others, standing exactly as they were now. It was a perfect, faultless rendering.

Bane suddenly wished that he had kept the shotgun and tried to fight his way out. 'How?' was all he could manage.

Smite pointed with one finger to his left eye. 'I told you,' he said, pulling down a part of the mask that was hidden from view, it covered the lower part of his nose and mouth completely. The Redemptionists mimicked their leader.

'I saw it,' said Smite, voice muffled by the mask.

Bane realised suddenly that it was a respirator. With frantic alarm, he remembered the hissing sound. Looking to his feet, he saw dense gas filling the room, exuding from the bases of the ornate lamps. As the gas, manifesting as a yellowish mist, grew higher, the lamps died and darkness rushed back at him.

'No,' Bane gasped as his legs turned to lead and he fell. Spittle forming on his lips, he raised his head and reached for Smite. White fury raged in Bane's head as one of the preacher's cohorts struck him savagely. A thick needle of pain bore into his skull and he was vaguely aware that his face was touching the floor.

He looked up as dark spots crept over his vision, and made out Smite standing over him, the book cradled lovingly in his talon-like grasp.

'There is much I wish to discuss with you,' he said, voice fading into gradual oblivion. 'But not yet.'

Blackness consumed Bane utterly. Smite disappeared into a blur of nothing, his voice trailing into the ether of unconsciousness.

'No. Not yet.'

A POUNDING HEADACHE woke Bane from his enforced slumber. His muscles were stiff and his head fogged up. Dazed, he reached out, vision still blurred, and touched the side of the cot on which he lay. Hard, like plascrete with musty sweat-stained sheets and clogged with dust. He rolled over onto his side, still trying to get his bearings. He remembered the gas, creeping up at his feet like a jaundiced mist and the masks arrayed about him, grinning, shining, grotesque.

Heaving his body up, Bane let both feet touch the floor. It was cold and hard. He realised his boots had been removed. Looking around he discovered he was in some kind of catacomb. Must be those that lay beneath the chapel. It was dark. Light streamed in weakly from latticed grates set into the ceiling, no bigger than the length and width of his forearm. He made out ornate arches that stretched right into the middle of the room. At the end of each was a face, not unlike those depicted on the Redemptor's masks. A tongue unfurled from each one. Bane swore they were mocking him.

Next to him, Bane noticed another cot. He caught his breath when he saw who lay in it. It was Alicia, sleeping soundly. He watched her chest rise and fall. On her

forehead was a bruise, harsh and purple against her pale
skin. Bane crouched down next to her and went to stroke
her hair. He hesitated, afraid to touch her should she be
only a dream. His hand was still shaking when he at last
found the courage to touch her skin and confirm she was
real.

Warm. That was good. He brushed away the pink hair
that partly shrouded her face. He moved it gently as a
father would for a daughter. She looked so innocent lying
there, alone in the cot. Bane was reminded that beneath
the scars, gang tats and bravura was just a sixteen year-old
girl. She, who had once wanted to be a part of one of the
most powerful and dangerous gangs of the Underhive but
who had then found the courage to defy them, was still
just a girl.

'I found you,' he whispered, bowing his head as he held
her hand. Now all he had to do was save her.

'She's been that way for days,' an unfamiliar voice said
from the shadows. Bane started and snatched back his
hand. He became alert, searching the dark for the speaker.

A figure stood a few feet from him. He was short and
had once been immaculately dressed. Fine robes, fur
trimmed, hung from his portly frame. They had once been
black but were greyed with wear, and torn and spattered
with filth and blood. The fine trim around the edges of the
robes was frayed in places or ripped away entirely. The
robes overlaid a deep crimson suit. Wide trousers were cut
short, also frayed and sporting several shallow tears. Thick
leather moccasins sat snugly on his feet. They did not look
like the footwear of your average Underhiver. He had an
air about him and stood upright and proud despite his
dishevelled appearance. He had a dark grey beard but the
rest of his head was completely bald. He peered at Bane
through a monocle, and the azure lens gave his left eye an
unearthly luminescence.

Bane could tell he was a guilder, by the timbre of his
voice, and the gold sovereign ring upon his finger

confirmed it. Although it was dark in the catacombs and Bane could not discern the exact details, he had seen enough guild rings in his time to know it bore a flattering resemblance of Lord Helmawr on the upper side, etched in profile and on the other the motif of that guilder's house, the family to which he belonged. But it was more than just a badge of office, a symbol of status – it had a practical application too.

The guild rings were encoded. Nano-chips within were better than any key. They granted access to parts of Hive Primus that the majority of the populace would never see. They allowed the guild to conduct clandestine meetings, ensure the safe passage of goods and sequester the services of certain official and unofficial bodies. Such a trinket was reserved for high-borns. No Underhive guilder could possess one. It meant this man had influence and wealth.

'Where are the others?' Bane demanded, standing up a little shakily.

'Two are in here with you.' The guilder gestured behind Bane. Gilligan slept fitfully on a cot, Jarla nestled next to him. Bane had not even noticed them. 'As for the rest,' the stranger continued, 'they are in the next room, awake but resting like you. You were struck very hard.'

Bane raised his left hand. There was a bump on his right temple and a spike of pain made him wince as he touched it.

'There was another empty cot, it didn't look like you were waking any time soon.'

'How long have we been down here?' Bane asked. He found his boots next to the bed and pulled them on.

'Myself? Or you and your party?'

'Both.' The response was terse. Bane was in no mood for the guilder's games. Most of those he had met in his life were selfish egotists, no action beneath them if it meant profit. Though how this particular guildsman had ended up at the mercy of a bunch of Redemptionists was something he intended to discover.

'I have been here for at least seven days, though that is
an estimate. We have been fed whilst incarcerated but
enclosed like this, there was no way to gauge the passage
of time accurately,' the guilder said.

Seven days was a long time to be held captive by out-
land fanatics. The guilder should have been dead by now.
Then Bane remembered something the crazed preacher,
Smite, had said. That he had been waiting for them. He
alluded to some kind of plan for them all. Now Bane and
the others were here. At first, Bane had just thought him
mad, but now…? Then there was the book.

'And us?' Bane asked, fixing his boots so they fitted
snugly and looking up.

'You were only out for a few hours.'

Bane paused and looked back down to the floor, trying
to think as his head throbbed painfully. 'Who are you?'
he asked at last, eyes narrowing suspiciously as he
regarded the guilder again. 'You're either brave or stupid,
coming in here alone. How do you know I'm any better
than those bastards above us?'

'A prisoner, like you. My name is Archimedes Vaxillian,'
he said. 'And to answer your second question, I am neither.'

Another figure, much larger, wearing a half-mesh emerald body glove, partly concealed by a heavy storm cloak,
emerged beside Archimedes.

'As you can see,' he said, gesturing to the man standing
beside him, 'I am not alone.'

The man was well-built with stimulant enhanced musculature rippling in his neck. His eyes were cold and hard.
An empty black pistol holster was strapped to his leg and
one arm was in a sling. The newcomer was a bodyguard,
through and through. A pretty good one too – all the
time they had been talking, Bane had not even heard
him.

'This,' added Archimedes, 'is Dietrich Meiser, my asso-
ciate.'

Bane feigned indifference. He looked back down at Alicia, slumbering quietly and his features softened.

'I assure you,' said Archimedes, 'she's as comfortable as we can make her. Now, if you don't mind, I have some questions.'

Bane looked back at the guilder, face set like stone. 'So do I,' he replied. 'Now, take me to the others.'

A LOW ARCH led out of the first chamber and into a larger one. The others waited, sitting quietly on wooden benches arrayed around the edge of the room. Bane felt their gaze on him. He had risked everything to come here, for his own selfish reasons and now they were all prisoners, at the whim of fanatical lunatics. Try as he might, he could not justify his actions. He had let them down.

MacDaur nodded a greeting at Bane. His deputy looked rough and his skin was grey. It seemed a nod was all he could manage. Mavro was nearby. He scowled as Bane walked past to sit down on a bench. Ratz crouched on the floor next to the doctor, staring vacantly.

Whether Bane liked it or not, all of them depended on him. He knew they had to get out of the chapel. The only safe haven was the Precinct House; all that mattered was getting there. True, they had escaped the plague for now, but it would catch them again. There was no way that a bunch of religious freaks could avert it, however righteous they believed their cause to be. Bane had no idea what the Redemptionists had in store for them, or how they fitted into Varlan Smite's plans.

'You're doing a lot of thinking lawman.' It was Nark. Bane had not seen him at first, sitting away from the group, smothered by the shadow cast by the door arch. The gang lord faced a set of stone steps that led up to a wooden trapdoor. It was the room's only exit. For once, Nark was without a Kalma-root between his lips; the Redemptors must have taken them. In fact, now Bane thought about it, he realised that all of his weapons were gone too. He checked for the pistols in his belt. The bolt pistol was missing, but he still had his service piece. They must have overlooked it; ironic, as it was the only weapon that had no use whatsoever.

'They've taken all the guns,' Nark confirmed. 'No way you're shooting your way out of this one.' He smiled languidly, leaning back against the wall as if already resigned to his fate. 'What have you done?' he asked mockingly.

'You shut the scav up,' Bane warned.

'You going to make me?' Nark said.

'Gentlemen,' said Archimedes. 'I suggest we refrain from killing each other, despite our differing… backgrounds. If the Redemptors had wanted us dead, we would be already. There may yet be a way out of this. Besides,' he added, 'I still have questions.'

Bane gave Nark a dark glance, to which the gang lord responded with a wry smile. 'You're a member of the Merchant Guild,' Bane said to Archimedes. 'So what the hell are you doing so far downhive?'

Archimedes took a seat. Meiser stood next to him. 'I don't know if you are aware,' the guilder began, 'but over the last few months, guilder caravans have been ambushed on an inordinate number of occasions, despite our best efforts to ensure the contrary. Supplies of Fresh, hive rations, munitions, and all and sundry were stolen.' Archimedes paused and leant forward to lend drama to his words. 'Our routes are secret, Watchman. No one knows of them but the guild. Even the recipients have no idea how the goods get to them. House Greim is but one of the houses hit by these attacks. I have been employed to root out the source of their dismay.'

'What? Taking out the attacking gang?' Bane was not convinced.

'No, of course not. By source, I mean the individual or individuals furnishing the Underhivers with our route plans. Guild activities, even those conducted at the highest level, require local contacts. It is not unheard of for such contacts to be *persuaded*, shall we say, to impart information. My enquiries were discreet, yet they attracted certain unwanted attention from extremists affiliated with House Delaque. My bodyguards and I were visiting a corpseyard, in a slum town called *Dreyzer Glut*.

'Healthy body parts, regardless of whether or not the owner is deceased, attract a high price uphive, particularly in the medical sector.' Archimedes glanced towards Mavro. The doctor, who had been looking at the guilder up to this point, averted his gaze and stared at the floor. 'I was questioning the yard master, unaware that he had hired protection, when a fight broke out. We were outgunned and I believed us to be in some peril. Then the firing stopped. At least it was not directed at us. At first, I thought the Delaques had turned on each other. It is a common occurrence. But I was wrong. They were firing at another enemy, one that had risen up around them from the very bodies being processed in the corpseyard.'

'I know Dreyzer Glut,' Bane said. 'It's on the opposite side of the dome.' 'There are hundreds of shanty towns between there and Former Glory, thousands could be infected.'

Archimedes nodded. 'I'm afraid your theory is correct. It became apparent that the plague was not restricted merely to the premises but had spread from outside.' Archimedes paused to wipe his brow, as if the memories were causing him to perspire. 'I travelled with two bodyguards originally. Trevallian was killed during our escape. Our only recourse was to try to find a way back uphive. We reached as far as this chapel. It's strange, but we all place false faith in holy symbols and believe they can protect us from evil. In truth, they seduce us. Lulled by their promises, promises of our own making and so it was that I was lulled, believing the chapel to be a haven, when it was anything but. And so here we are.'

Bane regarded the guilder thoughtfully. His story sounded plausible enough, but his instincts told him that guilders were not to be trusted. 'Why are you still here Archimedes? Why aren't your corpses charred on the floor of the chapel above, like those others?'

'Truthfully, I don't know.'

'Those flayed carcasses up there,' said Bane, 'they were killed recently. I could smell the stink of their flesh. I counted at least eight corpses. You didn't come here alone did you?'

'I don't know what you're talking about,' the guilder protested, a little uncertainly. He was hiding something. Whatever it was, it was bad. 'I've answered your questions, now you owe me the same courtesy. For instance, what is so important about that damn girl in the other room? Where're the rest of the enforcers? What are they doing about the outbreak?'

Bane opened his mouth to answer. A thick shaft of hazy light invading the room from above arrested his response. Bane looked up. A robed silhouette stood in the open trapdoor. He was big and had a conical shaped head. Leaning into the torch light, iron studs were revealed on a thick leather cowl that the Redemptor wore in lieu of a mask.

'Come,' his voice was so deep it was barely audible. 'The father wishes to speak with you.' It was directed at Bane.

He got to his feet. 'Seems all I'm doing these days is talking,' he said and walked slowly up the stairs to the light of the trapdoor.

BANE WAS TAKEN by the Redemptor who had identified himself as Deacon Raine, to an anteroom off the nave of the chapel. Raine left him there. Bane stood, hands bound with a leather strap, upon a circular, wooden platform. It was dark in the chamber, but Bane could see it was some kind of auditorium. Wooden seats arced around him in a semi-circle, three rows deep. Intersecting the semi-circle was a simple wooden podium, raised a few feet from ground level.

After a few moments, a figure stepped out of the gloom and onto the podium. As he did so, torches flared violently to life. Varlan Smite stood before him, a lectern nearby cradling his book. Alongside the preacher was Raine, arms folded. In the fiery light, shadows ran down his mask in sharp slashes. It made him look eerie, death-like. The audience of Redemptionists sat above like a wall of grinning, gleaming metal.

'What is this?' Bane demanded, trying to stay calm. It looked very much like a trial. 'What the hell am I do–'

Smite raised a finger, cutting Bane off.

'You are not here to ask questions lawmaker,' he said, in an unnervingly benign manner. 'You are here to answer them.' Smite smiled and approached him.

'Clearly you have fallen from the path of righteousness,' he began. 'Yet, you have survived the plague and reached this sanctuary. You have endured much, yes?'

Bane did not know how to respond. Did Smite want an answer? He was suddenly aware of the peril of his situation. The fact that the Redemptors were talking was good, but Smite was a madman with more than a trace of wyrd about him. Bane had to play this carefully, at least until he could gauge their intentions.

'We have suffered, yes,' he said.

'And through suffering do we begin the path to righteousness,' preached Smite. He turned to his congregation and swept his arm over them as if he were performing a benediction. For a moment, Bane thought he caught a glimpse of pink scar tissue, just visible beneath the mask. Smite turned back to face him and the Redemptionists nodded as one.

'Through suffering do we begin the path to righteousness.' It sounded like a mantra, a raft of dulcet voices without distinction.

'Tell me, lawmaker,' said Smite, drawing close. 'How far has the plague spread? Are all sinners reaching from beyond the grave to claim the damned that still walk and breathe?'

Bane was about to confess his ignorance, but thought better of it. 'The Underhive has all but been consumed,' he said. 'There are thousands of them.'

Smite turned his back to him, stroking his chin as if thinking.

'It is as I foresaw,' Smite muttered. 'An army of the dead that walks the earth.' He straightened up and faced the congregation but addressed Bane. 'There is one whom I seek,' he said. 'Come from the very Abyss itself. His will… drives them. You know of what I speak,' the preacher turned around to look Bane in the eye, as if examining him for any trace of deception.

At first, Bane had no idea what the crazed preacher was drivelling about, he thought it was more inane babble. Then he remembered the zombies at the Salvation. He remembered how they had paused outside the bar, deliberately gathering together as if waiting for something. As if waiting for instruction. There was something unearthly about the plague, the way it had grown and spread so quickly. Was it possible that there was more to it than a simple epidemic and this madman knew about it? Bane thought for a moment and decided to take a gamble. He spoke quietly, so just Smite could hear him. 'You must set me free. I have seen evidence of something driving these creatures. I must get a warning uphive and stop the contagion before it spreads further, before it cannot be stopped.'

Smite smiled. 'No,' he said, shaking his head. 'You cannot leave this place.'

Bane's heart thumped hard in alarm.

Smite retreated a little, shoulders sagging in resignation. He sighed. 'I had hoped you would be the one to lead me to him.' He turned away, talking to himself. 'My vision was so clear. After all the others that failed, all those who were unworthy. I had hope for this one.'

'Others? What others?' Bane interrupted.

But Smite was not listening. He was locked in his monologue. 'The time has arrived. This man's coming has heralded that, if nothing else,' he said, and turned around quickly to face Bane.

'Tell me, enforcer,' he said, 'who do you pray to when all seems lost and the darkness is closing in around you?'

'I...' Bane stuttered, bad memories springing unbidden into his mind. He wondered whether or nor Smite could sense them.

'Is not faith a lawmaker's greatest weapon?' Smite went on. 'His shield, his unswerving belief in what is truth and the power of the law.'

Bane closed his eyes, his head dropped and he spoke to the floor.

'I have no faith,' he admitted.

'Then you must be cleansed,' Smite concluded. 'Just like all the rest.'

Bane opened his eyes and saw black scorch marks beneath him. He had not noticed them before. He was losing. He had hoped that he could reason with the preacher, maybe try and trick him into letting him go. Now he could see that was impossible. He did not have what Smite wanted, knowledge of this *one* of whom he spoke. The preacher approached and looked deep into Bane's eyes. Bane realised, at that moment that Smite was certain of that fact too.

Bane had to do something before he became another scorch mark on the ground. Somehow he knew that if he went back to the catacombs, it would be a death sentence for them all.

'You listen to this madman?' he cried, addressing the throng suddenly, 'One that claims to see and hear thoughts and events yet to pass? You harbour a witch,' he said accusingly. Bane reasoned that Smite's will and prophecy kept the religious cult together. Perhaps if he could make them question, throw doubt onto their benefactor...

'I am blessed,' raged Smite, crushing Bane's hopes instantly with his fervour and zealous charisma. 'Given visions by powers from on high, to root out the sinful and purge the damned. And if they are at our gates, they will be judged.'

That was it, the last gambit. Bane had failed. It was over. There was only one course of action left. Go down fighting. He powered at Smite, leaning in with his shoulder for a body charge.

Deacon Raine stepped into his path and put him down hard with his huge bulk. Bane felt a shockwave of pain rush through his body.

Smite motioned to two Redemptors who stood nearby in shadowed alcoves. They grabbed Bane roughly by the arms and dragged him away.

'You will all be judged!' bellowed Smite, his voice ringing in Bane's ears like a death knell, as he was thrown back down into the catacombs.

BANE HIT THE stone floor hard, sprawled out on all fours, the trapdoor booming shut in his wake. MacDaur went to his side. 'Are you all right?' he breathed, an unhealthy rasp to his voice.

'I'll live,' Bane said, spitting out a gobbet of blood.

'I take it the negotiations didn't go well,' Nark said snidely.

Bane glared at him.

'What happened?' Archimedes asked, his tone fearful. Cracks were appearing in his, until now, composed façade.

'Smite is completely mad,' Bane replied, sitting back down on one of the benches, 'and I think he's a wyrd too, some kind of prescient telepath.'

'I thought the Redemption hunted and killed wyrds,' said Mavro.

'They do,' Bane replied. 'I tried to use that against him, but he has a hold over them, possibly some form of mental control. He's seen the plague in some kind of vision and fervently believes he's destined to go on some kind of crusade to crush the unholy, starting with the zombies.'

'Those frikkers are all crazy,' chipped in Nark.

'There's more,' Bane told them. 'He's looking for someone, said he'd come from the Abyss.' Bane flashed a glance at Ratz, who stared vacantly into space. He could not help thinking that whatever the Ratskin had unearthed was tied into this somehow. 'Smite thought I knew where this someone was, seemed like he'd asked before too.' Bane switched his gaze to Archimedes. The guilder was looking down, his head in his hands. Meiser remained impassive. 'I couldn't tell him what he wanted to know,' Bane concluded.

'So where does that leave us?' Mavro asked.

'Dead.' The voice of Archimedes was little more than a whisper.

'What?' asked Mavro. There was a flash of silver as the razor came out, flashing in the light. 'What do you mean? They spared Bane so maybe they'll just leave us here and go on their crusade. Once they're gone we can escape, get to the Precinct House.' The doctor was smiling. It was a deluded expression as he tried to convince himself they would be safe.

'No,' muttered Archimedes. He dropped his arms to the floor, defeated.

'What is it? What's wrong?' Bane asked.

Archimedes looked up. He was pale, the thin veneer of confidence he had maintained thus far, stripped away to reveal a haggard old man resigned to his fate.

'I lied,' he said, with remorse. 'We did not come here alone. When the neurone plague broke out, I mean *really* broke out, people fled in droves. Meiser, Trevallian and I were caught up in a mob as we tried to escape the Corpseyard. It was the mob that killed my bodyguard, crushed him to death as he fired on them, trying to protect me. In the end we allowed the wave of fleeing settlers to carry us. We came here. Some of those fleeing had heard about the priests canvassing the settlements, they knew this was where others were gathering,' the guilder said, eyes intent as he regarded Bane especially.

'We were not prepared for what we'd find here. The Redemptors herded us, like sump cattle, fifty people rammed in these chambers with no explanation as to what was going on.' Archimedes paused, as if dredging up the courage to speak further. 'It wasn't long before they took the first,' he said, his voice diminishing to a croak. 'The preacher questioned them about the plague, about the one he was seeking. Ignorance, fear and pleading were met with the torch. The bones you saw in the chapel are of the people Meiser and I came here with. One by one he took them, one by one they burned. The screams…' Archimedes swallowed hard, trying to fight back his discomfort. 'They killed over forty like that. Then he came to the girl,' he said, nodding at Bane.

'When he touched her, something happened. He grabbed her wrist tightly and shook. She bore the brunt of his convulsions, thrown about like a doll as he thrashed. Her head struck one of the cots as he sagged into a heap. His brethren hoisted him up. He was muttering incoherently about his book. I realised later that he had scribed whatever he had seen in them but the interrogations and the burnings stopped. There were just the three of us left, alone in the dark, waiting for someone to arrive. When I saw you, the way you were looking at her, I knew you were the one the preacher was waiting for, the one who'd have the answers. I knew that you'd placate him and we'd be released. Now I realise that isn't so, that we'll die in this place.' Archimedes fell silent, regarding Bane with hollow, life-less eyes.

'Smite is insane,' Bane said at last, 'He's ingratiated him-self into this cult, passing off his mutation as a blessing. He's no priest and I don't believe he would have let us go, even if I did have the answers he seeks – I saw it in his eyes.'

It was cold comfort, but the best he could do. Silence smothered the room, the direness of their fate sinking in.

'So that's it?' Mavro bawled. The doctor got to his feet, shaking his head as he raced up the stone steps to the trapdoor. He hammered on the toughened wood furi-ously, knuckles white.

'Listen to me,' he cried at the trapdoor. 'Listen, I can tell you what you want to know. Let me tell you,' he raged, thumping hard with the balls of his fists.

Bane got to his feet. 'Weren't you listening Mavro? It doesn't matter. Smite has no intention of letting us go. He never did.'

Mavro stopped hammering on the trapdoor. He turned around and looked at Bane with pleading eyes.

'Then what the hell does he want with us?' he whim-pered.

A heady stench filled the air, thick and cloying.

Nark sniffed. 'What is that smell?' His voice betrayed a hint of fear.

Bane took a lungful, coughed and wiped his mouth. 'Fuel,' he breathed, hawking a thick gobbet of blood and phlegm onto the floor. He looked up to the small grates above. Thin wisps of smoke were exuding through them, growing in density.

'Quickly,' said Bane. 'Clog those openings.'

There was a frantic bout of movement as the survivors tore urgently at their clothes, ripping off thin shreds from sleeves and tunics to staunch the flow of acrid smoke now surging into the chamber. Four separate grates were set into the ceiling. Bane, MacDaur, Nark and Mavro stood beneath each one, holding the makeshift wadding in place.

'So, what now lawman?' Nark asked, coughing.

Bane thought for a moment, knowing that he had to act fast. He looked up at the smoke issuing through the cracks in the trapdoor and felt the heat from the room above. Bane used the wadding to cover his mouth.

'What are you doing?' Mavro screamed. 'We'll be suffo-cated.'

'Soon that's not going to matter,' Bane called back at him with grim finality. 'Nark, with me.'

Nark knew when to argue and when to act without question. A lifetime in the Underhive had taught him that. He dropped the wadding and followed Bane into the anteroom.

Jarla was waking up, disturbed by the commotion, as Bane entered.

'What's happening?' she asked sleepily. Her eyes widened when she saw the smoke filling the other room.

'Get your father up,' Bane told her. 'We're getting out of here.'

Above the coughing and the sounds of frantic despera-tion as the others fought to stop the smoke getting in and choking them all, Bane heard the harsh *snap* of burning wood in the chapel as the fire took hold.

Jarla had got Gilligan to his feet. The old barman was haggard, needing more than just sleep. They were at the door when Bane took hold of one of the stone cots. Nark saw his plan and moved quickly to the other side.

Bane heaved. It was damn heavy but between them they lifted it. Bane's muscles tightened as he hefted the cot's weight. Thick cords of vein stood out on his arms and he felt the same tension in his neck. As he and Nark took the cot through the door, Bane heard another sound above the eager conflagration: chanting. Numerous voices in perfect harmony. It was a ritual, and they were the sacri-fice. Smite had wanted to anoint his crusade with blood.

Pushing the thoughts into the back of his mind, Bane drove on.

They were through the door. Smoke choked the room. It was difficult to see through the grey miasma. Bane found the stone stairway. He took a step and coughed up another lungful of phlegm and blood. He heaved another step. The chanting grew louder, insistently demanding his attention. He heard Nark, breathing hard, choking and spluttering intermittently. Bane was exhausted, his arms and legs burning as if they were ablaze.

They reached the top of the stairs. The heat from beyond the trapdoor was searing Bane's face. He could only just see it through the thick cloud of smoke.

'What are you doing?' Archimedes cried urgently. 'They could still be out there.'

'A chance I'm willing to take,' Bane returned and looked at Nark. 'Ready?' he growled, trying to keep his head low and shifting his body so he held the cot at the side.

'Do it,' Nark coughed.

Bane tensed his muscles and with a huge effort, swung the cot back like a battering ram. Nark followed his lead. As it came forward with crushing force he roared, Nark's own voice similarly defiant as the gang lord cried in unison. The cot smashed into the trapdoor with the blunt, decisive aggression of an uphive trans-rail shuttle. The wooden trapdoor exploded against its fury, huge scorched chunks of it blasting outwards into the flames beyond.

Bane and Nark let go of the cot and it crashed through the gaping wound where the trapdoor had been, splinters framing the void like shattered teeth. The backwash of heat and pressure threw them down hard, crushing them onto the stairway. The intensity quickly abated and fire licked at the edges of the hole, turning the splinter teeth into blackened nubs.

Bane got to his feet and raised his hand over his eyes to ward off the heat of the flames. He edged out of the trapdoor to look around the chapel. Fire crawled up the walls and smothered the floor. The wooden pews crackled and roared with it. Like a bubbling wave, the roof was consumed and dusty tapestries dripped like wax. A narrow channel led through the conflagration. The Redemptionists were gone.

Bane ducked back into the chamber, turned to the others who were cloudy silhouettes below him and bellowed furiously. 'Go, now!'

MacDaur went first, then Jarla and Mavro, who supported the ailing Gilligan. Then came Ratz, hooting and whooping, a macabre grin etched on his face as the flames danced in his eyes. Last of all were Archimedes and his bodyguard.

'Meiser,' Bane shouted at him, the bodyguard at first a shadow as he cut through the smoke. 'I need you to get Alicia.'

Archimedes, coughing and wheezing, was past Bane and almost through the hole, when he turned and gripped his shoulder. 'He stays with his me.' Meiser pushed Bane aside and followed his master out into the chapel.

Bane barrelled down the stairs, shoving Nark aside.

'Leave her lawman or you'll both be killed,' the gang lord cried after him from the top of the stairs.

Bane was not listening. He had not come this far just to let her go. He fought his way through the smoke, feeling with his hands. Coughing and spluttering, he found his way into the anteroom. It was wreathed in acrid, black smoke. Eyes watering, Bane found he was out of breath and could not drag any air into his lungs. He was choking. He fell to his knees, pressed his head right down until it touched the floor, his nose and mouth just below the deepening pall of suffocating smoke, and heaved air into his body. He crawled, knees and elbows raw as he pounded forward, heedlessly.

Reaching Alicia's cot, he dragged her to the floor. Lowering his head again, he took another breath. He heaved

Alicia onto his back and with a massive effort, stood up. Back bent, he staggered to where he thought the door was. In the billowing black tempest he might as well have been blind. After a few moments, a sudden panic gripped him. He could not find the door! In the smoke he could be right next to it and not see it. Pawing at the smoke madly, Bane felt a strong hand grip his shoulder and drag him out of the anteroom. Together they found the stairs, crawled up the first few and staggered up the rest. At the mouth of the trapdoor, fire sketched around it in a ragged circle, Bane saw his rescuer. It was Nark.

He could not keep the surprise from his face. Nark returned the look with grim indifference and slung Alicia's left arm over his right shoulder. Bane took the other side and they dragged her bodily out through the chapel as the flames tore into it. They surged outside and fell into a gasping, wheezing heap.

BANE WATCHED AS the chapel was devoured by fire, stone charring and cracking with the sheer heat of the blaze. He bent down to listen at Alicia's mouth, smoothing her hair out of the way. After a few seconds he heard her breathing. She was alive. He felt someone grasp his arm. It was Nark.

'Look,' he said.

Bane followed his gaze and noticed the others all looking in the same direction. His eyes narrowed and he made out the robed forms of the Redemptionists, disappearing into the darkness of the Underhive, heading towards what Smite believed was their destiny. Heading towards a horde of thousands of creatures without remorse, who felt no pain and devoured the flesh of the living.

'Told you they were crazy,' Nark said.

'So what now?' Archimedes asked.

Bane scowled at him, remembering how he had left Alicia to burn. Meiser returned his look with steel in his eyes. I'll deal with you later, Bane thought.

'Without any weapons, we have no choice,' he said eventually. 'We have to reach the Precinct House before the horde does.' Bane swung his gaze around to the gang lord. 'That includes you, Nark.'

Nark sighed and said, 'I'm gonna need a smoke.'

CHAPTER: NINE

BANE SAT ALONE, swathed in the grey light issuing through a wide crack in the roof. The constant dripping of the dysfunctional precipitator nagged at him. It was a huge device, rusted and dilapidated but still impressive. It dominated the vaulted ceiling of the disused refinery, reaching up with ancient pipes, a dormant gyroscopic engine at its core. Thick coils of armoured tubing twisted from it like exposed intestine, conjoined to multiple banks of moisture condensers. Trapped water vapour was fed up the tube to a confluence at the zenith of the mighty machine, where a huge pressure sealed vat still existed. It was almost empty. All it contained was rusty sludge.

Bane cradled a battered shotgun in his lap. He had found it in a warden's lockbox when he had checked out the refinery. It had a full load of ammo: six standard solid slugs, plus one in the breech. Not enough, but something was better than nothing.

They had put a few miles between themselves and the chapel. The Precinct House was not far away, but Bane's detour had made the journey more arduous. With little knowledge of how far the plague had spread uphive and what safe zones still existed, they had had to take the most oblique route. Fatigue had set in quickly and the disused water refinery had seemed safe enough.

The others were resting in an old labour dorm. Nark was look-out. None of them had any weapons, except Bane who carried the shotgun and his dysfunctional service pistol, a weapon tarnished by age. It was an item that epitomised his failue, the symbol of it tarnished by memory.

He had thought about asking MacDaur to keep watch. He trusted his deputy more, but he looked weak and needed rest. He had railed against Bane's decision at first. The young deputy hated the ganger. His vision of the law was an ideal, black and white, with no room for grey. Strange then, how he had turned a blind eye to Bane's misdemeanours. Maybe he had not noticed. Funny what you see and do not see when you want to. In the end, MacDaur relented and the gang lord dutifully agreed.

It was a risk. Nark might make a run for it, but Bane had seen the fear in his eyes, more than once. It seemed as if Nark was with them for the time being. What choice did he have? Out there, in the unknown darkness, predators stalked them. There was safety in numbers. Nark knew that; it was a dogma indoctrinated in every Underhive ganger. What would happen when they got closer to the Precinct House? Bane did not know. He resolved that was when the shotgun would come in most useful. He was taking Nark in, whether he liked it or not.

A sudden bout of the shakes made the shotgun jump from his lap. Bane breathed deeply and fought down nausea and the stimm-craving that felt like it was eating his gut. He felt sweat on his forehead.

There was someone else in the room with him. He made a fist to stop the shaking and gripped the shotgun quickly and raised it, aiming at the dark. His heart pounded, then, from the soft crump of their footfalls, Bane realised who it was. He lowered the weapon and went back to staring at the precipitator.

'You wish to talk, guilder?'

Archimedes sat down next to him on a packing crate. 'The girl is still unconscious,' he ventured.

Bane had left Alicia in the dorm. He had watched over her at first but found he could not do it for long. The sight of her like that was difficult to bear. He had left Jarla and Mavro to keep her safe and maintain the vigil in his absence.

'You never did explain why she is so important,' the guilder said.

'It's a long story,' Bane said after a few seconds. 'I see you have brought a friend,' he added.

Meiser's shadow loomed into the room. He stepped into the light, announcing wordlessly his presence and threat.

'Laconic as ever,' Bane gibed, turning to regard the bodyguard with a stony gaze. 'I haven't forgotten what happened in the chapel, guilder,' he said.

Archimedes ushered him away with a glance, Meiser disappearing into the shadows once more. Out of sight, but never far away. The guilder sighed. 'You have my apologies. In truth, I was afraid. Meiser is my only protection here in the slums.'

'We are but a few hundred feet from Hive City,' Bane countered.

'It is a far cry from civilisation. You know that.'

Bane sniffed his agreement.

'I didn't know I could trust you, or the company you keep. I had to look to my own interests,' Archimedes admitted.

'How guilder-like of you,' Bane returned darkly.

'You were an enforcer once, weren't you?' the guilder said, changing tack after a moment of thoughtful silence.

Bane nodded.

'It wasn't from the uniform that I knew,' Archimedes admitted. 'You could've stolen that, or bought it. I've heard of you. Captain Erik Bane, one of the finest.'

'Seems everyone has.' Bane's retort was caustic.

'You were disgraced, expelled from the service,' Archimedes continued.

'I know the story, I lived it. Is this history lesson going somewhere, Vaxillian?' Bane turned his head to look at him, eyes narrowed contemptuously.

'My point is, you were once a leader and you're leading these people now, like it or not. On a small level, I think it gives you back some of the dignity you've lost. Maybe by saving that girl in there, you can start to feel like a worthwhile human being again. Only there's a problem.'

'What's that?' Bane's voice was a little choked.

'When you reach the Precinct House, all that will become a fallacy as you're confronted by the very institution that cast you out.'

'For someone who I met barely a few hours ago, you seem to think you know a lot about me.' Bane stared off again into the shadows.

'It's my business to know about people, to make a reckoning of them quickly and to know when they're telling the truth,' he said. 'You are obviously the leader. You demonstrated that in the chapel but it is a burden you do not wish for. Why else do you sit here, alone in the shadows?'

'Maybe I came here to get some peace and gather my thoughts.' The insinuated request did not hold much weight, and Bane knew it.

'And leave the girl alone, who you braved the depths of the Underhive to save? I don't believe that. I've been talking with the others and I know what you did to try and get her back: all that you risked. No, you're here alone because you can't face them. You can't face their expectant faces, the pressure that their desire to survive puts upon you. Even that ganger gives you grudging respect,' Archimedes concluded.

Silence fell. It endured for a minute before Bane responded.

'Archimedes, why are you saying this? Even if everything you've said is true, what does it matter?' Bane asked, anger in his eyes as he regarded the guilder.

'Because what happens when we reach the Precinct House and they turn us away?' he said.

'I…' Bane had to admit, it had crossed his mind. All the Enforcement knew of him now was that he was a drunk, left to die in some backwater settlement. Truth was, most who once knew him probably thought he was dead.

'If we get to their borders,' Archimedes said, after a time, 'take me with you. I will ensure our presence is met with cooperation, if you cannot.'

Bane was open mouthed. So many hard truths, from a virtual stranger, were difficult to bear. Was his psyche so easy to disentangle? In the end, he nodded.

'Thank you,' the guilder said.

'What for?' Bane was incredulous.

'Your trust and now I shall trust you,' he added.

Bane sat up straighter. The confusion in his expression remained, but it was tempered with intrigue.

'House Greim was not the only caravan to lose its cargo,' Archimedes admitted. 'In fact, several different houses have suffered similar fates. It was believed that the caravans were operating on secret trade routes, away from the bad-zones and it wasn't supplies of Fresh and rations that were taken. It was all munitions. They were weapons, bought and sold by gangers throughout the Underhive. Some were mass-produced, due for shipping off-world,' Archimedes paused. 'The firepower in those caravans could furnish a small army and there was only one band of perpetrators.'

'The Razorheads,' Bane spat.

'Yes. How did you know?' Now it was Archimedes turn to be wrong-footed.

'Alicia, the girl in the other room, was once part of the gang. She wanted out. I went in to get her.'

Archimedes nodded and smiled as he began to under-stand her significance.

'She made it out, I didn't,' Bane continued. 'They held me for months – quite a prize to have an ex-enforcer as a captive, particularly one who had a history with them. I got out and found the Razors were all dead. I found the majority of the gang clustered together in some kind of central chamber. The weapons you spoke of were all there.'

'Dead?' Archimedes asked. 'Killed by whom?'

'I don't know. They didn't stay like that. They turned into those things we've been running from,' Bane said, looking at the precipitator as he remembered. I saw the sill beneath it, used to catch any residue run-off. 'I found two of them head first…' He remembered the water still at the Razorheads' lair; remembered thinking it must have pumped throughout the complex. The hooded figure through the bars of his cell wasn't one of them. Couldn't be.

'What is it?' Archimedes asked. Bane had been thinking for about a minute.

Bane regarded the guilder. 'I think it was deliberate,' he said.

'What?'

'The plague. I think it started with the Razorheads, that the neurone disease was somehow made into a chemical and fed into their water supply. It was the only way to guarantee they were all infected,' Bane explained.

'But who could do that? Just infiltrate their stronghold and poison them and why, why start a plague to do it?' Archimedes said.

'The Razor's had an ally, who kept their identity secret,' Bane began.

'The one giving them the trade routes?' Archimedes ventured, catching on.

'Yes. But they were double-crossed. Whoever it was wanted the Razorheads' dead for some reason. The neurone plague would kill them before they even realised,' Bane surmised.

'But who?' the guilder insisted. 'My investigations produced nothing, not even a lead.'

Bane shook his head and looked away again. He crashed back to earth after his euphoric sleuthing. 'I don't know.'

'And the way it has spread. You and I both know there is something unnatural at work. What about this *one* the preacher spoke of?'

Bane sighed in exasperation and defeat. 'I don't know,' he repeated. 'The best thing to do right now, is to get to the Precinct House and present our findings to the–'

An urgent cry interrupted Bane mid-sentence. It was Jarla's voice. 'Alicia,' he breathed. He barrelled into the labour dorm without caution. He saw Alicia lying on one of the bunks. She was shaking, arms and legs thrashing as if of their own volition. Her eyes were closed as if by some kind of dream reflex. Spittle frothed on her lips. MacDaur was doing his best to hold her down, but he was weak and ready to collapse. Fruitlessly, the deputy Watchman tried to grasp an arm, but Alicia's muscle spasms wrenched it away and it struck him hard in the face. MacDaur fell back, blood streaming from his mouth.

'Alicia, it's all right,' Bane soothed, holding her arms. His grip was stronger than MacDaur's but still she thrashed, her body convulsing. Bane winced as her knee dug into his back.

'Meiser,' he cried. Archimedes had reached the end of the corridor, his bodyguard stepped into the labour dorm after him. The bodyguard flashed a glance at the guilder, who nodded nearly imperceptibly. He covered the distance to the bunk in three long strides and pushed Alicia down. She stopped thrashing, but she quivered, as if tiny jolts of electricity were going through her.

'What's wrong with her?' Jarla asked with a horrified expression.

'She's having a seizure,' Bane said. 'Mavro!' As the doctor caught Bane's gaze, he backed off, shaking his head.

'Help her,' Bane urged, aware that if she did not stop soon she was likely to break bones and maybe even hurt the one she carried.

'I'm not a doctor anymore, you said so yourself,' Mavro protested.

'Do it,' Bane bellowed. 'Get the scav over here and give her something.'

Mavro felt strong fingers grip his shoulder. It was Nark. He had not even heard him approach. He must have returned from look-out duty when he heard the commotion.

'Get over there,' he hissed into Mavro's ear, his tone threatening.

Mavro shrugged Nark's hand away. He got to the bunk and started fiddling around inside his long coat, looking for a sedative.

'Hurry up,' Bane urged, panting as he fought with Alicia. Meiser showed no sign of discomfort or labour. He just held her, staring as if into space. He had not even broken a sweat.

Mavro kept on digging, nodding profusely and then exhaling his relief as he found what he sought. It was a vial of copper coloured fluid. He produced a syringe, plunged the needle into the vial and drew a measure out. He held it up to the weak yellow halogen light in the dorm, flicked it and squeezed out a fountain of the stuff, removing any air bubbles. Mavro gripped Alicia's arm. 'Keep her still,' he breathed, wiping sweat from his brow with his sleeve. He bit his lip as he brought the needle close.

'Just calm her down, right?' Bane said. 'If that shit gets her hooked, the plague will be the least of your worries.'

'It's mild,' he breathed, returning Bane's gaze. 'It'll relax the muscles; that's all, I swear.'

Bane nodded. Mavro concentrated on his work again. He turned Alicia's left wrist over, smacked it a few times and plunged the needle in, pumping in the fluid. They waited, still she bucked and thrashed. The muscles in Bane's arms and wrists were burning.

'Thought you said it would relax her?' Bane said.

'Give it time to get through her system,' Mavro said. He shrank away from her, eyes fixed on her body, watching the infinitesimal reaction of her nerve endings as the chemical took hold. Slowly, the thrashing stopped, first the body, then the arms and finally the legs. She was still.

Meiser removed his hand from her stomach.

Bane released his grip. He had been holding her so tight that two dark bruises had blossomed on her skin. He felt shame gnaw at him but he crushed it.

'Thank you,' he rasped breathlessly.

Meiser nodded, his dark eyes unfathomable and went to stand over by his master again.

Bane looked at Alicia, wiping the froth from her lips. The room settled down as everyone started to relax. Bane slumped in one corner, eyes on Alicia. Two lives were at stake. He prayed she was not badly injured, her or her child. Nark's voice arrested his thoughts.

'We have a problem,' he whispered, eyes on the others.

'What is it?'

'I found something.'

Nark led Bane to the back of the room and pointed to a bunk. The light hanging over it was smashed, plastek shards littering the floor covered by a thin patina of dust. It made that part of the room dark, almost black. It looked innocuous, pretty much like the rest of the labour dorm – just another bunk, one of twenty-four arranged in three columns of eight ranks. There was a strip light for every four bunks, casting yellow and weak light. The walls and floor were grey and bare, and dust clogging the air. One door led to the rest of the complex, another led in from the precipitator room. Standing there, in the bland room, Bane had no idea what Nark was talking about.

'What am I looking at?'

Nark reached onto the bunk and dragged back the coarse top sheet.

A dark patch, about the size of a balled fist was visible beneath. It had been concealed.

'What is it?' Bane looked back as he said it, but no one else was paying them any attention.

'Smell it.' Nark said.

'What?' Bane looked up at him, incredulous.

'Smell it and you'll see,' Nark repeated.

Casting the gang lord a wary glance, Bane knelt down and sniffed the under sheeting. It was much thinner, a virtually thread bare cotton that had soaked through with the dark substance staining it.

'Blood,' Bane said.

'Not just blood. It's dead blood,' Nark corrected.

Bane knew instantly what Nark was driving at. 'This could've been here before we arrived.'

'It's fresh,' countered the gang lord.

Bane closed his eyes.

'It's not your girl,' Nark said. 'Someone has covered this up.'

'I know.' They had been in the refinery for two hours and people had slept as soon as they had found the labour dorm. Even Bane had been out of it for twenty minutes or so, plenty of time for someone to cough up a load of blood and conceal it. He remembered the blood on the walls of the Razorheads' lair; how it was congealed, how it had not spread like it should. It was a symptom. It left only one possible conclusion. 'Someone has been infected.'

'Yep. So what do you plan on doing about it?' Nark asked.

Bane thought for a moment. 'Nothing.'

'There's blood on this damn sheet, Bane,' Nark whispered, urgently. 'Someone in here got bit and whoever it is wants to keep it secret. Now I know it isn't me,' he said, eyes wide and insistent, 'and you haven't been in here since we arrived, so that rules you out, but it could be any one of those other frikkers.'

Bane held Nark's gaze.

'Nark, we keep this to ourselves,' Bane urged. 'If the rest find out it will get real ugly, real fast.'

'No scavving way,' said Nark, shaking his head and walking away before walking back. 'No way.'

Bane grabbed his shoulders. He was vaguely aware of some of the others taking notice of them. 'We can't linger here. Infected or not, we have to get to the Precinct House. We won't survive outside and we can't risk the enforcers finding out. If they knew, they might kill us all.'

Nark shrugged himself free of Bane's grasp and walked back and forth, trying to decide what to do. A few of the other survivors were stirring.

'Judging by the blood, the neurone plague is already fairly advanced,' Bane continued. 'It's going to be impossible to tell who has and who hasn't been infected.'

'And what if they turn?' Nark asked.

'Then we'll know,' Bane said simply. 'We stick to the plan. We get to the Precinct House and try and figure it out then – it's a hell of a lot safer there than it is here.'

Nark was not convinced but Bane had the gun and that made him the boss. If only he and Bane knew about the infection, that gave him an edge over the rest – it could mean the difference between survival and the alternative. He remembered Skudd, screaming wildly as they tore him apart. In the end, Nark nodded his compliance.

'One thing,' he said, quietly.

Bane's eyes narrowed suspiciously. No way was he letting Nark go.

'I'll come with you,' he said, 'but anyone looks at me in a way I don't like, I won't hesitate in putting them down.'

Nark walked away just as Archimedes approached. He pushed past the guilder with a meaningful glance and sat pensively in a corner where he could see everyone.

'What was that all about?' asked Archimedes.

Bane had already covered the bed back up. 'Nothing,' he lied.

SENTINEL LIGHTS, LOFTY and powerful, blazed into the gripping darkness of the Underhive fringe. It was known as the Frontier Land, which lay between the Underhive and Hive City, and in truth was neither.

Such was the ferocity of the lamp array, the blackness seemed to wither and retreat before it. It was white, absolute white, no more greys or grimy yellows. In a world in which darkness was more commonplace than light and where shadows provided anonymity and safe passage, such a beacon was a warning. A more potent one than any sign could muster.

Each light array was fixed to a hexagonal metal tower, buttressed where it connected into the sector power supply. Thick steel plates were riveted around the base, the heavy armour designed to prevent siphoning from energy-thieves and charge-vendors. This avenue of illumination, several hundred metres long, had two lamp arrays every twenty metres, each consisting of eighteen separate units, combined in three blazing strips of six, was merely the outer reaches of the approach to the Precinct House and from there to Hive City.

The lamps framed a long strip of cracked tarcrete, warning chevrons – yellow industrial, blast resistant paint – delineated it. The runway led to the Precinct House. Massive, like a fortress, the outer wall surged high into the false firmament. Winking lights bedecked its sleek, grey surface, angular shapes of reinforced plascrete jutting out from it at intervals. Razorwire wreathed the tops of the walls, so dense and thick it looked like black wool. Exacerbating the bastion-like image was a thick metal door, more like a drawbridge, set into the very centre of the wall. Upon it was wrought the symbol of the Enforcement, a clenched fist, an effigy of violent intent to would-be perpetrators of lawlessness. Bolts driven into the door, roughly the size of a man's fist, furthered the sense of impenetrability.

The wall was nearly a hundred metres across and bore three watchtowers. Huge search lights contained within each one strafed the ground beyond the runway, their beams grainy white, illuminating the periphery of the Precinct House's immediate domain.

The Precinct House was situated at an urban confluence. Its mighty wall filled a breech that led through to Hive City. Beyond it was a gulf of blackness where the level fell away to nothing. The Precinct House defended a comparatively narrow strip and the only access for several miles across. Behind its lofty walls, the multitudinous towers of Hive City soared, spikes of metal, rectangles on rectangles and jutting platforms whose winking guide lights were like distant stars. Vast plateaus stretched out between the towers; residential districts, private offices and empty domiciles. A steel monorail line snaked between them. The multiple, conjoined cars flashed like silver as it raced through the blackness, azure neon blurring. Gradually, the higher they rose, the lights of Hive City gave way, smothered by industrial gases, diffused into a luminous haze.

Bane crouched just beyond the range of the probing search lamps in the shadow of a disused fuel stack, long since dormant and decayed. He was thinking.

'What are we waiting for?' Mavro hissed, his impatience growing as he cast frequent anxious looks behind him into the threatening dark.

'We can't just walk right up to the gate and knock,' Bane returned without averting his gaze.

'Why not?'

'Because they'd be just as likely to shoot us as to ignore us completely,' MacDaur returned. He was crouching next to Bane. He had perked up a little, but still looked rough. No one wanted to get within the safety of those walls more than he did.

After a few moments, waiting as the search lamp made another pass, casting them all in monochrome white, Bane spoke.

'I'm going in alone,' he decided. Archimedes rested a hand on his arm. He too was at the head of the group with Meiser poised behind him.

'What if you can't gain us passage?' he asked quietly. 'You'll only get one chance at this. Let me come with you.'

Bane turned to him. The experience in the chapel had obviously changed him. He did not know of anyone in his trade that was so willing to put themselves in danger for others.

'If you come,' said Bane, 'you come alone.' He didn't need to look at Meiser to know the bodyguard's expression had darkened.

Archimedes looked into Bane's eyes, searching them. After a few seconds, he found what he was looking for and nodded.

'Alright then.' Bane turned around to face the group. Nark's face stood out, waiting at the back of the group. His eyes held suspicion and a readiness to act. Bane did not want to leave him alone, unwatched, but he had no choice. He had to take the gang lord at his word. There was distance between Nark and the rest, who huddled together.

MacDaur and Meiser carried Alicia between them on a makeshift gurney. Jarla stayed dutifully with her father behind them. Gilligan leaned heavily on his crutch. To their left, a little further back were Mavro and Ratz.

As the Ratskin came closer, nudged along by the doctor, in sight of the massive Precinct House walls, his expression changed. Bane saw a creeping dread infect his face, all trace of blissful, ignorant catatonia extinguished.

Ratz screamed, a terrible wrenching noise that made Bane wince.

He shuffled back, about to turn and run.

Nark grabbed him. Ratz struggled, flashing fevered glances at the forbidding structure before them. He pointed, looking at Nark, trying to get his attention, to get him to understand. His mouth open and closed constantly as if he were trying to utter something.

'What the hell is wrong with him?' Nark asked, strong enough to hold him still. 'Snap out of it,' he urged.

Bane gripped Ratz by the shoulders, forcing him to look at his face. 'What is it?' he asked slowly and firmly. 'What have you seen?' Ratz tried to look past him but he blocked his view. The Ratskin's mouth opened and closed. He was growing more hysterical, gasping for breath, clenching and unclenching his fists. He started wailing.

'Mavro,' Bane called, 'we need to shut him up.'

The doctor shook his head, reluctant to get involved. Fear and mistrust were etched on his face for all to see.

'Get over here, right now,' Bane said.

There was a flash of movement and the incoherent wailing ceased. Nark stood over Ratz, rubbing his knuckles. A thick, purplish bruise was already blossoming beneath the outlander's left eye. 'You wanted him to shut up,' Nark said nonchalantly. 'He's shut up. At least he isn't dead.'

Bane held the gang lord's gaze a moment longer and then turned to Mavro. 'You watch him. Drug him if you have to.' The doctor dared not disobey and nodded.

'And you,' Bane added, scowling at Nark.

The gang lord gripped Bane's arm and pulled him close. 'I helped you out of that damned chapel. I helped you get this far,' he snarled.

'I know that.' Bane went to move away, but Nark increased his grip and held him closer.

'I'm taking you in, Nark,' Bane said, shotgun raised to the gang lord's gut.

Nark felt it but ignored it. It was not the first time he had had a gun pointed at him. 'You make sure *they* know that,' he said. He had no chance out there in the dark, at least not unarmed. Trapped here with an infected, whose identity he did not know, heading to the bastion of his enemy, it was a bad situation. Maybe if he had a gun...

Bane cocked the shotgun with a dull, metallic click and met Nark's intense, desperate stare. He looked down at his arm; Nark held him a moment longer and then let go.

'I'll do what I can,' Bane said solemnly. 'You have my word.'

Bane moved to where MacDaur, Archimedes and Meiser waited. He unslung the shotgun and gave it to his deputy.

'Best chance is if we go ahead unarmed,' he said, trying to push the Ratskin's psychotic episode to the back of his mind. Something did not sit right, but there was no time to investigate it. The zombies could be close and they needed to get inside the Precinct House quickly. 'Don't want to provide them with an easy excuse to shoot us.' He leant over and spoke so that only MacDaur heard.

'You got seven shots,' he whispered. 'If he runs,' he added, eyeing Nark surreptitiously, 'incapacitate him, but don't kill him. Are we clear?'

MacDaur took a moment on that one. He would like nothing more than to shoot the dirty ganger, but he respected Bane's command. 'Clear,' he said.

Bane looked at Archimedes. 'Are you ready?'

'Ready.' The guilder took a breath and smoothed his worn robes.

Bane caught Nark's gaze. 'Everyone stays here,' he ordered. 'MacDaur is in charge.' He got to his feet. 'Raise your hands,' he said as he and Archimedes started forward.

Archimedes nodded. Following Bane's lead, he raised his arms, palms facing out. They walked slowly towards the lit tarcrete runway.

'AHEAD, TO THE left of the door. You see that?' Bane gestured with a head movement towards what looked like little more than a jutting square of plascrete.

'Yes,' Archimedes breathed.

'It's a sentry station. Four enforcers man it. There are two inside a concealed gun nest above; a narrow slit gives them a wide field of fire. It's likely that they have a high-calibre riot-stubber. It's loud and they might fire a warning shot.'

'I understand,' Archimedes replied.

'Walk towards it.'

Archimedes swallowed hard.

'Eyes front,' said Bane. 'We're in range of the search lamps.'

Within three seconds of the two men walking into the effective range of the probing lights, a throaty crackle emitted from a vox-speaker concealed within two wall cavities.

'Halt!' The tinny voice was threatening, riddled with partial static.

'Do as they say,' Bane hissed urgently.

'Identify,' the vox voice continued.

'Erik Bane. Watchman, Former Glory,' Bane responded.

'Archimedes Vaxillian, guilder.' He saw the black, gun-metal glint of the riot-stubber's barrel nose. He felt as if a target was being burned into his chest even as he spoke.

'No Underhiver may advance beyond this border without authorisation,' the voice crackled.

'Please,' Bane began and then chastised himself inwardly.

'The Enforcement does not respond to pleas of mercy. Remove your presence from the immediate district or face lethal action.'

This was a Sector Precinct House. They were different to local Precinct Houses. It guarded a major route into the Hive City, one of the few points on this level with some measure of protection. Bane knew he had to tread very carefully.

'We bring news from downhive. A neural plague outbreak has engulfed many of the lower domes and threatens the upper levels,' Bane said. 'I once served at this precinct,' he continued. 'Service number six-five-three-three-two-one-one.' It was a risk, hopefully at the very least it would give them pause, something to corroborate. They were still custodians of the law, after all.

A minute's silence persisted. It felt like half-an-hour in the tense atmosphere. There was a loud crackle and a dull click as the vox link was terminated.

'Eyes on the sentry station,' Bane muttered to the guilder.

Another long minute of charged silence passed before two figures emerged from the sentry post. A door slid open in the flat, dull grey, revealing a black rectangle.

One of the enforcers held a portable vox caster. They were both armed with combat shotguns. The one without the vox had his weapon raised and trained on Bane and Archimedes.

'Approach,' the porto-vox crackled.

Slowly, Bane and Archimedes walked towards the two enforcers who had moved to within ten metres of the station.

At a safe distance away from the enforcers, the vox crackled again. 'Halt.'

The enforcer with the vox let it hang by his side and pulled out a bolt pistol in preference to his primary weapon, which enabled him to vox and shoot if necessary. Together with his shotgun-toting partner, they advanced. At three metres they stopped.

The one with the pistol raised his free hand and twirled it around in the air, fore finger extended in a gesture for them to turn around in a circle. They complied willingly. The enforcer with the pistol brought out a scanner to check for hidden weapons.

'Throw down your arms,' he said. He was speaking through a respirator. It was standard procedure; gas attacks were common. His voice came rasping and distorted through the device. The effect made it cold and impersonal.

Bane wondered briefly if he had sounded like that when he had worn one. 'We are unarmed,' he said, aware of his thumping heart.

The shotgun armed enforcer raised his weapon and cranked a round into the chamber. The crunch of the loading mechanism made Bane feel sick. He remembered the service pistol. They must have read it on the scanner.

'Wait,' he said, turning around slowly, pulling up the jacket at his back, revealing the weapon. 'It's dysfunctional,' he added, easing the pistol out so they could see. 'No threat.' He tossed it behind him and it landed a short distance from the enforcer with the scanner. Keeping his hands raised, Bane turned back around, catching the ident-plate on both men's carapaces: Mackavay and Holpen. He did not recognise them, but it had been a long time. In three years faces changed, people died, and there were many enforcers in his precinct.

Mackavay, who held the scanner picked up the pistol. He examined it briefly, before pocketing it in a side pouch. He scanned them again.

'Clean,' he said in a monotone. The shotgun armed enforcer, Holpen, lowered his weapon from a kill to a ready position, waist height, cradled easily in two hands. Mackavay holstered the bolt pistol.

'State your business,' he barked.

'I and a group of survivors have fled the Underhive,' Bane began. 'A neurone plague is sweeping through it and I believe thousands could already be infected. It is imperative we be allowed inside this facility and a message be sent to Hive City Precincts to stem it before it boils over into the general populous.'

Mackavay regarded Bane impassively.

'Please, there isn't much time,' Bane urged. 'There are more survivors beyond those stacks, most need urgent medical attention.'

Mackavay clicked a comm-bead attached to the side of his helmet, a personal voxponder. His shadowed eyes, white slashes through his helmet slits, stared ahead. 'Be advised, additional targets located in vicinity, sub-sector three-three-two-point-one horizontal, six-six-nine-point-three vertical. Threat level unknown.'

'Threat? There is no threat,' Bane implored. 'They're unarmed civilians.' That was a lie but he could explain the details later. Right now, they needed access.

Beyond the two enforcers, Bane heard the whirr of an automated pintle-mount. The riot-stubber, training behind them on the co-ordinates Mackavay had provided. He watched as two of the search lamps flashed over to the stacks and rested there: two overlapping ellipses of intense, stark white.

'This is the Enforcement,' the main vox-emitter chirped again. 'Be advised, step into the lamp halo or you will be fired upon. I repeat: you will be fired upon.'

Bane looked back and felt paralysed. He prayed Mac-Daur would remember his training or the heavy stubber would shred him, Alicia and all of them without mercy.

There was another brief spell of silence in the wake of the vox command until MacDaur emerged, shotgun held above his head, palms out in a gesture of compliance. He waited there alone.

'Lay down your arms.'

MacDaur obeyed and stepped forward. The others came out after him, Alicia borne on a stretcher by Meiser and Mavro, fear of imminent death compelling the doctor into action. Gilligan stumbled out, Jarla supporting him as best she could. Then there was Nark, the unconscious form of Ratz slung over his shoulder.

'Advance.' The vox commanded.

The group moved to within fifteen metres of the enforcers, before the vox instructed them to stop. Mackavay had his pistol out again. Holpen had the shotgun at kill position.

'We are in need of your help. I can vouch for them, I was an enforcer–' Bane's plea was cut off by Mackavay.

'We know who you are citizen. Erik Bane is a drunk and an addict; a disgrace to the Enforcement. You will take these civilians and return to the hole you came from. The Enforcement will waste no further time on drunken delusions,' he said. 'You have thee minutes.'

Bane was dumbstruck. His fears were realised. He might not know the two men before him, but clearly they knew of him and his disgrace.

Mackavay tapped the comm-bead again. 'Trespassers have been advised. A standard protocol three minute extrication order has been issued. Prepare to fire in,' he paused to check something in his helmet pict, 'one-seven-three seconds and counting.'

'No, wait. You have to believe me,' Bane urged.

'Back away to thirty metres, or I will shoot.' It was Holpen.

Bane found himself backing away. He could not believe what was happening. He had not expected a happy home coming, but this…

'Wait,' Archimedes said. 'I am a Guilder. Here is my badge of office.' He showed Mackavay the guilder ring.

The enforcer looked at it and thought for a moment as the counter in his helmet pict-display ticked ominously downward. Mackavay tapped the comm-bead.

'Belay last command, pending my authorisation,' he said. He produced the scanner and held it over Archimedes's hand, logging the signature of the guild ring. 'Authenticated,' he said after a few seconds, reading off the scanner's low-res display. He sounded almost disappointed.

Archimedes gave an inward sigh of relief, but outwardly maintained his false aura of calm. 'By order of Necromundan Guild Law I demand safe passage granted to my person and those in my charge,' he said.

Mackavay did not hesitate. He nodded to Holpen, who lowered his shotgun back to ready position. He tapped the comm-bead.

'Nine to transport through the gate,' he uttered. 'Scratch extrication. I repeat; scratch extrication.' Behind him, the riot-stubber's pintle-mount powered down.

Bane sighed with relief and clapped Archimedes on the back.

'Let's just get inside,' muttered the guilder, looking back to eye the forbidding dark behind them.

THE GREAT DOOR to the Precinct House ground open slowly and inexorably. Churning servos protested in dull metallic baritones. Released pneumatic pressure hissed as interlocking pistons extended. It took two minutes for the massive gate to open fully across the tarcrete approach runway. It did so in a dense *thunk* of heavy metal, and kicked up dust and grit.

In the gloom inside, there came a throaty engine rumble, low and powerful. Bright flare lamps banished the semi-dark, a rigid silhouette framed in the backwash from the lights. A transport, not entirely unlike the *Bull*, grumbled into view. It was slightly bigger with a thick dozer plate on the front. It ground towards them noisily.

The survivors gathered together. Despite their suspicions, the prospect of survival and safety was enough to compel them. The transport took two minutes to reach them, from its emergence in the gateway, to the access door sliding open. Two enforcers waited within. As Bane entered, helping to carry Alicia with MacDaur, he saw an indent-plate. It was Vincent, one of his team at Toomis Pre-fab, three years ago.

'Vincent,' Bane said after he got Alicia comfortable. He sat next to him. The enforcer gave no response. 'Vince, it's me, Erik,' Bane tried again as the last of the survivors got inside. The door shut. There was a brief spell of darkness, before crimson internal lighting and activation runes on the driver chamber pict-display illuminated the transport space.

'Vin–'

'Please refrain from all communication,' Vincent responded tersely, eyes front, monitoring the display.

Bane sat back as the transport's engine rumbled to life. He looked at Alicia, pale and thin on the Enforcement stretcher. Webbing held her in place. Vincent's words echoing in his mind, Bane had never felt the burden of his guilt more than at that moment.

CHAPTER: TEN

THE HOLDING AREA was a grey rockcrete rectangle. Broad pillars bore down from the ceiling into steam-riveted steel supports. Walls, cracked and split in places, sported the occasional errant bullet hole. Overhead, strip lights exuded a dirty yellow glare. Shadows crept into the recesses of the room against the weak light. A battered looking couch of deep green synth-leather, sat in one corner. Small holes pockmarked the surface that was ingrained with years of sweat and grime.

Ratz and Mavro sat on it. The Ratskin was still out cold from Nark's punch. A large bruise had blackened in the time between the survivors arriving inside the Precinct House and being ushered quickly and silently into the holding area.

Next to the couch was an ancient looking caffeine-vending unit. It dispensed one choice of beverage – foul tasting, extra-strength caffeine in reconstituted paper cones. The entire room reeked of it, that and the stale stink of narco-stick emissions. The smell clung to the atmosphere like a second skin.

MacDaur and Bane sat in the middle of the room on low stools, around a metal table of similar stature. The table had head-shaped dents in places; Bane also thought he could make out the impression of three knuckles from a fist. A dark patch in one corner and a trail of fainter spatter marks could have been blood. Clearly the room was used for 'informal' interrogations too.

Meiser stood a short distance away from the table. The taciturn bodyguard waited patiently beside his master, who sat in a high-backed chair, covered in a similar shoddy synth-leather to the couch. Like everyone, the guilder was quiet, contemplating what lay ahead for them all.

The silent unease was broken only by the intermittent *thwump* of three ceiling rotator fans operating languidly above them. Strange, but they did not seem to perpetuate anything approximating a breeze. They were just a noise, and one that exacerbated the anxiety they were all feeling.

Bane eyed them speculatively, as if in the drone of their slovenly spinning blades, he would find the answers to the questions dogging him and the unexplainable unease gnawing at him. The sense of elation they should have been feeling and the relief at their apparent escape to a place of safety, had been crushed by doubt and a growing tension at the enforcers' wall of silence.

Bane had requested to be taken to the head of the facility. It was imperative that Hive City be warned of the impending plague horde. His request was met with characteristic stone-walling. He should have expected it. That was the Enforcer way: minimal communication. The survivors were an unknown factor. Their reports of a mass, potentially epidemic, bio-hazardous incident were unsubstantiated. In their position, he would have exercised caution, possibly suspicion. Yet still he was uneasy.

'This place is a frikking dump,' Nark said. He sat on a chair bolted to the floor and situated at the edge of the room, swathed in shadow. 'Is that what you're thinking lawman?'

Bane looked over at him. It was the first time anyone had spoken since they had arrived. 'Not exactly,' he answered.

'Yeah, didn't think so. Shall I tell you what I was thinking?'

'Does it matter what I say?'

Nark ignored him. 'I'm thinking where the hell are our medical checks? I'm thinking, why haven't your girl and the big guy in there,' he thumbed over to a thick black curtain across the room opposite the battered couch, 'been treated yet? We've been here almost an hour and so far we've been told precisely zilch. Personally I'm worried about what the scav these bastards are gonna do to me,' he concluded, staring intently at Bane, eyes hooded by the shadows. Bane returned a stony glare. He was aware that everyone except Ratz was watching them.

'I'm betting *that* was what you were thinking – with the exception of the latter, of course,' the gang lord added, sitting up to emphasise his point.

'I don't know Nark. I don't have the answers,' Bane replied, 'but don't pretend you care about these people. One act of selflessness doesn't eradicate a lifetime of past sins.'

'Past sins, eh?' Nark said, a sarcastic smile creasing his clean features. 'Well you'd know all about that wouldn't you?'

'You know nothing about me, ganger.' Bane's tone was hostile but he checked it quickly. 'I told you back at the gate, I'd do what I could for you and I will, so shut the frik up. You're not helping.'

Nark stared for a moment longer, sniffed derisively and slumped back into the shadows.

Bane got to his feet and eyed MacDaur. 'Watch them,' he mouthed with quick glances at Mavro and Nark in turn. The doc had grown skittish again, tapping his foot incessantly and flicking the razor over his fingers.

MacDaur followed his gaze and nodded. The deputy was almost grey. The second wind he had got earlier, possibly fuelled by the prospect of safety at last, had evaporated. He was breathing hard.

'You all right, MacDaur?' Bane whispered, keen not to draw too much attention.

'Yeah,' MacDaur rasped unconvincingly.

Bane regarded him for a moment, searching his face.

'Don't do that to me,' MacDaur said, mustering a stronger tone, 'I'm ok, just tired.'

'I need you to stay with me, MacDaur,' Bane said.

The deputy nodded. 'I will, Bane.'

Bane put a hand on his shoulder and squeezed a little. 'Soon as I speak to the Sector Judge, I'll get a medicae in here, ok?' Bane's attempt at reassurance fell a little short. 'It's nearly over.' That was not convincing either.

Bane walked over to Archimedes. The bodyguard observed him as if he was little more than an inanimate object, but did not block him. It seemed he had his trust – for now. The guilder looked drained and was deep in thought. When he saw Bane approach, he kept his voice low.

'Is this normal procedure?' he asked. 'To be kept here like this. I don't trust the ganger either, but selfish or not, he has a point.'

'Just stay calm,' Bane said. 'I will get a medicae to treat the injured and find out what's going to happen to us. You think that guild ring of yours can swing us any more slack?'

'It's done all it can. Friends in high places have little marketable value on the frontier. Perhaps if I could get into Hive City…'

'I thought so. Hopefully it won't come to that.'

'He doesn't look so good,' Archimedes said, looking at MacDaur.

'He's fine,' he said. 'Adrenaline's been keeping him going for a while, has all of us to one degree or another. He's just coming down from it, that's all.'

With that, Bane walked away, over to the black flexi-plas curtain. He drew it aside slowly revealing an antechamber. There were three bunks where patrolmen could catch some shut-eye. Aside from that it was bare, with strip lamps on the wall next to each bunk. A fan, much like those in the main room, hummed noisily above. When Bane entered, it was dark.

Errant light washed in from the adjoining room. Jarla sat hunched between two bunks. She looked up at Bane. Her eyes were sad and tired, faintly red as if she had been crying. On either side of her, Gilligan and Alicia were slumbering silhouettes.

'You ok?' Bane asked quietly, sinking down to one knee. The room was so small that he was almost next to her without approaching further.

'I'm fine,' said Jarla, her voice betraying her emotions. 'Just tired, that's all.'

Bane paused for a moment. 'How are Alicia and your father,' he asked.

'Not sure.' She rubbed her eyes and brushed her hair away where it was stuck to her face. 'They're still out.'

Bane thought about taking a look at them but stopped himself. No point. Nothing he could do right now.

'Just make sure they're comfortable. I'll get some help soon, ok?'

'Ok,' Jarla answered meekly. 'Can you close the curtain?' she added, shielding her eyes. 'I'm very tired.'

Bane got to his feet, 'Sure.' He drew the curtain shut again and turned to find Mavro in his face. The doctor had a wild look in his eye.

'What's taking so long, Bane?' he hissed. 'Nark said it already. Don't you think it's odd that we're still holed up in here?'

Bane shrugged dismissively. 'Enforcement protocols take time Mavro. This isn't a medical facility. Right now, I'm more concerned about warning Hive City garrisons. Now,' he said, leaning in close, 'Sit… back… down.'

The doc backed away and was about to protest when the entrance door, a grey metal plate, slid open. An enforcer stepped in, wearing half armour – a black cara-pace shoulder guard and vambraces. His hair was cropped close and dark brown in colour, the same as his eyes. Like most enforcers, he had perfected the steely gaze. The rank on his arm denoted him as proctor, a low rank in the Enforcement. A side-arm was strapped to his torso.

'You two,' he said, voice low and aggressive. He indicated Bane and Nark and then stepped aside to reveal the open door. The intimation was obvious. Bane gave Nark a look and the two men walked towards the door. Half way, Nark caught up with Bane and hissed in his ear.

'Remember what you said.'

Bane nodded. The two men reached the opening and went through, followed by the proctor, the door swishing shut in their wake.

'Finally,' said Mavro, sitting back on the couch, 'some action.'

'Yes,' breathed Archimedes. Suddenly the room felt less like a holding area and more like a tomb. 'Let's hope it's of the benevolent variety.'

ON THE OTHER side of the doorway there was a narrow corridor. They had walked along it on their way to the holding room, two armed enforcers flanking them either end of the column. An access panel had led them in through a subterranean vehicle yard where the transport had parked. Other than that, they had seen precious little of the facility. Clearly, they were not to be trusted.

The corridor was lit by a long crimson strip light that stretched its entire length. Nark was out first. As soon as the door was shut and he set foot in the corridor again, a combat shotgun was thrust into his face. Two enforcers were waiting for him, armed and in full armour. The one who did not have Nark at gunpoint punched him hard in the gut.

Nark buckled and coughed but did not go down.

'Hey!' Bane began, but he shut up when he felt cold steel in his back.

'Not your concern,' said the proctor, voice thick with meaning and menace. He gripped Bane's shoulder and pulled him back out of the way. Bane could only watch.

'You bastards,' Nark growled as he straightened, spitting at the guard who had struck him. The second guard pulled a bolt pistol and smacked the stock of his weapon across Nark's back, putting him down on his knees.

Bane shrugged off the proctor and tried to intervene. The enforcer turned the bolt pistol on Bane. The proctor then stepped between them, blocking Bane with his arm.

'Grakken Nark,' he intoned with a voice like a prophecy, 'you are under arrest and will be taken to the cells until a full account of your crimes can be scribed. There you will await trial.'

'Wait,' Bane said sternly. Despite his feelings towards Nark, he had given him his word. Were it not for the gang lord's actions, Alicia would be dead. He owed him that much. 'There is mitigating evidence in his favour.' His tone demanded the proctor's attention.

'This is an Enforcement matter. We are fully aware of this Underhiver's transgressions. Your testimony has no bearing,' he said.

'He was brought here in my custody. I am still a Watchman damn it,' Bane snarled, trying to keep his temper in check. The proctor had all of what, five maybe six years service and here he was, quoting the law at Bane as if he was a common citizen. Then it struck him. That was all he was to them, a common citizen, no different from Mavro or Gilligan, or even Nark, except he had not committed any offences they knew of.

The proctor turned, ignoring the dawning realisation on Bane's face. 'Take him away,' he ordered, the two enforcers who shoved Nark in the gut, urging him to rise.

'Wait,' Bane spluttered a desperate edge to his voice. 'You don't understand.'

'I don't think they're listening Bane,' said the gang lord, getting warily to his feet and wiping blood away from his mouth. Once he was up, the two enforcers ushered Nark down the corridor.

'Erik Bane, follow me,' the proctor said, walking in the opposite direction. Bane did as ordered, following silently.

At the end of the corridor, bypassing the entrance port which the survivors had entered by from outside, was a small hexagonal antechamber. Shimmering blue energy crackled at the doorway – a force shield. The proctor hammered an access code on a panel next to it. The shimmering energy diminished into nothing. He pressed a second panel beneath. Servos whirred dulcetly and the lifter platform came slowly into view, as if the ceiling of the chamber was gradually descending. After a few minutes it docked at their floor with a hiss of released pneumatic pressure. The proctor gestured Bane inside with a sweep of his arm.

Bane stepped onto the platform, a halo of white lights winking around the edges. There was the faintest clunk of metal on metal as the locking clamps disengaged and the platform began rising again.

'Command centre,' the proctor intoned and the lifter picked up speed. He turned to look at Bane, face impassive. 'You've been granted an audience with the Sector Judge of this facility,' he said.

As they rose, Bane noticed various chambers visible through clear plexi-glass. In numerous offices, enforcers filed reports, checked crime statistics and planned patrols. Training rooms were filled with cadets learning unarmed combat techniques tutored by veterans. On a gun range, bolt pistols and combat shotguns barked and roared and plastek targets daubed with simplistic black icons of menacing lawbreakers exploded in curious, violent harmony. One window provided a view out into the vehicle depot yard where transports waited, tech-adepts toiling beneath engines, stripping and reassembling weapon arrays.

Soon, the glimpses into the facility at large ceased and Bane was left to contemplate a gun metal void as he felt the levels swishing by. He felt time eking along with it. As the lifter gradually came to a halt, the force shield evaporated and a wide barren corridor of azure-stained steel was revealed. Bane only hoped it was not too late.

THE WIDE CORRIDOR leading to the Precinct House's command centre had a slight upward incline. On either wall were statues of ex-judges, either dead or retired, displayed in full armoured regalia, often carrying a power maul aloft like a banner. All of it was propaganda, a perception of justice. Anyone who had served as long as Bane knew that. But it was important for morale, and for aspirations, however lofty and untenable.

Reminded of those ideals once more, Bane felt a renewed pang of guilt as he approached a large set of bronzed double doors, the Enforcer insignia engraved onto them. Two enforcers waited dutifully on either side, their armour slightly more ornate than those officers in the field. Both were ten-year veterans, as indicated by the rank insignia wrought upon their brocaded shoulder guards.

On reaching the door, Bane's guards nodded to the others, about faced and left without a word, leaving Bane wondering what to do next. He did not have to wait long. The doors slowly edged open with a dull, metal shriek. Bane entered.

The command centre was dark. A vast square office space was lined with blinking charts on the walls, describing sectors of the Underhive and Hive City in detail, including trade routes and known hide-outs of criminal elements. Another statue was set into a cavity space, several metres tall. Beneath it was a bronze scroll; an epitaph with a roll of honour.

The names of fallen enforcers were painstakingly etched beneath. Bane traced the names with his finger, eyes narrowed to make them out. He felt his stomach lurch when he came across a certain cluster: Nabedde, Heske, Lorimir, Rannon and Keller. All of them had died at Toomis Pre-fab, the night Bane had killed Alcana Ran-Lo. Keller was the last one to fall. It happened when they made their escape. A lucky shot struck a fuel cell, causing it to explode. Keller's insides were vaporised in the blast swell and he had died instantly. Five men dead in what was supposed to be a routine mission, a mission where they had the upper hand. Something had gone wrong. They had been betrayed and the price paid was dear.

'I still remember that night, as I'm sure you do,' said a familiar voice from the shadows. Bane turned and realised someone was sitting at a large ops-desk in the middle of the room. Until that point, he had thought the Sector Judge was in some anteroom, trying to make him sweat before he announced his presence. In fact he had been there the whole time, watching him.

'Do I know you?' Bane asked.

The figure was nothing more than a silhouette, backlit by a large hive schematic, while an emerald under glow threw wan light beneath his chin from a display pict on the elliptical ops-desk below. The silhouette's hand moved slightly, pressing an activation rune and lighting set in alcoves about the room stuttered weakly into life.

'Better than anyone,' he said. Even in the wan glow of the half-powered globe-lamps, Bane recognised who it was.

'Mathias,' Bane gasped. Before him was his old proctor, Mathias Vaughn, wounded on the night of the ambush at Toomis Pre-fab. He was almost exactly as Bane remembered him, though he looked a little older and more haggard around the eyes and face.

'How are you, Erik?' Vaughn got up from his command chair. He wore a simple black suit, machine pressed, no buttons or lapels to speak of, save for a silver badge over his left breast. The shirt collar had a small square cut into it at its curvature at the throat and there were slits in the cuffs. He carried no visible weapons. As he approached, Bane noticed he walked with a limp.

Vaughn extended his hand. Bane took it out of instinct and the two men shook hands. 'It's good to see you,' he said, though his eyes told Bane different. The old training, however dulled by vice, never went away.

Bane sniffed his amusement at that. 'You're lying, but thanks anyway. Why the perpetual darkness?'

'Nursing a headache. Ever the detective, eh?' Vaughn remarked.

'Three years to Sector Judge,' said Bane. 'That's fast track advancement.'

'Arrest records speak for themselves,' Vaughn explained. 'After you... left, I assumed command of the precinct and became captain. A year later I was Sector Judge, and I've busted a lot of heads, even disabled,' he added, tapping the injured leg. 'But I won't be here much longer.' Vaughn walked to the ops-desk again and pressed a silver panel on its surface. There was a hiss of pressure release and the panel arched up forty-five degrees, revealing a decanter and two glasses. 'Fresh pure?' he asked, 'I've had it alcoholically treated, so it's got a kick even you'll appreciate.'

Bane smarted at that, not sure if it was meant as a gibe.

'What do you mean, you won't be here much longer?' he asked.

Vaughn poured himself and Bane a glass. 'I'm being promoted, to Hive City Judge.'

Bane couldn't disguise his shock. He masked it quickly, refusing the glass.

'I hope in this role, I'll be able to do more for the citizens of Necromunda,' Vaughn added.

'Never pegged you as altruistic, Mathias. I always thought you just wanted to put away scum,' Bane said.

'This way, I can make a *real* difference.'

'Rubbing shoulders with the elite of Hive Primus, you'll be at Helmawr's table before you know it,' Bane returned.

Vaughn smirked at that and drained his glass. 'You didn't come here from the squalor of Former Glory – that's where they dumped you, isn't it? – to reminisce over old times and debate the merits of my career. What do you want Bane?'

That was more like it. Truth. It was a rare quality, but when Bane saw it he knew it for what it was. He was surprised Vaughn was being so cordial, but then he knew Vaughn's captains would have submitted preliminary reports.

'An epidemic of neurone plague has afflicted a significant section of the Underhive. I've not seen it for certain but from what I can gather, there must be hundreds of thousands of plague zombies heading this way,' Bane said. 'They pose a serious threat to Hive City, unless stopped.'

Vaughn's demeanour changed. Whatever he had been told, it was not this. Despite Vaughn's feelings towards him, Bane guessed he still trusted his judgement, at least when he was not drunk or high on stimms.

'This had better not be some spook-induced fantasy, Erik,' Vaughn warned, tapping a sequence of activation runes on the ops-desk. The pict display behind him shimmered and changed to a schematic of the Underhive.

'I'm clean,' Bane said vehemently, 'and if you don't believe me, I've got a House Greim guilder at ground level willing to back me up.'

'I know of the company you keep,' Vaughn said darkly, looking up from the ops-desk. 'That ganger, for instance?'

'I brought Nark here to be submitted to Enforcement justice,' Bane protested. 'In the end he came willingly and he saved the life of an innocent.'

Vaughn's eyes narrowed but he gave no indication of what conclusion he had reached about the gang lord. 'What sectors are infected?'

Bane stepped up to the ops-desk, reviewed the schematic carefully and pointed. 'Former Glory here, to

Dreyzer's Glut. The horde has passed through this broad area. All of it.' It encompassed roughly half the Underhive.

'The horde,' Vaughn intoned.

'I wasn't kidding when I said there are hundreds of thousands, Mathias.'

Vaughn's expression was hard like stone. 'How did this start?' he asked beneath his breath.

'I'm not certain,' Bane admitted, 'but I think it began way downhive, with the Razorheads.'

'What?' Vaughn's hand went involuntarily to his injured leg.

'I was their prisoner, Mathias,' Bane explained. 'When I got out, I found them all dead. Only they were infected with the neurone plague. I think their water still was tainted.'

'Deliberately?'

'That's not all,' Bane said. 'They were planning something, getting tips from an insider with the guild. They had a huge stockpile of guns. I found them all, racked and stacked in their lair. Enough to make an assault on a frikking city.'

'You think the guilders, the legitimate guilders, orchestrated this to pay them back?' Vaughn asked.

Bane shook his head. 'No. They trusted whoever did this to them, at least as far as Razors trust anyone. They had to get close enough to infect the still. You didn't see that place Vaughn. It was like a fortress. Besides, tainting water supplies? That's not guilder style. No, there's something very wrong about all of this, something that doesn't add up. I just can't put my finger on it.'

Vaughn licked his lips. 'Very well,' he decided after a moment, 'regardless of the source, something has to be done to quell the epidemic right now. I'll send a communique to Hive City and get them to send troops. Meanwhile, I'll put the garrison on high alert.'

Bane nodded. He was tired. Only now, after he had done what he needed to do, did he feel it fully. He sagged.

'You need some rest,' Vaughn observed. 'Rudius, my aide, will escort you back to the holding area. I'll get a medicae to see your people as soon as you've returned.'

'Thank you,' Bane said. He was about to leave when Vaughn stopped him. 'Erik,' he said. 'I believe this is yours.' He held Bane's service pistol in his hand, produced from a hidden drawer in the ops-desk.

Bane took it without saying anything. He had had it this long; it seemed strange to refuse it now. He looked up at Vaughn and nodded his thanks.

'One of my officers said they confiscated it. I've had it checked. It's harmless, won't fire,' he said, regarding the antique weapon. 'A shame to let such a nice piece fall into disrepair.'

Bane tucked the pistol away, without a word but he felt the accusation as he walked back over to the door. The lights were dimming again as Bane approached it. He turned. 'Mathias.'

'Yes, Erik?' Vaughn looked up from the ops-desk, in the middle of establishing comm-links to Hive City.

'They're coming. Make sure your men are ready.'

'I will.' Vaughn's tone was earnest.

The doors behind Bane opened. As he stepped through them he looked back at Mathias, his frame blackened by the semi-darkness now drenching the room, and was struck by a sudden sense of déjà vu.

The doors ground shut with a clang, arresting Bane's thoughts – old memories, nothing more. Rudius was waiting, tight-lipped and stoic.

'I know the way,' Bane growled and thudded down the corridor to the lifter.

HE COULD SENSE them amongst the throng of thickening, putrefying bodies, sense their minds, arrayed about him like rotting fruit. They were empty shells, their old memories and any semblance of humanity diminishing into a vast, oblivious void. Instinct now reigned in their subconscious, fuelling their animalistic desires: a boiling maelstrom of hate and hunger. It was intoxicating.

He was still weak and pain rushed into his body with every movement. Only a few were under his thrall, two dozen – no more. Just the closest. They formed a shallow, circular cordon around him, their shuffling gait conducted in mind-compelled unison. He shuffled with them, a dark, wizened figure, leaning heavily on a staff, tapping the life energy of the weakest to perpetuate his broken body. As he walked, he felt his long coat, encrusted with filth and dried matter, trailing in the dirt behind him. He wiped a tangled strand of lank, grey hair from his face and smoothed his glabrous scalp, reaching out with his mind. One of *their* number, one of the survivors he had been pursuing, had been tainted.

Nascent urges within them had acted like a guidestone, bringing him this far. He could feel the infection running through the victim's blood stream, dissolving living tissue, eradicating sense synapses in the brain. Micro electrical impulses and thought centres shut down, as instinct and the desire to feed became absolute. The wizened figure revelled in it. The infected was close, which meant that he was close.

His euphoria was short-lived as he felt a spike of pain in his gut. He tasted necrotic blood on his lips. His hold on the creatures wavered; there was an infinitesimal pause as indecision crept into their debased consciousnesses. Refocusing his mind, he reaffirmed his mental grip. The creatures immediately around him shuffled on, dragging broken limbs, their agonised moans a constant, macabre chorus.

Too close, he thought. His ordeals in the Abyss were draining, and without the artefact to focus his powers... It was all he could do to keep them under control but it was just enough. A few, driven by his will, were enough to compel the rest of the horde. He had studied them, experimented at length. They were like sump cattle, gathering together out of some primal instinct. Where one leads, others follow. It began humbly, at first. He had only a few dozen, as he toured the devastated settlements downhive. Slowly the numbers grew, and now he had many thousands. He cast his gaze over a sea of the living dead, corpse heads bobbing in a plague-ridden tide. They stretched far and wide. He was at the heart of them. He was their indomitable will.

A vast structure loomed ahead. An avenue of blaring lights illuminated a runway leading up to it. A massive wall barred the horde's advance. Even in the wizened figure's mind-sight, it looked formidable. It was close and preparations needed to be made. A smile cracked his lips. There was a gate that was worked from within. If *he* could be manipulated…

He was back amongst the horde, the Precinct House just coming into view as little more than a huge, unfocused shape. Absently, he stroked the hair on a decapitated head tied to a belt around his waist. He stopped walking and the cohorts surrounding him stopped as well. The rest of the horde moved slowly onward; grey, decaying bodies carrying shovels, swords, rusted pipes and guns. His army.

The head on his belt was that of a Redemptor priest. Varlan Smite, he had announced himself as. It wore a gilded mask that covered the top half of the face, jaw slack, mouth open wide.

Another figure came into view. Taller than most of the zombies and bedecked in Redemptor robes it looked much like the now headless priest. He wore a conical mask that left his chin and mouth exposed, and carried a massive eviscerator in both hands. Its saw-toothed chain blades were stained black with chunks of ripped flesh between them. There was a gaping hole in his chest, flesh ragged and bloody at the edges where it had been torn. The wizened figure marvelled at the steadily putrefying organs exposed within and the matter-slick broken rib bones. He watched as the Redemptor kneeled, as he would before a king.

The wizened figure gripped the hair on Smite's head and raised it up to the kneeling Redemptor's face. The severed head made it easier. The Redemptors had been strongly indoctrinated to follow the priest's will – even in death his fanaticism clung to them like a persistent, unmovable mind stench. This way, he would meet little or no resistance.

The eyes of the decapitated head flared a green, ugly light and a low, rasping voice exuded through the mouth as the wizened figure spoke through it like some horrifying vox-caster. All the while his lips remained shut.

'What is your name?' came the voice through the head's mouth, which neither opened nor closed throughout the exchange, just gaped hideously.

'Deacon Raine,' said the Redemptor dully, his lolling tongue mumbling.

'And whom do you serve?' It was like a mantra, enabling the wizened figure to establish deep control.

'I serve you.'

The wizened man pushed the head closer and the baleful fires in the eyes lit Raine's face. His dead eyes stared at them, hypnotised.

'I have a special task for you, Deacon Raine.'

Through the head, the wizened figure gave his orders. At the end of it, Raine got to his feet, hefted the deadly eviscerator and made off into the horde, full of implanted purpose. Then the wizened figure was moving again.

All his endeavours had led him to this point. The artefact he sought was within; months of hiding in the shadows, feeding off rats to build his meagre strength, gradually exerting his influence over the one who had claimed it for his own. Soon it would all come too fruition.

Soon, very soon.

* * *

THE RETURN JOURNEY to the holding area was conducted in silence. Rudius, the proctor-aide was unreadable. Bane wished he had Varlan Smite's precognitive powers, perhaps then he could get an inkling of what was going on in Rudius's mind. Bane knew truth, he could read it as easily as any legal edict, and something nagged him. What he had seen was a mere simulacrum of the truth, not actual truth. What the enforcers were hiding bothered him. The audience with Vaughn had done little to allay Bane's fears. Maybe there was something...

Bane dismissed the idea. He was tired and overwrought. His imagination was running wild, perhaps a symptom of the stimm deprivation – he had never gone this long without before. Paranoia during withdrawal was not uncommon. He had seen it plenty of times in the dregs he had shovelled off the streets. No, he was still an officer of the law. He dealt in facts. Vaughn was sending the communicae to Hive City and that was all that mattered.

The lifter touched down, arresting Bane's thoughts. An armoured enforcer waited beyond the shimmering azure of the force shield. He stood unmoving, like one of the statues from the command centre. The shield dissipated and Bane stepped into the crimson-flushed corridor. Rudius remained in the lifter. He waited until the force shield had re-engaged before he spoke.

'A medicae will be sent shortly,' he intoned without emotion. 'Officer Hagenbak will escort you back to the holding area.'

'I feel safer already,' Bane muttered. 'Lead on.'

'You first,' Hagenbak growled.

THE DOOR TO the holding area slid open. As Bane entered, he was surprised to see that a medicae was already there. Another enforcer was present, standing next to the door. His ident-plate read, Trakkner. Bane stepped through, aware of Hagenbak following behind him. It seemed like a lot of muscle. The door slid shut. Bane suddenly felt vulnerable. This was not the safe haven he had envisaged.

'We have two injured in that anteroom, over there,' Bane said, gesturing to the flexi-plas curtain. It was drawn. He assumed Gil, Jarla and Alicia were still inside. The medicae was examining Ratz, who was still unconscious, though Doc Mavro had shifted and was now trying to look inconspicuous in one corner of the room. Everyone else was as he had left them. Bane noticed that Trakkner kept his gaze on Meiser at all times.

'Rest assured, we'll get to them,' the medicae responded. He did not look up and was intent on his work.

He was younger than Bane and slight of build compared to the other enforcers, obviously not indoctrinated on the same exercise and diet regimen endured by the frontline peacekeepers. He wore a plain grey suit with a charcoal shirt. Mousy brown hair framed a youthful face, drawn and pale. One of his eyes was an augmetic – it whirred and clicked, cycling through examination protocols. Insignia on his arm identified him as scientific staff: Kepke. There was no medical insignia on his clothes. He had a brown bag with him. It was open and Bane could see chemical solutions and syringes within. Kepke delved into it and produced a syringe containing a black liquid.

Kepke had a micro-bead attached via minute-pins into his ears, easily overlooked. He was muttering something. The micro-bead was duel feed – transmitting and receiving.

Bane watched intently as Kepke carefully manipulated the syringe. The liquid inside was filled with tiny bubbles. His attention back on Kepke's communication, Bane made out some words. 'He's the one.'

There was a pause. Receiving instruction. Bane felt his heart hammering again. He cast a sideways glance at Trakkner who was no longer looking at Meiser. He had his eyes on Ratz. The tension was palpable. He even felt it from Hagenbak behind him. Bane shifted slightly, show-ing his side to the officer behind him. Another sideways glance. Hagenbak was edgy as scav. They all were.

'What is that?' Bane asked.

Kepke looked up briefly. 'Just a mild sedative,' he said, smacking Ratz's arm to get a vein up. It was not hard as the Ratskin was skinny as hell.

'Sedative? He's unconscious.'

'It contains a pain-nullifying agent,' Kepke explained. 'Judging by the size of that bruise, he'll have quite a headache when he wakes.' He lined up the syringe. Put in the needle. His hands were shaking.

'Stop!' Bane cried, reaching out, grabbing the medicae's wrist and wrenching the syringe out of Ratz's arm. As soon as he did so, Hagenbak put a combat shotgun in his face. A round was cranked into the chamber.

'Don't move,' he warned.

Trakkner had pulled his gun and trained it on Meiser. 'And don't you even twitch,' he told the bodyguard. Meiser remained immobile. His gaze was fixed on Trakkner's gun, hands clenched into fists.

Kepke shook his wrist free of Bane's grasp and wiped his sweating forehead with a quivering hand. When he put the needle in Ratz's arm, the Ratskin woke up. His eyes were glazed at first and he seemed unaware of the syringe in his arm. It made the medicae hesitate. When Ratz saw the enforcers he went crazy.

He kicked Kepke in the stomach who doubled over, falling back. The Ratskin smacked the syringe out of his arm, clambered, spider-like, onto the back of the couch and tried to scale the wall, scratching at it with fevered fingers.

'They took it, they took it!' he screamed, pointing at Hagenbak and then at Trakkner.

'Shut him up!' Hagenbak bellowed, switching his gun between Bane and the Ratskin.

'Take your gun out of my face and I'll try,' Bane snarled.

Hagenbak held his gaze for a second and took the gun off Bane. 'Do it.'

Bane went over to the Ratskin, putting himself between Ratz and the enforcers.

'They took it!' he raged, clambering up the walls, only to slide back down, only to try and claw his way up them again.

'Ratz,' Bane said urgently, holding the side of his head, forcing the Ratskin to focus on him. 'Ratz,' he repeated. 'Calm down.'

'You shut him up, right now,' Hagenbak bawled.

Bane ignored the threat. 'Ratz,' he said again, quietly. The Ratskin was sobbing. 'What is it? What was taken from you?'

'What are you saying to him?' It was Trakkner, getting closer and taking his eyes off Meiser. Meiser watched him all the way. He unclenched his fists.

Ratz sobbed, his breathing growing erratic. He clenched Bane's arms so hard his fingers drew blood. Bane winced but ignored the pain. Ratz was the key to all of this.

'What was taken?' he repeated. 'What did you find in the outlands, Ratz?'

For the briefest moment, Bane saw a flash of clarity in Ratz's eyes. The catatonia vanished and Ratz spoke calmly in a normal voice.

'A crown,' he said. 'The Black Crown of Karloth Valois.'

'What?' Bane said. He could not believe what he was hearing. Valois was a legend. He did not think he was real.

Ratz stared ahead, glassy-eyed again. He could not answer. He was dead.

Hagenbak knew it too. Bane was suddenly aware of the man behind him, or more specifically, Hagenbak's combat shotgun aimed at his head. Funny, but live a life where people aim guns at you on a regular basis and you get a kind of sixth sense about it. The way Bane figured it,

he had about three seconds: two for the enforcer to hesitate and make a decision, another for him to pull a
trigger. It was obvious. They had come to find out what
Ratz knew, that he was the one they needed to kill first.
Make sure of the kill. Then they would kill the rest of
them.

Everything Bane had done, the battles he had fought to
get here, the distance he had travelled. He had kept them
alive, he had got Alicia out. To be executed on his knees
after all he had been through did not seem fair.

Time slowed. Bane closed his eyes. He reckoned he
could hear Hagenbak squeezing the trigger. Any millisec-
ond now, there would be an explosion of noise and it
would be over, all of his struggles for nothing.

The shot did not come. Hagenbak cried out. Bane
turned and saw Mavro on the enforcer's back, hacking at
his exposed neck with his razorblade. Trakkner went to
intervene, taking his eyes off Meiser. Big mistake.

The bodyguard moved quickly and silently. He
clamped one massive arm around Trakkner's neck even as
the enforcer turned to help his comrade. He should have
killed Meiser first. It was a natural reaction – to go to the
assistance of a brother-in-arms. It proved a fatal decision.
With one arm, Meiser broke Trakkner's neck, wrenching
it so hard, the skin bruised and reddened instantly, the
flesh around the neck slightly distended, overlapping in
hideously misshapen furrows.

Meiser did not stop.

Hagenbak mashed Mavro into the wall. The doc
squealed and let go, dropping the razorblade. Hagenbak
turned his gun on the others, blood streaming down his
neck where Mavro had cut him.

Bane had one of the metal stools in his hand, about to
throw it. There was no way he could make it before
Hagenbak fired, but what the hell.

Thunder roared, resonating off the walls and fire flared.

Bane threw the stool.

Hagenbak went down. The stool missed him by a fraction and clattered against the wall behind him, removing great chunks of loose rockcrete, showering Mavro with dust and grit.

The enforcer was dead. A hole in his chest had opened up his armour. Massive blast burns scorched away the black lacquer of the carapace, revealing the cold metal beneath.

Mavro was next to him, dumped on his ass. He sat, legs splayed, specs of Hagenbak's blood decorating his face. He had his hands raised up, palms facing forward.

'He was going to kill us,' the doctor said plaintively. 'I know that look.'

Bane turned his attention to Meiser. The bodyguard stood over Hagenbak's body, Trakkner's bolt pistol sidearm smoking in one hand.

'Thank you,' Bane said breathlessly.

Meiser nodded and turned the pistol on Kepke. The medicae was slowly crawling away on his hands and knees.

'You,' Meiser intoned. It was the first time Bane had heard him speak – even his voice was scary. Kepke stopped and looked at Meiser, his faced etched with terror.

Meiser gestured behind him. 'Open this door, right now.'

CHAPTER: ELEVEN

THE RUNWAY LAMPS flared brightly in the blackness, the search lamps illuminating farther patches of it in grainy white.

Nothing.

Silence deafened the outer reaches of the Precinct House. Ever since the civilians had arrived, an eerie void of sound had descended. It was unnatural, enough even to shake the iron resolve of an enforcer.

'You hear what those civilians were saying?' asked Holpen, peering through an observation slit. His eyes narrowed, becoming slivers through his helmet visor, as he regarded the silent darkness.

The two men were still on sentry duty, but their shift was coming to an end. It was not unknown for those on long duty details, particularly sentry, to develop mild paranoia. They called it 'watch fever'. Holpen and Mackavay were as tough as they came and neither had ever suffered from it. Tonight though, felt different.

'Some,' said Mackavay. 'Something about a plague, a horde of the living dead.' Mackavay sat on a metal bench, checking the load of his combat shotgun. 'Sounds like grade-A shit to me.' His tone was dismissive and he did not even look up from what he was doing.

'Yeah, that's what I heard.'

Mackavay looked up, sensing the enforcer's unease. 'Why?'

'You think there's any truth to it?' asked Holpen.

'Not our concern,' Mackavay said. 'Don't place too much faith in paranoid ramblings.'

'Seem quiet to you?' Holpen asked.

'A little.' Mackavay laid the shotgun against the bench. 'Why, what's the problem, Holpen?'

'Not sure, I just got this strange feeling.'

'What?' Mackavay got to his feet and walked to the observation slit.

'Shit,' Holpen hissed.

'What is it, damn it?' Mackavay was getting agitated.

Holpen turned, grim-faced. 'The runway lights are out.'

'That's impossible; the power cables are protected by sheet steel.' Mackavay shouldered Holpen aside to look through the observation slit. 'And buried under six metres of…' Mackavay's words died on his lips. Darkness greeted him. All the lamps were down.

Mackavay got on the internal vox.

'This is Mackavay. We have a power outage at the runway. Divert probe lamps to within twenty metres of the wall,' he barked.

Holpen took up his position at the observation slit again. He watched as the lamps drew in, their long grainy beams becoming tighter and more focused. They ranged, quickly from side to side, illuminating the immediate area beyond the wall.

'I don't like this,' Mackavay hissed, taking up his shotgun and cranking a round into the chamber.

'I can see something,' Holpen said urgently.

'What is it?'

Holpen peered intently into the shadows beyond the range of the search lamps. 'Can't be certain,' he said. 'Get those lamps to fifty metres.'

Mackavay ordered it on the vox and the lamps ranged further out.

'What the–' Holpen breathed.

'What?' Mackavay was sweating in his armour.

'People,' Holpen said. 'Lots of people.'

'People? What, rioters? More civilians?' Mackavay asked urgently. He moved to the back of the watch station by a hatch which led across a yard into the facility itself. Mackavay dragged his stool over to a bio-scanner and flicked it on. It powered up with a dull hum. A few seconds and a circular screen lit up in washed-out green. It was delineated into three metre blocks, stretching out a hundred metres from the station. A darker green line pulsed out from a central point, surging out in a semi-circular wave. The scanner was devised to register any heat signatures.

'I'm getting nothing on this thing,' Mackavay said.

'I'm frikking telling you Mackavay, I can see them with my own two… oh no.'

The crowd had got closer, steadily advancing towards the wall. The lamps still strafed over them. Holpen thought he could make out details. He reached for a pair of magnoculars. He aimed them at the crowd and waited for one of the lamps to strafe over the area he was looking at.

'The scanner must be malfunctioning,' Mackavay said, working at the machine's dials and activator runes.

'It's not malfunctioning.'

'That's not possible. Those people would have to be…' Mackavay realised the truth and suppressed a queasy sensation in his gut.

'Vox the stubber nests,' Holpen said urgently, throwing down the magnoculars, unhitching the observation slit and pushing his shotgun through. 'Vox them now!' he cried, thunder booming inside the tiny room as he fired.

'It won't open from the inside,' Kepke protested.

Bane reached over to him and yanked him to his feet. 'Do as he says,' he growled.

Kepke stared for a moment and then hurried over to the door, casting fearful glances at Trakkner and Hagenbak.

Using the tips of his fingers, Kepke prised off a panel set into the door. The medicae took a small card from his pocket, metal and rectangular – micro wiring and circuit boards made it look like some kind of tech – and pressed it into the panel. An access key lit within the panelled compartment, next to the tech card. Kepke was about to touch it when Bane stopped him.

'Hold on,' he told him. He looked at MacDaur. The deputy still resembled something that had just crawled from the Abyss, but he was slightly more alert after the brief mêlée.

'You ok?' Bane asked.

MacDaur nodded.

Bane crouched down, took Hagenbak's bolt pistol and tucked it in his pants. Then he took the shotgun from where it had fallen and tossed it to MacDaur. 'You're with me,' Bane said.

'What are you going to do?' Mavro asked, getting to his feet and wiping the blood from his face.

'Going back to the command centre,' Bane said.

'And the rest of us?' asked Archimedes. 'What are we supposed to do?'

'You and Meiser are getting out of the Precinct House. Something is badly wrong here and I need you to get a message to Hive City.' As if to emphasise Bane's point, a warning siren sounded in the room.

'A drill?' Archimedes asked.

The overhead strip lights flickered and went out. The whirring fans ground to a slow stop. Green emergency lighting crackled around the edges of the room.

'No. That's for real,' Bane said, moving quickly over to Trakkner's body. He picked up the shotgun, walked up to Mavro and pressed the weapon firmly into his hands. Mavro opened his mouth, about to protest but Bane's wagging finger stopped him.

'Just point and pull the trigger,' Bane said. He did not want to leave Mavro with the gun, but more enforcers might come looking for them and those that were left needed protection.

'Ok,' said Bane. 'Open it.'

Kepke pressed the rune and the door opened. The warning sirens grew abruptly louder. Meiser looked outside, quickly scanning both sides of the corridor.

'Clear,' he said, voice low.

Bane still remembered the warning protocols. He paused at the threshold of the room.

'The walls have been breached,' he said. 'The precinct is under attack.'

'Attack?' said Archimedes. 'By what? This place is a fortress.'

'What do you think, guilder?'

'Oh,' he muttered breathlessly. 'Oh hell.'

'That's right. Now, let's get moving,' Bane told them, 'You too,' he added, giving Kepke a nudge. 'You're first out.'

Bane was the last to go. 'Keep your head Mavro,' he warned.

The doctor nodded. The shotgun looked awkward in his hands. 'You're coming back, right?'

'I hope so.' Bane gave the black flexi-plas curtain a last look. Alicia was still unconscious. He thought about going back and seeing her one last time. It might be his last chance... No, they were getting out of this, one way or another. She'd be safe. Teeth gritted, Bane stepped out. The door slid shut behind him.

Out in the corridor, the sirens were deafening. Mac-Daur was about to head towards the lifter at the far end. Bane grabbed his arm.

'Not that way,' he said. 'It's voice activated and probably mag-locked. Without the access protocols to open the shielding, we're going nowhere.'

MacDaur nodded.

Bane headed in the opposite direction, the way they had come. He gestured over his shoulder for them to follow. Kepke the medicae went next, MacDaur's shotgun in his back. Archimedes followed and then Meiser.

About halfway down, they reached a junction. To the right was a hatch where a sloping ramp led to the subterranean vehicle yard.

Bane turned, pointed in the direction of the yard and shook his head. It was a dead end, blocked by another shielded lifter. Bane knew it led up to the cells. They must have taken Nark that way. Even in the crimson light, Bane thought he could detect a dark patch on the floor – Nark's blood. It did not sit well with him to leave him like that. In all the confusion, maybe there was another way. Another doorway, on the left led further into the lower section of the Precinct House. A crimson access panel throbbed quietly next to it.

Bane waited until they had clustered around the door, the faint hum of the shield, even at such close proximity, obliterated by the keening sirens. Only Meiser remained at the junction, watching the corridor carefully, bolt pistol raised. Bane got hold of Kepke. He shouted right in his ear. 'Access code, right now.'

Kepke winced in pain, tapping frantically at a pad by the access panel. He typed a sequence and it turned emerald. Bane shoved the medicae out of the way and looked at MacDaur. The deputy nodded; eyes on the door, shotgun at the ready. Bane hit the rune.

Nothing. The room was empty, some kind of storage area, just a few plastek crates and some metal drums, harbouring fusion-dried meals and fuel. Racking lined the outer walls on two sides. There was another door at the far end and a hatch in the centre. Bane waved MacDaur inside and the rest followed. Bane closed the door and shot out the access panel. The brass casing hit the ground amidst a shower of sparks and seared metal. With the door sealed, the wailing sirens dulled in volume.

'Don't want anybody following,' Bane said, cranking a fresh round into the bolt pistol's breach. It never hurt to be prepared. 'Ok,' he said, addressing the group. 'The way I see it, if there's an assault on the gate then most of the enforcers will be mustering there to repel it. In theory they shouldn't use these channels,' he said and then turned to face Kepke who was shaking.

'Am I right?' Bane asked.

Kepke nodded.

'Thought so. This is some kind of service wing. From what I remember, we can get to stores, vehicle yard, cells too. That hatch,' Bane said, pointing to the one in the middle of the room, 'leads to a freight access tunnel. There'll be a rail line down there and a freight-loader. You'll need to wire it, as there's no other way down the tunnel.'

'No problem,' Meiser said.

'Take the loader about two hundred metres down the tunnel. There should be a gantry. Find that and on the left side of the tunnel wall is another hatch. Two hundred metres down another length of tunnel and you'll be in the vehicle yard, opposite side to where we came in,' Bane explained. 'Take a transport and get the scav out. I assume you can drive,' he added, switching his gaze to Meiser.

'One or two-handed?' he said.

Bane had to check himself; that almost sounded like an attempt at humour.

'All right, you ready?' he asked Archimedes.

'Yes,' the guilder answered calmly. Together, they went over to the hatch and crouched down by it, Meiser too, while MacDaur watched the medicae.

The hatch was mag-locked, but done manually, not coded. It was designed to keep people out, not in. Bane cranked a hexagonal panel, fixed on top of the hatch. He rotated it through six revolutions and the mag-locks disengaged. Gripping the hexagonal plate, Bane lifted the hatch. It creaked open. Darkness beckoned from within.

A ladder was illuminated by the dim light of the store room.

'The ladder leads to a platform,' Bane told the guilder. 'The freight-loader should be right next to it.'

Archimedes looked at him, eyes narrowed. 'How do you know all this?'

Bane grew solemn for a moment. 'This used to be my precinct.'

'So it wasn't just the institution that rejected you that you were confronting by coming here,' Archimedes said. 'It was the very people that actually threw you into the cold and left you for dead.'

'I deserved it,' Bane said, holding Archimedes's gaze. 'Still do.'

'Not in my eyes, enforcer.'

Bane nodded his thanks. 'We haven't much time,' he said. 'Once you get into the tunnel and I lock the hatch, there's no going back. It only opens from this side. It's manual, so tech won't help.'

'I understand,' Archimedes replied.

'One last thing,' Bane added with a glance at Meiser, 'if anyone tries to stop you, kill them.'

The bodyguard's dark expression told Bane all he needed to know, although he felt MacDaur shift uncomfortably nearby.

Archimedes got to his feet and held out his hand. 'Good luck, Bane,' he said. 'I hope to see you on the other side.'

'It's Erik,' Bane said, 'and you too.'

Meiser was first into the hatchway, tucking his bolt pistol in his shoulder holster. Slowly, he descended into the gloom. Archimedes followed after him, with one last glance at Bane and the others, eyes fearful but resolute. The hatch closed for the final time and Archimedes and Meiser were gone.

Bane re-engaged the locks with a dull metallic *thunk*. He looked at MacDaur. 'Let's go.'

Through the back door to the store room was another, longer chamber. This one was filled with machine parts and a metal bench stretched half the length of the room, with a battered set of tank tracks laid on top of it. A huge metallic disc dominated the centre of the room. It looked as if it was mounted on some kind of rotating crank and raised up about a metre off the floor. Four access hatches were cut into it. More racking on the walls was piled with engines, fuel converters, capacitors and coolant units. A large ramp on the left led down to a massive concertina door, another route to the subterranean vehicle yard. There was another door that Bane was interested in.

As Bane walked over to it, he stopped just in front of the ramp. There were boot prints, faint but definitely fresh, overlaying the tread tracks. He crouched and scooped up some of the dirt from the print with his fingers.

'What is it?' MacDaur hissed.

'Not sure,' Bane muttered, getting back to his feet. 'No time for that now. Let's move.' He rushed to the door.

They were right outside it when MacDaur spoke again.

'Meiser just killed those men without even thinking,' he said.

'I know,' Bane returned darkly. He stopped and turned to look at the deputy, 'and we might have to do that too. Kill the enforcers.'

MacDaur licked his lips and looked uncertain. He believed in the law and what it stood for. He had not been a peace keeper long enough to get jaded. The idea of attacking the enforcers, even homicidal ones, must have been close to anathema for him.

'They're not all corrupt,' Bane said. 'In fact I'm not even sure those two back in the holding area knew whatever the hell is going on in here.' Bane gave Kepke a glance, but the medicae was saying nothing. 'They had a mission, to make sure they had the right ratskin – the one that found the crown and then to find out what he knew and kill him.'

'What the hell was that in that syringe?'

Bane gave Kepke another glance. Still nothing. Silence was his best policy now. 'Nerve toxin, internal haemorrhaging serum, who knows? Whatever it was, I don't think it got into his system. He just… died.'

'Inked saline solution, loaded with additional oxygen molecules,' Kepke muttered, deciding to speak after all. Perhaps, in some warped part of his fear-addled mind, he thought this was helping. That it might grant him leniency.

'What?'

'Inked salt water. That's what was in the syringe,' he said meekly.

'I didn't ask,' Bane snarled, turning back to his deputy. 'The Enforcers are our enemy here, MacDaur. That's all you need to know.' Bane put his hand over the door's access panel. He looked back at the medicae. 'You first.'

Bane pushed Kepke out into a broad stairway where rough rockcrete walls and bare metal greeted them. The air stank of dust and sweat. There was only one direction: up. They took it, Kepke leading, until they reached a platform about ten metres up. Another stairway led higher. MacDaur was about to mount the stairs when Bane's voice stopped him.

'No,' he said, 'I want to check something first.' He advanced towards a door that led off the platform. It was split on a diagonal and heavily reinforced, but with shorted-out servos. There was a metre wide split in it, enough room to creep through.

Bane edged through first, bolt pistol leading the way. Kepke came next, urged by the muzzle of MacDaur's shotgun. They entered a small guard room. A pict screen displayed a view of another room beyond. No sign of any guards, just a table, two chairs and a battered caffeine vendor in one corner of the room. A weapons cabinet stood alongside. Bane had seen enough to know it would be locked. A door to the other room in the viewer was open, servos shorted. Behind a second door opposite, Bane detected a faint hum – active shielding. It must lead to the lifter.

MacDaur saw the room in the pict, a long bare metal corridor, six doors along each side facing one another. 'Cells?' he asked, his tone was confused at first, then, as realisation dawned, he scowled.

'I owe him, MacDaur,' Bane replied. 'Watch Kepke.'

As soon as he stepped through the doorway, he felt the echoing resonance as his boots struck bare metal and he knew something was wrong. The access panel to the door had been prised off and wiring hung out of it like intestines. He walked slowly, checking each cell in turn and holding his gun in front in a two-handed grip, one palm beneath the stock to steady it. The strip light was weak and made the corridor gloomy. Emerald light from activator rune panels washed over him, turning his skin green.

The fifth door on the left side was open, just a crack, but definitely in recent use. Bane readjusted his grip. He smelled something like copper. Bane got his foot inside the crack of the door. He edged it open, very slowly. The copper stink grew stronger. Then he saw why.

There were two bodies inside, both enforcers. One had a shiv embedded in his neck. He guessed that Nark must have made it en route and kept it hidden. A fountain of arterial blood decorated the wall. The other corpse had a hole in its chest and two sets of blood spatter on its face. It was a close-range shot. The wound was cauterised, skin burned black at the edges. He had been thrown back by the impact; there were drag marks where his heels had caught on the floor. The enforcer with the shiv in his neck must have bled out. It would have hurt like hell and was probably the worst three and a half minutes of his life.

There was no sign of Nark. Both side-arms were gone. They must have stowed the shotguns in the weapons cabinet. Bane was surprised Nark had not taken them.

Maybe he did not have time, or maybe he preferred pistols.

Bane left the cell and saw a wrecked terminal. He was not sure what Nark was looking for. A pict display showed the outside of the Precinct House. The gate was open, and the only way to do that was from the inside. Bane gaped in horror.

The zombie horde was pouring through. Sporadic flashes lit up the dark – most of the lamps were out – as the enforcers discharged their weapons. They were hopelessly outnumbered. Stubber nests raged, bullet casings falling like metal rain. Bane watched as an enforcer was torn from his position. He had got close to toss a grenade. Bane watched as he was dragged into the horde. His mouth opened in a silent scream.

Bane looked away. It had come to guerrilla fighting, back into the facility when the wall garrison fell. Had Nark somehow accessed the gate mechanism from this terminal? Was that even possible? Gangers were wily bastards, learned a lot of stuff from embittered ex-officials. He could have got the guard's access protocols. It was possible. The only certainty was that time was running out.

Bane went back into the guard room. 'We go up,' he said. 'No more stops.'

WIRING THE LOADER had been easy. The vehicle filled the freight corridor as it went, effectively blocked it off from the boarding platform. Meiser stood at the controls, set the drive-shifter to med-power and with a lurch of metal and the whirr of servos activating, the loader started to move, quickly picking up speed.

The bodyguard had to yank on the brakes with a little urgency as they over shot the hatch, two hundred metres down. No apology. Instead he hammered the access console that opened the entry port and he and Archimedes got out onto another platform.

'This must be it,' Archimedes muttered, gazing down at the strip lit tunnel they had just traversed. Crackling energy spiking across the loader's tram line, threw azure flashes onto the walls. The shadows it caused took on a grim aspect.

'Get that hatch open,' he said, turning back to Meiser.

The bodyguard stalked forward. He gripped the hexagonal plate of the hatch. It did not budge. He put the weight of his shoulder into it. Still nothing.

'We may have a problem,' he rumbled.

AFTER MORE FLIGHTS of stairs than Bane cared to count, he was sweating and his muscles burned. MacDaur looked worse. Bane eyed him for a moment. He got hold of Kepke by the collar again. 'I'm your babysitter now,' he snarled in his ear. He pointed to a door at the top of the stairway. The rune gleamed red. 'You know what to do.'

Kepke opened the door to the corridor which led to the command centre. Bane shoved the medicae through it, half-expecting a challenge from the guards at the far end. He was fully prepared to use Kepke as a human shield if necessary.

The challenge did not come because the guards were not there. Bane tramped down the corridor, a hand on Kepke's collar all the way. MacDaur followed slowly behind.

Bane eyed every alcove and every doorway and vent, expecting an ambush at any moment. It did not come. When he reached the bronzed double doors at the end, they started to open as if they had been waiting for his approach.

Now he was really freaked out.

A void of half-dark pervaded in the command chamber. It seemed to draw them inside, against their will.

THE SENTRY STATION was completely overrun. Mackavay watched the grisly scene on a pict-viewer in disbelief as the zombies swarmed inside. They had fled the sentry station as soon as the zombies had got close. The power relay that gave life to the runway outside was dead and the sentry station door protocols were out. The creatures had literally torn their way inside. Together with Holpen, he had sealed the access port that led from the station annex to the wall and beyond, with the help of a tech. He had welded it shut. No use taking chances.

Mackavay switched the viewer to another area of the wall and then another and another. The zombies were swelling up against its length and breadth, like a living tide of decay. They clawed ineffectually at the heavily armoured wall, moaning and hissing and crawling onto the bodies of those creatures that had reached the wall first. They were crushed against the massing horde.

Heavy stubber fire raged in his ears. Holpen and four other enforcers who stood in the yard with them winced against the deafening barrage. The gun nests must be getting hot. How many must they have slain? How many more were there?

'We need to assemble all the men,' Mackavay said to Holpen. 'Relay to all watch captains and sound the alarm.'

Mackavay looked back at the viewer, which abruptly died. Static roared across it violently. They heard a sound. It was the gate. Servos squealed as it ground slowly, inexorably open. He could hear the horrible cacophony of groans grow suddenly louder.

'Oh no,' he breathed.

Dead eyes, unblinking and cold regarded him from the widening void beyond the gate. There must have been thousands of them.

'Get more troops,' Mackavay urged. 'Get them, right now.'

He watched, almost petrified as the horde surged through. Twenty enforcers armed with suppression shields rushed to meet the zombies. Tech's working feverishly at the gate controls had managed to stop them from opening it any further. It was possible they could cover the breach.

The enforcers locked shields, dug in hard and pressed into the emerging masses. The creatures snarled and raged as the enforcers impacted against them, clawing at the shields.

Mackavay came to his senses and led Holpen and the others towards the men blocking the breach, shooting any creatures that squeezed through. One of them leapt, or was maybe thrown, right over the shield wall. Bolt pistol cracking, Mackavay shot it in mid-air. He was a few metres away from the suppression shields when a high-pitched metallic shriek tore out from the undead mass.

Sparks flew, bright and angry in the shadows of the outer yard and one of the enforcers in the wall fell, his suppression shield torn in two. More sparks, the flash of metal and blood, and another enforcer died. Mackavay saw the source of the power outage. A huge, hooded figure, dressed in the robes of the Redemption, wielded a massive eviscerator in two hands and was carving up the rest of the wall.

The zombies swarmed around him through the breach he had created. The other enforcers tried to close ranks but were too late and another suppression shield fell. Corpse hands dragged him down, his muffled screams crushed as the horde smothered him. Steel flashed again and blood rained as another shield went down. Mackavay took aim at the Redemptor, but the round hit a zombie instead. He fired another as he retreated but other zombies were closing. His bolt pistol blazed in his hand as he tore them down. He heard the booming retort of combat shotguns. Holpen and the other enforcers were firing too.

Mackavay backed off. Only six of the original shield bearers remained. Their defiance was short-lived. The horde overran them and they sank beneath it. Mackavay heard a scream to his left. He tried to get another shot at the hulking Redemptor, but he was gone, lost amidst the horde that had swarmed around him as they filled the yard. Above, gun nests roared and flared but the horde was not thinning. There was another scream, closer this time.

'Spread your shots,' Mackavay barked, trying to assert his authority and fighting the blind panic that threatened to unman him. 'Keep a tight cordon of fire.' His men were not listening. He just wanted to get away, to wake from the nightmare.

In their flight, the retreating enforcers became separated. The zombies were everywhere and it was difficult to differentiate where the enforcers were. Mackavay thought he caught a glimpse of a helmet disappear beneath the mass. He heard the grunts and moans of the horde as they snapped and clawed at their prey.

Only Holpen stood next to him now. He saw him out of the corner of his eye, face etched with desperation, lit by the staccato blast flare of his bolt pistol. Sirens were wailing in the air. They screamed for him to flee. Mackavay felt cold rockcrete at his back: the Precinct House gate.

'Keep them back!' the enforcer bellowed above the din to Holpen, whirling to examine the access plate. He hammered in the access protocols. Too fast. He had made a mistake. There was another scream. It sounded a little like Holpen. He hammered the protocols again. Green light. The door was opening. He was about to step through when strong hands gripped his arms, head and neck. He managed to squirm round. A thousand pitiless corpse faces regarded him. The door opened fully. Mackavay realised his error even as they tore apart his armour.

'What have I done?' he breathed, before all light was blotted out and he sank like his comrades into darkness.

CHAPTER: TWELVE

MEISER WAS SWEATING by the time he wrenched the access port open. The thick metal pipe clanged as he threw it aside. He had used it to lever the portal wide enough for him and Archimedes to squeeze through. He was exhausted from the effort and it had taken valuable time.

The long tunnel that led down into the subterranean vehicle yard beckoned. From there they could make their way to the surface, appear on the opposite side of the Precinct House beyond the wall, and head to Hive City.

Archimedes eyed the gloom warily. A cable array of yellowish lamps lit the way poorly. It was very quiet, very still. 'I don't like it,' the guilder breathed. It was cold in the lower levels away from the heat ducts, and his breath misted the air.

'I'll go first,' Meiser grunted, keeping the bolt pistol close to his body. An outstretched grip was fine with another hand for support, helped accuracy and balance, but one-handed it was weak, easy to knock loose and the weight quickly made the arm ache. Meiser decided to conserve his strength.

The bodyguard moved slowly. Stout buttresses ran up the curved edges of the tunnel. They protruded a metre or so out; room enough for someone to hide in the half-light. Meiser took no chances and checked every alcove, waving Archimedes up after him. Two hundred metres of tunnel, same routine each time. It was slow going.

The lighting died. Meiser stopped and remained still. He gestured for Archimedes to do the same.

'What's going on?' the guilder hissed as loud as he dared.

'Don't know,' said Meiser. They stayed like that for several minutes. For Archimedes, it felt like hours, perception of time distorted by the sudden darkness. Meiser knew the duration exactly. He listened hard. Nothing. If anyone was there, waiting to ambush them, he would have heard them. There is no way anyone can stay that still for that long, without giving themselves away.

'Keep moving,' he rasped. Only about thirty metres left. He could see the faint oval of light coming from the vehicle yard. It must run on a separate power feed, he thought.

Something moved ahead, a group of hunched shadows, undulating like a wave of blackness. In the dark, it was difficult to see anything. Meiser edged closer, gun outstretched. Twenty metres away and he could hear noises: sucking, tearing, licking. Ten metres away and in the half light, Meiser saw a bloody hand flop out of a huddled mass that looked like scraps of entwined cloth. The hand twitched as something gnawed at the arm. A face appeared in the huddle of apparently conjoined rags, alerted by the bodyguard's approach. It was withered, grey and decaying. It snarled when it saw him, strips of torn flesh spilling from rotten teeth.

Meiser backed off, pushing Archimedes behind one of the alcoves. 'Stay there,' he warned.

Two plague zombies surged towards him, leaving the remains of their half devoured prey – an enforcer, probably a sentry, his armour cracked and split, his flesh...

The bolt pistol roared, lighting up the tunnel. Meiser hit the first zombie in the gut. Another shot to the head and it fell. The second took one in the neck and another in the head – its cranium exploded with the impact. In a matter of seconds they were inert carcasses, lying on the tunnel floor. Meiser was about to advance when the bundle of rags moved again. It alone formed the bulk of the obstruction – another plague zombie, but much, much bigger, stooping to fit in the tunnel. It was some kind of mutated ganger. Goliath tats were prominent on its decaying arms and chest. Its size came from stimm-enhancement, which reacted with the neurone toxin from the zombie plague to create a whole different breed of monster. Its musculature was impossibly developed, with hands that could wrap around Meiser's torso and a tiny diseased head on top of slab-like shoulders.

Meiser fired once, twice. It took a hit to the right temple – a glancing blow that did not even slow it. The creature rushed forward with all the momentum of a freight transport. Meiser winced in pain as the freak flung its arms around him and pounded the bodyguard into the hard rockcrete of the tunnel wall. The sudden impact jarred all the way down the bodyguard's spine and he cried out. Meiser's good arm was pinned at his side and he yelled in pain as the sling was torn off the injured one.

The creature pitched him off his feet and Meiser had to ram his elbow up into the zombie's chin to stop it from biting him. Spikes of agony shot into him and white slashes invaded his vision. Panting for breath, Meiser managed to wrap his finger around the trigger of the bolt pistol. It was buried somewhere in the creature's drug-fuelled bulk. He pulled the trigger, five, six times.

The muzzle flare, even buried as it was between them, lit up the tunnel – Meiser's snarling visage described in stark light and shadows. Archimedes watched, huddled next to the opposite buttress, as the zombie's back exploded outward in a mass of flying bone and gore.

Still it held on.

Meiser felt its grip loosen, and pulled his knees up between his torso and the zombie's chest. He got his palm up, under the creature's chin and pushed. It leaned back a fraction, froth and gore-soaked spittle flying. Meiser got his feet against the thing's chest and kicked hard. It still gripped his body but he got the bolt pistol free. Roaring, it came back at him, only this time Meiser jammed the pistol into the zombie's snarling mouth. He fired three times.

Archimedes ducked down, closing his eyes and covering his ears. The shots came like gargantuan hammer blows, resounding in his head. When he opened his eyes, clearing smoke infected the part of the tunnel they had fought in. Meiser was slumped on the floor breathing hard, his injured arm limp at his side. The freak was down, most of its head missing – rotting graffiti on the tunnel wall.

Meiser wrenched himself to his feet and wiped a swathe of blood off his face and neck with the sleeve of his bodyglove. He looked over to the tunnel mouth.

About a metre away from the tunnel exit a figure stepped into the light. It was a silhouette, crouched, bent up and old looking. But there was something about it, something powerful. Meiser felt the hackles on the back of his neck rising.

No way back.

The figure was coming closer, its movements slow and awkward. Meiser held up the gun. He was weak from his exertions and it wavered slightly in his grasp. He pulled the trigger and heard an ominous click. Empty. He tossed it to the ground. His heart thundered. 'Get behind me.'

Archimedes obeyed.

Meiser had been his bodyguard for nearly six years. They had been through some tough situations. The Corpseyard at Dreyzer's Glut was one of the toughest, so tough he had lost Trevallian, another long-serving henchman. But Meiser, like always, had got him out alive. In all those years, through all those life or death moments Meiser had never, ever shown fear, not even in his voice, until now.

THE WORLD WAS *dark and undefined, as if shrouded by a dense fog. Hunger gnawed at the infected's brain, driven by debased instinct. Only the scantest thread of humanity remained, a barely recognisable memory trace embedded deep in a withering psyche. The stink of flesh filled their nostrils, awakening a primal craving. It was unbearable.*

Sweet soft flesh…
So sweet…
They longed to taste it.
Sanity ebbing away…
The plague… Impossible to resist…

CHAPTER: THIRTEEN

BANE ALMOST TRIPPED on the first body. It was one of the guards, still wearing his armour, although there were no visible wounds. A shotgun lay nearby. Another body was further inside the room, little more than a bulky shadow in the gloom. Again, no wounds and a gun laying nearby.

Bane stooped over the first guard, thrusting Kepke just in front of him. MacDaur waited just behind. Bane could hear his deputy's laboured breathing. Tentatively, Bane pulled the guard's head back. There was a loud crack as his neck snapped. He had barely touched him. Bane winced when he heard it. Heart thumping, he held both sides of the guard's helmet and carefully pulled it free. It came off easily, as if his head had grown too small for it. Bane gave a sharp intake of breath.

The guard looked like he had been dead for years. His skin was thin, like parchment and bluish veins showed through. His cheekbones poked upwards like miniature peninsulas. The eye sockets were black and sunken, pupils white and glassy. His lips were sloughed away to reveal blackened gums and teeth. The tongue was a black and withered strip of flesh.

Bane rolled him over. Air, his final breath, escaped in a long and tortured rasp. The foetid stench of it washed over Bane and he gagged. It was as if the life had been literally drained out of him. Bane got to his feet and looked

over at the ops-desk. It was hidden completely by the
darkness, unnaturally so. Even the light washing in from
the outer corridor seemed to abate at this threshold, as if
it was afraid to penetrate further.

'Get up,' Bane hissed. Kepke was on his knees, vomiting
quietly in the corner. He wiped his mouth and obeyed.
Bane turned to MacDaur. The deputy was keeping it
together, just. Bane gestured to his left, indicating that
MacDaur should circle. The deputy followed his gaze,
moving slowly, wearily.

Together, taking Bane's lead, the three men edged
towards the ops-desk, penetrating the rim of the darkness. As they did, the door began closing.

Kepke cried out, looking back urgently, about to flee.
Bane gripped his wrist hard, arresting his flight.

'No time,' he whispered.

In seconds the doors slammed shut and darkness
engulfed them. Just the strip lights overhead to guide
them with their dull green luminescence.

Bane waited, allowing his eyes to adjust. Slowly, a figure began to materialise, a hazy silhouette.

'I know you're there,' Bane said, trying to keep his voice
calm and level.

Another moment of silence.

'Ever the detective.' The voice was familiar, but cor-
rupted somehow, as if two people were speaking at once.

The light on the ops-desk flared. Harsh and white, the
sudden illumination made Bane squint but he resisted
the temptation to look away.

Lit from beneath by such stark light, Vaughn's face
looked haunted. Deep shadows pooled in his eyes,
cheeks, around his mouth and beneath his nose. He
looked somehow older, even in the short time since their
last meeting.

He wore a crown. Jet black, the crown shimmered like
living metal. It was hooded at the back. It extended all
the way round to the front, ending in two raised edges,

like spikes. All manner of grotesque metal artifice was attached to it. A grinning, daemonic visage regarded Bane from between the raised spikes.

So this was what Ratz had ventured into the Abyss to retrieve. This was what the Enforcers had stolen.

Bane heard voices in the void as he stood facing off against his old proctor, sibilant, soothing yet urgent. Not Vaughn, his mouth was shut tight, as if stitched. He was listening. Bane realised it was the voice of the crown's owner, Karloth Valois, infamous zombie master, a nightmare tale to scare hive children to sleep. Except the nightmare was real; the very evidence of it was before him. Bane knew that it was not Nark who had opened the gate but Valois, through his willing pawn, Mathias Vaughn.

Bane took a step forward, waving MacDaur behind him. Vaughn's raised hand stopped him. There was pain etched on the Judge's face as he struggled for control. His eyes were fixed tight, teeth set in a grimace. The hand clenched into a fist.

Vaughn opened his eyes, awareness returning, the pain gone.

'You opened the gates,' Bane said, his tone accusatory. The bolt pistol was low, held in line with his waist, pointing down. He should kill Vaughn now, but he had questions and he did not know what Vaughn, or rather Valois, could do. The desiccated corpses of the guards stayed his hand for now.

'In a manner of speaking, I suppose I did,' Vaughn returned.

Bane licked his lips, not sure what to do. 'Vaughn,' he said, 'fight it. Give up the crown and we'll get you help. Valois has seduced you. You don't know your own mind.'

Vaughn threw his head back and laughed. The sound boomed around the chamber like maniacal thunder. Recovering his composure, he looked back at Bane. 'I was seduced by nothing,' he said, lip curling into a sneer. 'I wore the crown willingly.'

'You're a good man at heart, Vaughn,' Bane continued, edging the gun up. 'I know this isn't you.'

Vaughn's face grew suddenly solemn. 'For someone who was once regarded as a formidable detective, you are disappointing Erik,' said Vaughn. 'I thought you'd realised it when first we met not more than an hour ago, in this very room.'

Bane looked on, confusion and disbelief warring in his mind.

'You paused, as you left. I was... *aware* of it.'

Realisation dawned finally in Bane's mind and with the weight of it the bolt pistol sagged in his grasp.

'The hooded figure,' he said, eyes wide, 'It was *you*.' Vaughn sniffed his amusement and smiled broadly. 'But that would mean...' Bane continued.

'That I was the leak, the one providing... information to the Razorheads,' Vaughn said. He took great sadistic pleasure in it, pleasure in watching Bane crushed by the truth. 'That night in Toomis Pre-fab. You remember it, yes?' He was still smiling.

Bane felt his legs weaken. He dropped the pistol – didn't even hear it fall – and put out a hand to steady himself.

'No.' The word was barely a rasped breath.

'Our intelligence led us to believe we were the ones who had the upper hand, and yet we were ambushed,' Vaughn continued, delighting in every moment. He began walking from around the ops-desk, still framed by the harsh light. He waited until he was face-to-face with his old captain before he spoke again.

'You were supposed to die in that ambush,' Vaughn whispered darkly, 'but something altogether more satisfying happened instead. You killed that girl. Alcana Ran-Lo was her name, wasn't it? An enforcer slaying the child of a high-born in a botched mission he himself had orchestrated. What other penalty could there be but expulsion? And for someone like you, who lived and died by the very institution that spat you out like poison, that was worse than death. So followed your predictable slide. Wash-out. Drunk. Addict.' He dwelt on each word, letting it sink in, making it hurt. 'You were as good as dead, better even.'

'I trusted you Vaughn. You defended me,' Bane blathered, eyes on the floor as if shamed. Then he looked up, right into Vaughn's eyes. 'You were shot, I saw it.'

Vaughn smirked. 'A small price to pay,' he said, getting close. 'Power, Bane, that is what I craved, like you crave stimms. You were a good detective, great in fact. I knew I couldn't keep my… associations from you forever. You blocked my ascension and were getting close to ruining everything.'

'And your comrades, the other enforcers who died and were injured, what of them?' Bane fostered his anger and felt it building.

'Come now Bane, you and I are familiar with collateral damage.'

Bane clenched his fist. All he had to do was reach up, grip Vaughn's throat and crush the life out of him with his bare hands. Then he remembered the dead guards and his fist unclenched. Vaughn was a vessel, a vessel for Valois's power. It was primal, beyond Bane's comprehension. He could feel it, crackling beneath the surface, pricking at his skin. He was in trouble.

'And the Razors?' Bane hissed. He heard something moving behind him. 'Were they collateral damage too?'

'Inadvertently, I let them grow too powerful. They had to be destroyed,' he explained. 'It was easy to taint their water still. They trusted me.' He could not resist smirking at that. 'As I'm sure you realised, it fed the entire complex. Once they were infected, the plague would do its work,' he said.

Bane stared in disbelief.

'They were a loose end,' Vaughn said. 'Just like this Precinct House. There is evidence here that can link me to the Razorheads and certain personnel I was forced to take into my confidence. The plague will see to them,' he added, nodding. 'This,' he said, pointing to the crown, 'told me what to do.'

'You're deluded,' Bane said. 'This may have been your plan at the start, your corrupt will, but it is the whim of Valois you serve now.'

Vaughn ignored him. 'The zombie horde will overrun this entire facility. No one will escape, no one. I will be the only survivor. A desperate rearguard action to Hive City, my internment as Sector Judge bathed in courageous glory as I personally rally the defences.'

'You're crazy,' Bane snarled. 'The plague will ravage Hive City.'

'An unfortunate necessity,' Vaughn returned. 'It will abate eventually, and in the rejuvenation of those sectors doubtlessly afflicted, with me at the helm, I will shine and thus garner more favour with the ruling elite of the Spire. This,' he said, spreading his arms wide, 'is all that stands in my way. All of you, everyone in this Precinct House, must die.'

Bane heard Kepke yelp and get to his feet from where he had been cowering. He felt the power inside Vaughn before he saw it. He dropped to his knees out of instinct, the same instinct that had kept him alive this long.

'All must die,' Vaughn raged, outstretching his arm.

Now Bane saw it. The dark power seemed to manifest in slow motion. Black energy, like miniature forks of malevolent lightning, crackled over and between Vaughn's fingers. They shuddered, the movement minute and urgent. Steadily the forks arced and merged, forming a dark nimbus of reckless energy. The nimbus swelled, consuming Vaughn's entire hand until it exploded outward in a coruscating bolt of black lightning.

Bane felt the backwash of power sear the skin on his face, streaking across the room until it struck Kepke as he fled towards the door. The medicae's death screams wrenched time back to normal. The blast wave lifted him off his feet, a flare of dark energy lighting up the air around him, casting him in stark silhouette. Tendrils of evil power raced over his body, probing, coursing, eking the very life out of his puny body.

Kepke's scream died. His steaming corpse lay on its back and smoke funnelled from the mouth like some extinguished fuel stack. His skin was withered, aged impossibly in seconds. Bane suddenly wished he had the same faith Smite had been so fond of. Maybe he would have prayed. Instead, he reached for the bolt pistol lying on the floor.

He raised the gun, half-expecting Vaughn to turn his borrowed power onto him but the blast of dark energy did not come. Vaughn staggered back. Bane fired and the first shot missed as the ex-proctor fell against the ops-desk. His psychic exertions had taken something out of him. Bane swung his pistol around as Vaughn clambered around the edge of the ops-desk, face wracked with pain as he tried to focus.

'This madness ends now,' Bane cried. He was about to fire when someone crushed him into the floor from behind. The bolt pistol boomed, the shell impacting into the ceiling. Bane caught a glance of Vaughn disappearing further into the room beyond the ops-desk, before he was crushed down completely. His wrist smashed against the hard floor and the bolt pistol spiralled from his grasp. Bane struggled and threw an elbow into his assailant's gut. It got his arm free. He backhanded and felt connection with bone. The weight lifted for a moment. Bane used the time to roll onto his back, blocking a grasping hand reaching for his throat. Bane stared into the eyes of his attacker.

MacDaur's face was drained of colour, his eyes a glassy void. He snarled as he fought, spittle flecking Bane's face.

MacDaur was the infected and he had at last succumbed to the plague. Not MacDaur, Bane thought.

MacDaur got a hand around Bane's throat and squeezed, the deputy's nails digging into flesh. Bane head-butted him and felt MacDaur's neck jerk back. The deputy's grip weakened. Bane drove his knee up into MacDaur's stomach, using his free hand to throw him off his body. The deputy skidded across the floor. The bolt pistol was right next to him. Dazedly he saw it and picked it up. Bane sat up and crawled backward on his elbows, kicking with his feet for more purchase. He saw the gun. MacDaur's slackjawed expression showed no emotion.

'MacDaur, don't do this!' Bane pleaded. He felt the wall at his back. No where to run. He felt something else too, digging into him: his service pistol. Bane wrenched the pistol out from behind him, took aim and pulled the trigger. The pistol's report resonated around the room. The bullet hit MacDaur in the chest and he fell, his weapon clattering down with him.

Bane sagged against the wall. Vaughn was gone. There was a concealed lifter at the back of the room that Vaughn must have used to escape. Bane got to his feet and went over to MacDaur. The deputy was breathing heavily. Breathing?

Bane dropped to his knees and held MacDaur's head up into the light. The glassy expression had vanished. He must have been controlled by Vaughn's – or rather Valois's – will. It was not MacDaur who was infected. Maybe none of them were. Maybe the infected was already dead. Bane looked down at his deputy, his friend, and was horrified. He could not speak. MacDaur was dying, blood staining his clothes in a growing crimson blossom.

'Bane,' MacDaur breathed, blood flecking his lips as he spoke.

Bane leant down. 'Easy MacDaur, easy,' he said, his voice choking.

He had driven him to this. MacDaur was an idealist. He had believed in the law and what it stood for. He had believed in him. Those ideals were shattered. Bane had seen to that. He had been adamant that they should head for the Precinct house. His damned redemption, so precious to him, had led only to death, maybe for them all, and many more besides.

'Bane,' MacDaur said again, voice growing weaker.

Bane put his ear to MacDaur's lips. 'Yes.' His voice was barely a whisper.

MacDaur's final words were spoken defiantly. He arched his neck up as he said them. They used up the last of his fading strength. 'Get him.' MacDaur's head sagged back down. He was dead.

Bane closed his eyes tight. He cradled MacDaur's head for a moment as he crushed his feelings of remorse deep down within him. He let the deputy go and got up. No way forward. The lifter would be keyed into his old proctor's voice signature. He had to go back. One way or another, Vaughn would pay.

BANE SHOT THE lock on the door mechanism using the bolt pistol. The service pistol firing once was a miracle. He doubted it would fire again. He heaved the doors free by hand. Rage fuelling him, he got them open. He hurled himself down the corridor. He noticed that the lifter at the end was plate sealed. He made for the stairwell entrance instead. As he reached it, there was another thought dogging his mind. He had believed MacDaur was the infected. It was one of the reasons he had taken him, to get him away from Alicia. He had thought he could handle it, hoped MacDaur could stave it off for long enough for him to take Vaughn down. But it was not MacDaur, so who was it?

Bane's mind was racing when he opened the hatch that led to the stairway. He bolted through heedlessly. It was unlike him. His emotions were making him careless.

When he saw the bolt pistol in his face, he realised his mistake.

The enforcer smashed Bane into the wall, smacking the bolt pistol from his grasp. Another smashed the hatch shut. Bane had surprised them, but they had been ready enough to act quickly.

The second enforcer pressed his forearm across Bane's neck and pinned him against the wall. With his free hand, he held Bane's chin. 'He's not one of them,' the enforcer growled, letting Bane go. The bolt pistol was still in his face.

'Who the hell are you?' the first enforcer snarled.

'His name is Erik Bane,' said a familiar voice. Bane looked over to its origin. He recognised Vincent. 'He's an escaped prisoner.'

'You don't understand,' Bane began as the second enforcer grabbed his arm to restrain him. The other enforcer holstered his weapon, grabbing Bane's other arm. Bane did not resist. There were too many of them. 'Judge Vaughn,' he said, grimacing as the enforcer twisting his arm around his back turned him around and pressed his face against the wall. At least the gun was out of his face. 'He's the one behind this attack,' Bane snarled.

'Judge Vaughn is the head of this facility,' Vincent countered. 'The zombie horde came after you arrived,' he added accusingly.

Vincent got close and took out his pistol. 'You're under arrest Bane.'

'Release him,' ordered another voice.

The enforcers hesitated.

'I said let him go.' They relented. Even Vincent backed off.

Bane turned to face his apparent ally. In the half-light of the stairwell, he cast a large shadow. He towered over Bane – a wall of carapace and muscle. A sergeant's rank pin was fixed to his armour. The patchwork of scars on the lower part of his face was unmistakable. 'Dugan,' said Bane, more than a little relieved as he recognised his old heavy weapon specialist.

'Bane,' the massive enforcer returned.

'Judge Vaughn opened the gates,' Bane said quickly. 'He admitted it to me himself.'

Dugan could not hide his shock. 'What do you mean?'

'I don't have time to explain. Vaughn is the one who started the plague. He'd been giving information to the Razorheads and he killed them with the neurone virus to cover his tracks. He's been playing all of us: you, me, this entire precinct.' It sounded crazy. Bane was not even sure he believed himself, now he had said it out loud.

'What?' Dugan wasn't buying it. He looked over to Vincent and the other enforcers.

'Wait,' Bane urged, holding up his hands and backing up as far as he could. 'You think this zombie attack is a coincidence? Vaughn came into possession of an arte-fact, something an outlander salvaged from the Abyss.'

'The Abyss? Bane, what the hell has this got to do with Vaughn?' Dugan's face crumpled in confusion. He shook his head. 'When I heard you'd been brought in, that you saved some civilians, I thought you'd changed but you're still a frikking stimm-head, full of paranoid scenarios.' He looked at Vincent. 'Take him.'

They went to grab him again, but this time Bane resisted. He managed to pull Vincent's gun, punch him in the stomach and spin him around to make a human shield. He put the bolt pistol to Vincent's forehead.

'Listen to me,' Bane urged.

Dugan showed Bane his palms, a glance at the other two telling them to back off. Bane was desperate, he looked like a lunatic.

'Take it easy,' said Dugan.

'Vaughn is dirty. The corruption goes way back,' Bane tried to sound adamant. 'He even staged the ambush of Toomis Pre-fab.'

Dugan shook his head again. 'Bane, that night was tragic, but there was nothing we could've done. It just went bad.' He took a step forward.

'Keep back,' Bane warned, pressing the pistol harder, his arm around Vincent's neck. He took the opportunity to look around. Four enforcers on this level: Dugan, Vincent and the two who had restrained him. There was a heavy stubber rig stowed in the corner, next to the hatchway. One level down, there were five more. Two had suppression shields, another carried a flamer. One enforcer was working on a vox unit. It looked like he was trying to get a signal and he kept sending out an acknowledgement message. The fifth was at the door where presumably the enforcer's had entered. He was a tech-adept, just finished welding the lock. He heard a scratching sound – low and insistent – coming from outside.

'What the hell are you doing in here anyway?' Bane asked.

Dugan licked his lips, trying to stay calm. 'We got trapped,' he admitted. 'The zombie horde flooded the outer yard and penetrated the central structure of the facility. We were forced to retreat into the stairwell. The creatures migrated upwards for some reason.'

Bane looked back at Dugan.

'They're heading towards Vaughn. He has the crown of Karloth Valois.'

'That's insane.'

'They are coming for it, Dugan,' Bane urged. 'How else do you explain this? You've got good instincts, always did. Tell me you don't think there's something unusual happening here.'

Dugan regarded his old mentor, trying to decide. There was doubt, Bane saw it in his face. 'Behind me, down a corridor, is the command centre,' Bane said. 'Inside you'll find four bodies. One of them belongs to MacDaur, my deputy. I shot him because he was under Vaughn's control when he used the crown. As for the other three,

Vaughn turned Valois's powers on them too. I'll let you judge for yourself on that one.' Bane was breathing hard. He needed Dugan to believe him, it was his only chance of getting to Alicia and the others.

Dugan was agitated, old feelings warring with current duty. 'Even if what you say is true,' he said, 'and I'm not saying I believe you,' he warned. 'How could he do it? How is it even possible?'

'I don't know how, but he did. I saw it with my own eyes,' Bane said. 'Do I look jacked up on stimms to you? If you don't believe me, go and check. But do it quickly.'

Dugan regarded Bane a little longer and then turned to the second enforcer. 'Gant,' he said. 'Go check it out.'

'Are you crazy?' Vincent hissed, through gritted teeth.

Bane yanked his arm hard, making Vincent choke. 'Shut up,' he hissed, dragging him aside, so Gant could get through the hatch.

It took ten minutes for Gant to return. In the charged silence, broken by the steady clawing from beyond the door, it felt like ten hours.

'He's right,' said Gant breathlessly. 'I checked the ops-desk too. The gate protocols were activated from that station. I saw the command edict on the pict display.'

'What about Judge Vaughn?' Dugan asked.

'No sign of him, sergeant.'

Dugan looked into space, the revelations of the last few seconds wracking his mind. He made his decision. He turned to Bane.

'Let him go,' he said. 'I believe you.'

Bane hesitated.

'You have my word, there'll be no reprisals.'

Bane waited a moment more, searching Dugan's face. He let Vincent go. The enforcer coughed and spluttered as he hurried away.

Bane turned the pistol over and handed it out to Dugan, stock first. The sergeant holstered it. 'What now?' he asked.

'I need your help,' said Bane.

Dugan maintained his gaze and waited for more.

'The civilians I came in with,' Bane said, 'I need to reach them. They are in the lower levels of the facility. I need a way down.'

Dugan's face was a mix of annoyance and disbelief. 'And I'm to provide that help, am I? You've probably noticed Bane, we have a slight situation here ourselves. I'm trying to guarantee egress for as many of my men as possible.'

'She's a girl, Dugan, barely sixteen, just like Alcana,' Bane said, his voice betraying his emotions for a moment. It was selfish, Bane knew that, but it might be the only thing salvageable from this whole mess. 'In all the years you knew me as your captain, did I ever let you down?'

Dugan licked his lips. 'Just once,' he said.

'Then let me make amends,' Bane said earnestly. 'Trust me Dugan, as you once did, as I trusted you all those years–'

'Don't listen to him, sergeant,' raged Vincent. 'He's full of crap. No respect for the force, no respect for himself–'

'Shut up, Vincent,' Dugan bellowed. He searched Bane's eyes, like his old captain had always taught him to. Then he nodded.

'What do you need?'

'Get me to the ground level holding room. I'll do the rest,' Bane said.

'We've been trying to open up communications with other units,' Dugan explained. 'When the horde attacked we were split up. We believe that small pockets of enforcers still exist around the facility. If we can reconnoitre with enough of them, we might be able to breach a way through the horde, mount a significant assault...' Dugan's voice trailed off.

'What...' Bane began. Dugan raised his hand.

'You hear that?' Dugan said.

'Hear what?' Bane asked.

'The scratching... It's stopped.'

Dugan was right. There was only silence coming from beyond the sealed door. The tech-adept pressed his ear against it. A sudden high-pitched shrieking made him fall back. Sparks lit up the area around the door as a churning blade was pushed through the welded lock. Another second and the door came down, right on top of the tech-adept.

'Shields!' Dugan cried as he saw the zombies pouring inside.

Two enforcers raced forward, leaping over the tech-adept and smashing their suppression shields into the zombies. The vox operator followed closely behind, yanked the door off the fallen tech-adept and dragged him to safety.

Something flashed in the dark and there was the sound of churning metal and the guttural noise of a fuel-powered weapon. One of the enforcers with a suppression shield cried out. He spun ninety degrees. His arm was severed at the elbow and it flew off and down into the stairwell void below. He dropped his shield and was pitched over the side. He hit the lowest floor with a wet crunching sound.

A huge figure stepped through the doorway, dressed in brown robes, a conical mask covering his face and head. In his hands he held an eviscerator. The teeth of the deadly weapon whirred as he came forward, spitting out chunks of chewed flesh and splattering blood. Bane recognised him. It was Deacon Raine. it seemed that Smite's crusade had faired badly.

Raine was about to lay waste to the other suppression shield when the flamer came forward and ignited the entire area in front of his comrade. Raine and a dozen other zombies fighting to get through, burned. The Redemptor thrashed and turned and several zombies lost body parts as they came under his whirring chain blade. Several more were pushed over the side, burning like parchment as they fell. But Raine did not fall. He came forward, forcing the shield and flamer to back off.

Dugan and the other enforcers unhitched their weapons with unerring synchronicity and fired. Raine took six hits and went down. The flame-seared void created in his wake soon filled as the zombies continued to pour in. Vincent leapt down the first set of stairs and took up the fallen shield. Together with the other shield-bearing enforcer, and with gouts of fire from the flamer, they forced the horde back.

'Can we go up?' Dugan asked, turning to Gant.

The enforcer shook his head. 'I'm not sure. I didn't see any exits.'

'There's nothing,' said Bane. 'Apart from this hatch, the whole place is sealed including the lifter to the lower levels.'

Dugan swore under his breath. 'Then here's where we make our stand.'

'Dugan,' Bane said urgently, 'I've got to get to those people.'

Dugan thought for a moment. He heard something and looked down.

'You won't make it that way,' he said. In the darkness below, in the bowels of the stairwell, empty eyes regarded them balefully. A terrible groan carried up towards them, uttered by many voices. Dugan tracked higher up, aware of the zombies pounding on the suppression shields as they tried to force their way in. His gaze rested a few levels below.

'There's a lifter in the cells,' Bane said.

Dugan looked back at him. 'The protocol is halcyon four-four-three-two-three-six.'

Bane started off, aware that he did not have much time.

'Wait,' said Dugan. 'Zan, Renkner, go with him.'

Bane met Dugan's gaze. 'You'll never make it alone,' the massive enforcer said and handed Bane his bolt pistol. Bane nodded his thanks.

Zan and Renkner were already heading down. The shields were keeping the zombies back. The vox operator had abandoned his position and was firing shotgun bursts past them into the throng. Gant was strapping on the heavy stubber rig.

'Once you're through, we'll back up, seal the command corridor and try to wait it out,' Dugan said.

Bane regarded his old friend one last time.

'I won't forget you, Dugan.'

The heavy stubber raged as Gant washed the lower floors with it. The noise was deafening.

Dugan's face was grim. There was no way they could fight off the zombies. They did not have time to seal the hatch to the upper corridor, either. 'Go,' Dugan said.

Bane ran down the stairway, shotgun retorts and barking stubber fire in his ears as he went. Zan waited for him. Renkner discharged his shotgun into the gathering horde below until Bane was through. They followed quickly, sealing the door shut behind them.

On the other side, Bane breathed hard, his back to the wall as he regarded the cells and the plate door that led to the lifter. He heard the muffled fire, urgently barked orders and said a prayer for Dugan and his men.

The lifter hummed as it tracked down the facility.

'It's good to see you again, Zan,' Bane said, breaking the silence.

The weapon's specialist stood with Renkner at the front of the lifter, ready to be first out.

'You too, captain,' he replied.

'I don't know what we'll face down there,' Bane said.

'Neither do I,' Zan returned, 'but we'll get you to that holding area.'

The lifter slowed its ascent. A few more seconds and they touched down. The transit noise ebbed and died. Beyond the crackling azure of the force shield, it looked quiet. Renkner deactivated it. The crimson lighting in the corridor persisted.

'Ready?' Bane hissed, taking out the bolt pistol.

Zan and Renkner nodded. They moved out.

They were a few feet from the first corner when they heard the familiar shuffling gait of the zombies. Just one, it loped around the corner. It looked sluggish, it probably had not fed recently. Its clothes were ragged but it wore an apron and had a cleaver in one hand – a flesh vendor. The zombie snarled when it saw them, revealing rotten, jagged teeth. Renkner went down on one knee and blasted it with his combat shotgun. The creature's head exploded.

A low groaning sound – several voices – emanated from where the creature had emerged.

'Go!' Bane ordered and the three of them raced to the corner. Eight more zombies were shambling towards them, alerted by the gunfire. Zan stepped forward and a burst from his flamer torched four of them. Renkner took another and Bane shot down two more. A final flamer burst finished them off. Long shadows stretched into the corridor. Another four zombies came around the corner.

Bane heard a noise behind him. Five more zombies were coming through from the workshop and the store room. The bolt pistol blazed in his grasp. Three went down. Renkner shot the other two. Zan doused the corridor ahead, torching the group in front.

'We've got to move,' he said urgently. They pressed forward. Already more zombies were appearing in the corridor ahead and behind in greater numbers. They reached the holding room door. Bane hammered on it as Zan lit up the corridor ahead and then turned to hose the way behind. Renkner picked off the stragglers that Zan missed.

'Mavro,' Bane cried, 'Mavro, it's Bane, open the damn door.'

Zan's flamer ran out of fuel and died. He slung it down and pulled out his bolt pistol. There were at least twenty zombies at either end of the corridor and they were closing. Renkner was out too. He wielded the shotgun like a hammer as the first zombie reached out for him, smashing its skull. He waded in against another and battered it down. Three more came at him. He took down the first but the other two grabbed him. Then another came, and another. Renkner was dragged down, screaming.

Bane hammered at the door with renewed vigour. Zan had his back to him, picking off zombies on either side, with controlled bursts. The door opened. Zan was grabbed. As a zombie bit down into his shoulder he cried out in pain and pushed Bane inside. Then he hammered the rune that sealed the door. Bane watched as the door slid shut, desperate to try and help him, desperate to do something, but he knew that Zan was gone.

'What… What happened?' blathered Mavro, shotgun quaking in his hands.

Bane was already heading over to the synth-leather couch as he spoke. 'Vaughn, the judge who is head of this Precinct House, started the zombie plague. The entire facility is overrun.'

'What do we do?' Mavro asked.

Bane ignored him and took one end of the couch and started dragging. There was a sudden, heavy thud against the door and then another. 'Help me lift this,' Bane told Mavro. He put the shotgun down and raced over to the couch. When he realised they were dragging it across the door, he said, 'That's our only way out. Why are we barricading it?'

'There's no way out that way.'

Mavro didn't seem to register what Bane was saying. 'But we need to keep it clear,' he said. 'What if you've been bitten?'

'I haven't,' Bane snarled, then felt his face drain of colour and his legs waver. It was not MacDaur. It could not be Mavro, so that only left… His gaze wandered over to the black plexi-curtain where he'd left Alicia, Gilligan and Jarla.

CHAPTER: FOURTEEN

THE LIFTER CONCEALED in the Command Centre's ante-room, bore Vaughn quickly and silently to the very bowels of the complex. There was only room for one, Vaughn had it designed that way. It was his emergency exit. Once the lifter stopped, Vaughn deactivated the azure force shield and shot the controls with his sidearm. There would be no going back.

Egression from the lifter platform led Vaughn to a short tunnel. It was low and unlit. He had stashed a tube flare within it and it blazed as he stooped to make his way through. A mag-locked hatchway was at the end of the tunnel. Pneumatic pressure hissed as Vaughn punched in the runic sequence. Vaughn entered and then pushed the door closed. It was metre thick plas-steel on seldom used bolt hinges. He was sweating by the time it clanged shut.

He was in the freight tunnel. The hatchway he had exited from was concealed, impossible to see with the naked eye. Looking around in the gloomy light, he noticed that the freight loader had moved from its docking position. It blocked off the entire corridor and prevented him seeing further. It did not matter. Vaughn used the flare to locate another partially hidden panel in the tunnel wall. He struck it with his fist and the panel opened, revealing another keypad. He hammered a code and with the whirring of concealed servos a small metal bridge, just wide enough for one, extended across the freight loader's tracks. It fed into a port on the opposite side.

Vaughn walked across the bridge to the other side and was surprised to see that the exit to the vehicle yard had been forced open. He pulled out his sidearm. For a moment, he thought about using the crown. Even in the short time it had been in his possession it had granted him a certain awareness. He could sense things, usually people, and read their intentions. But he dismissed the idea. The crown was slung in a small pack over his shoulder, strapped to a concealed harness on his suit. He would not need it. He doubted anyone would have got this far in order to escape. Even so, Vaughn walked into the tunnel cautiously.

When he reached the end, he saw the corpses of three of the plague victims. They had been shot in the head. One of them, a big one, was a real mess. A few metres further down, he saw another two bodies. One of them was dressed in what had once been fine apparel. On his finger he wore a guild ring. Vaughn's heart thumped when he realised he must be one of the prisoners. Had they escaped? Surely that was impossible. Another corpse lay next to him in a bodyglove – probably a bodyguard. Vaughn's anxiety heightened when he got closer. Something had sucked the life from them.

With no time to investigate further, Vaughn hurried on, less self-assured than before. He got into the vehicle yard, glancing at every shadow and every imagined movement from the corner of his eye. Not far, not far. He saw his transport up ahead. There was no sign of anyone. It was eerily quiet. He reached the access hatch and punched in the entry codes on a rune panel. The door slid open and Vaughn stepped inside.

Dim, emerald lighting flickered on immediately as his presence was detected by the transport's onboard entry protocols. It took only a second for them to kick in, a crackling hum accompanying their activation. It took only two more seconds, as the door slid shut behind him, for Vaughn to realise he was not alone.

A silhouette at the back of the transport regarded him in the greenish light. It sat facing him on one of the metal bunks, normally occupied by Enforcer riot specialists. All the others were empty, save that one.

Vaughn was reaching for his sidearm when a voice stopped him.

'Stop,' it said. It had to be the silhouette talking, yet the voice was inside Vaughn's head. He was compelled to obey.

The figure stood up. He stepped forward and approached him. In the semi-darkness, Vaughn thought he saw his eyes flash red. He was old, his skin a pale, translucent pink that looked as if it might tear apart. Purple lips held a sneer of contempt and ragged strands of grey, wasted hair dangled from his balding pate. When he spoke, his mouth was a pit of eternal black, an unending void into which Vaughn felt himself falling.

'That,' uttered Karloth Valois, pointing a bony finger at the pack on Vaughn's back, 'is mine.'

'PICK UP THE shotgun,' Bane ordered as he raced across the room, bolt pistol out and raised ready to fire. He reached the curtain in seconds, but it was not nearly fast enough. Wrenching the black plexi-plas aside, he saw Alicia lying on her cot. Ripping his gaze across, he saw Jarla stooped over her father. She was little more than a semi-detailed shadow. It looked like she was kissing Gilligan's forehead. Bane exhaled his relief and lowered the gun. Maybe he had been wrong, maybe it was not any of them who had contracted the virus. It could have been Nark. He prayed it was not Archimedes or Meiser.

'Jarla,' he said quietly, aware of a jittery Mavro just behind him. 'Jarla,' he said again, when she did not respond. It sounded like she was chewing something.

Bane's heart quickened. He held out his hand. 'Jarla,' he said for a third time, bringing the bolt pistol back up. He touched her shoulder.

Jarla whirled around, her blood-smeared visage contorted with anger as she snarled at him. Haunting green light illuminated her face, shadows pooling like slime in the sunken recesses. Bane hesitated. Out of the corner of his eye, he saw Gilligan's ruined visage in the gloom. Jarla sprang at him, claws flailing. Bane fired, pulling the trigger as he backed away instinctively into the holding room. He hit the thing that used to be Jarla in the chest. The impact smashed her against the wall. It barely slowed her and she was on her feet quickly, possessed of a fevered zeal and came at them again. This time Bane was ready. One shot bored a hole in her forehead and she fell to the ground.

Bane moved into the room. He knew Gilligan was already dead so he went over to him, put the gun to the old barman's temple and closed his eyes. 'I'm sorry,' he breathed. 'Can't risk the infection spreading.' Bane pulled the trigger.

Bane went to Alicia, flashing a glance to see what Mavro was doing. The doc gripped the shotgun tight in both hands. His face was contorted with fear. He might snap at any moment.

'Ease up, Mavro,' Bane said soothingly. 'Jarla's dead.'

'What about her?' he breathed, nodding towards Alicia.

Bane could not see any wounds. Jarla must have started with her father when she turned. Tentatively, Bane moved his hand towards Alicia, about to check for concealed injuries. His hand was shaking. He looked back down at her and realised she was stirring. Bane sank to his knees and set down the bolt pistol.

'Alicia,' he said softly.

Slowly she opened her eyes.

'Bane?' her voice was croaky and weak and she squinted as she looked at him.

Bane felt tears welling in his eyes. She was alive and awake, at last. He had begun to doubt she ever would be. When he replied, he found he could barely speak. 'You're awake,' he said.

'You came back for me.'

'I told you I would,' Bane said, caressing her forehead.

'What's happening? Where are we? I couldn't find the Salvation. Some bastard jumped me.' She sounded agitated and still very groggy.

'Don't worry, you're safe,' Bane lied. 'I'm taking you out of here.' He picked her up in his arms and took her out of the room. 'Close it,' he said quietly to Mavro.

The pounding from beyond the door had grown insistent. Bane set Alicia down in the synth-leather chair, where Nark had been sitting. He wondered briefly whether or not the gang lord had escaped. Deep down, he hoped he had made it.

Alicia had little idea of what was happening. Bane was glad of it. At the thunder that raged beyond the room – the pounding fists of the horde – Bane gritted his teeth. The hammering continued and he was out of ideas.

Bane noticed a blanket, worn with holes, slung on the chair. He draped it over Alicia. 'Keep warm, you're still weak from whatever those bastards drugged you with,' he said.

After making sure Alicia was comfortable, Bane rose wearily. Mavro was at the caffeine vendor, trying to rip it up off the floor.

'Leave it,' Bane said.

Dents were appearing in the plate metal door. Bane looked over at Alicia again and felt his despair redouble. It had all been for nothing.

'So what now?' asked the doctor. 'Can we fight our way out? Do you have enough bullets for that?'

Bane discharged the clip form the bolt pistol and counted the rounds.

'There's just enough,' he said, his voice low and tinged
with a grim finality. He met Mavro's gaze. 'But not to fight
our way free.'

'How many are left?' Mavro's voice was choking – he
knew what Bane was saying, just did not want to admit it.

'Three.'

KARLOTH VALOIS EMERGED from the subterranean vehicle
yard. All around him, the zombies stumbled in loose
groups. Most of the enforcers were dead. Certainly, there
were none out here in the open. Without prey and his
direction, the creatures were purposeless. Some had
already started wandering back into the Underhive. Of
the rest, he doubted there were many left. A sea of diseased and decaying zombie corpses clogged part of the
gate, festering.

Valois headed to the gate, the black crown on his forehead. He had always intended for the enforcers to find it.
There in the Precinct house it was safe, it could be found.
The zombie horde was nothing but a device; one he had
implanted into Vaughn's subconscious, making him
believe it served his own ends. It had, up to a point. The
zombie horde had concealed his advance – within their
rotting ranks he was virtually invisible and they had protected him. Only the heathen wyrd, Smite, had been able
to detect him. The priest's derangement, a side-effect of
his raw powers, had eliminated him as a threat.

The army of the dead was nothing more than a distrac-
tion, a way in. Retrieval of the crown was all that
mattered. It had called to him on the fringes of the Abyss,
where he lay broken, believed to be dead. When Vaughn's
henchmen took it and he assumed ownership, his lust for
power – already a nascent contagion eating him from
within – had made it easy to manipulate him. Once the
wheels were set in motion, they could not be stopped.

There would be no assault on Hive City. He was still
weak and had exhausted much of his power to get this

far, to destroy those two in the tunnel as well as loan Vaughn some of his abilities through the crown to ensure he rendezvoused with him in the vehicle yard – albeit, without the judge's knowledge. No, he would not press his advantage. Most of the zombies were dead. He had little energy left to control those that remained. Valois had no desire to alert the rest of Necromunda to his presence, nor the numerous bounty hunters and zealots that still bayed for his blood. Varlan Smite was a fool and a mindless fanatic, but the other servants of the Redemption and the many independent wrydhunters were not so stupid.

Valois approached the gate. Raising his hand, a group of zombies milling around in front of the gate, parted. Valois stepped through. As he did, the zombies clustered back together. the crown atop his head, Valois released them from his influence and sinking into the scattered hordes, became lost in darkness.

CHAPTER: FIFTEEN

THE HAMMERING ON the holding area door grew louder, more insistent. Part of it bent inwards, at last yielding to the furious attention of the zombies.

The three survivors huddled together at the back of the room. Bane held Alicia in his arms. Mavro cowered nearby, holding the shotgun like a security blanket. He rocked back and forth, eyes never leaving the door, wincing at every blow.

'That door is plas-steel. How can they get in?' he whimpered.

'It's not that tough,' Bane replied, 'With enough repeated force, it'll give. Remember, there are hive gangers amongst the horde, some of whom have augmetics, others are stimmed up to hell and back. Enough fists that feel no pain hit that door and it will give.'

'I still have this,' Mavro offered, voice brightening but not enough to be convincing as he offered the shotgun.

Bane looked at the doctor. He had hated him. Bane was in no doubt, he'd fuelled his own stimm addiction but Mavro had made it so easy. He had lost count of the number of times that he had tried to kick his habit and Mavro had always been there to 'rescue' him from the even worse hell that was existence without them. Yet now Bane regarded him with pity. He was scum, but he had come through for him. Despite his cowardice and his self-serving attitude, he had come through. So what Bane said next, he said with compassion.

'I'm sorry Mavro, it's not enough. When the time comes I promise I'll make it quick.'

Mavro licked his lips and was about to say something but shrank back into himself again, instead.

Bane looked up. The hammering stopped. Silence descended. He heard something else – further away – dulled by rockcrete and metal. It could have been gunfire. They stayed like that for another five minutes. The only sound was their desperate breathing. None of them dared to speak, unsure what was going to happen next.

Something was moving outside. The hammering started up again. Bane's heart sank, hopes crushed. The dents became larger, and a clanking noise accompanied the dull hammering sound, as if made by tools. The left corner pulled away from the door frame with the shriek of tearing metal. The door's hinges came shortly afterward. In the gloom beyond the doorway, Bane saw shadows – the zombies, it had to be.

He looked down at Alicia as the door fell onto the floor with a resonating clang. He pulled her close – out of the corner of his eye he saw Mavro had put the barrel of the shotgun into his mouth – and moved the bolt pistol so she did not see it, resting the muzzle against the side of her head, cushioned by her ragged, pink hair so she did not feel the coldness of the metal. He whispered into her ear, 'Close your eyes.'

'Thought I'd forgotten you eh, lawman?' said a familiar voice.

Bane looked up and saw Nark.

The gang lord stood before him, twin autopistols holstered at his hips. Behind him, a big ganger – even bigger than Skudd – hefted a huge pneumatic vice which he had used to rip the door open. There were others, at least four more Bane could see, all heavily armed. Some bore the tattoo of the Sabres, others a hammer, a third a chain clenched in a fist. Bane suddenly remembered what Nark had told him in the cab of the *Bull*, about some of the gangs he controlled, the Ironhammers, the Jack-ratchets and the Sabres.

'I knew you'd be pleased to see me,' Nark said, 'but I didn't expect tears.' He smiled but it was a dark smile, one without humour.

'I thought you…' Bane began.

'I did,' Nark told him. 'Shivved those two frikkers in the cells and got the hell out through the vehicle yard. My men were waiting, just like I knew they would be. I couldn't get close, thanks to the horde, or the enforcers when we arrived here,' Nark explained. 'But once I was out and the enforcers and the horde were knocking the crap out of each other and a window of opportunity presented itself.'

Bane dimly recalled the boot prints in the workshop. Nark's. He had not made the connection, until now.

'What about the zombies?'

'Most of 'em are dead, but there's still a few of the more persistent frikkers roaming around the complex,' Nark explained. 'And I have no desire to go toe-to-toe with what's left. They were pretty light in the outer yard and who knows how many are infesting the entire building? So, let's get you the hell out of here.'

Nark held out his hand. Bane took it and got up. Two other gangers came forward, helping Mavro to his feet. Another moved towards Alicia.

'No,' Bane said, whirling to face him. The ganger glanced at Nark. The gang lord nodded and the ganger backed off. Bane picked Alicia up, taking her in his arms as a father cradles a child. He looked back at Nark.

'I've got her,' Bane said.

'I've cleared a route through to the vehicle yard,' Nark told him as they moved out of the holding room. 'There's a transport. Use it. Get to Hive City and tell them what's happened.'

They walked down the crimson-lit corridor, now the site of much carnage. A group of gangers stood ready, weapons primed at one end; others lined the walls en route. When they reached the exit to the subterranean vehicle yard, Bane stopped and turned to Nark. He was about to speak when the gang lord stopped him.

'You saved my life, Bane,' he said. 'Even stood up to those bastard enforcers to vouch for me. As far as I'm concerned, we're even. Our paths meet again and things'll be different,' he warned.

Bane nodded and was about to walk through into the vehicle yard when he stopped again. 'You've probably saved a lot of lives,' he said.

Nark smiled, slipped a kalma-root between his lips and fired it up. 'They won't thank me.'

EPILOGUE

THE AMBER LAMPS of the docking ports flicked by, illuminating Bane's face in sporadic, ephemeral flashes as he sped past in the limousine speeder. He was dressed in a crisp suit of dark azure with a small Enforcer motif stitched at the breast. Black boots ran up to his knees and shone dully in the ambient light. He wore his service pistol, gleaming with a renewed lustre. The black transport navigated the many jutting platforms and coasted through the access tunnels.

Bane looked out of the plexi-glass window from the opulent crimson leather seats within the transport and saw the cloud of pollution that delineated Hive Primus's lower levels fade away. He even saw the giant banks of precipitators as they vented false rain onto the hundreds of levels below. He watched the moisture saturated air spill over the shiny hull of his transport, flicking across the Hive City Judge emblem emblazoned in silver on the side. His own reflection looked back at him: shaved, clean and alert.

A vox was playing inside the transport. It was a news edict, pumped into the many Hive City factorums and in domiciles throughout the higher echelons of Necromundan society.

'Enforcement teams from beta and delta sectors have finally put down the zombie horde threatening the borders of Hive City. There are still no reports as to how this outbreak of zombie plague occurred in such close proximity to Hive City, but it has been confirmed that the remnants of the plague not already destroyed have been driven into the Underhive. Suspicion still remains as to the Enforcement's involvement in the outbreak, though at this time there is no investigation pending.'

Bane turned off the vox. In the end, only a small section of the Underhive had been affected, some few hundred thousand. Had the affliction reached Hive City and the teeming millions living there, things would have been very different. It was thanks to his intervention that the zombie horde had been crushed. Nark was right, there were still many remaining and they were dangerous. Bane had grieved when he had heard of the deaths of Archimedes and Meiser but he had achieved what they could not. It had meant his re-instatement into the Enforcement, albeit in a non-active capacity as Hive City Judge, where Bane knew there was an opening. He used the knowledge he had gained of Vaughn's plan and the corruption evident in the system, to act as leverage. That and his heroic actions, immortalised and embellished by the Necromundan Chronicle, had guaranteed his tenure as well as a few other concessions Bane had insisted upon.

As far as anyone else was concerned, other than those privy to secrets behind closed doors, Vaughn's body was never found, assumed lost amidst the burning pyres that littered the Precinct House's grounds. Of course, Bane knew differently. Vaughn's desiccated remains had been found in his personal transport and burned along with everyone else. The black crown, it seemed, was missing too. Nor was there any mention of Nark's involvement. Life was different in the Underhive, but some things, the exchange of information, the adage that 'knowledge is power' and those with it wield the power, still held true.

Something had happened at the Precinct House, something other than the zombie invasion and Vaughn's corrupt undertakings, something that no one knew about or could cover up. Bane had felt a presence there, overlying everything. It was unnatural. He had even heard it, talking to Vaughn through the crown. He remembered the words of Varlan Smite, that he was looking for someone, an individual he had seen in his visions. Bane had no doubt that this individual was the very person who had infiltrated the Precinct House and had killed Vaughn – Archimedes and Meiser too. The life draining effects were unmistakeable. Bane had his suspicions, but as yet, no fresh evidence had come to light. In any case, he dared not voice them.

The transport slowed, arresting Bane from his reverie as it reached its destination. Levelling out, the transport moved horizontally, merging with the docking platform upon which amber warning lights flashed silently.

The vox crackled and Bane's driver said, 'We have arrived, sir.'

'Thank you,' Bane returned and pressed the exit rune on the cab's interior. A hiss of pneumatic pressure and the cab door opened. As Bane got out, his driver held out a grey storm coat. Bane took it, said his thanks and walked across the platform, clutching the storm coat about him as he was buffeted by turbine winds. At the end of the platform there was an ornate doorway. Bane passed through it and found himself at the site of Alcana Ran-Lo's memoriam. He had been granted special permission to visit it, here in the Spire. It was one of his concessions.

Bane delved inside the jacket of his suit and produced a wax candle. The memoriam was simple, considering Alcana's heritage. A holo-pict image of her face revolved in mid-air inside the small chamber. In the recesses of the chamber there were two guards, enveloped by the shadows. Another figure was at the back of the room and would have been invisible were it not for the winking lights from a visual and cranial implant. Bane ignored the guards and the cyborg, took his candle to an igniter set into the wall and lit it.

He approached one of the platforms slowly, eyes on the image of Alcana revolving in the holo-pict. He set the candle down carefully and closed his eyes, whispering a prayer.

'Rest in peace,' he muttered, opening his eyes and stepping away. When he turned around, a figure was waiting for him at the doorway. Bane smiled and went over to meet her.

Outside the memoriam, Alicia hugged him long and hard.

'Easy,' said Bane. 'I'm an old man remember.'

She withdrew from the embrace and smiled. She looked different. The pink hair remained, but it was straight and cut short. The gang tatts were erased and the piercings were gone. She wore a simple jade suit with a long grey storm coat, flapping in the breeze. She still bore the scars of her injuries but they would fade. She no longer ran with a gang, no longer had to survive in the Underhive. She had a job at a merchant shipping firm in the lowest part of the Spire. That was the last of Bane's concessions. He kept an eye on her and made sure she was safe and well looked after. He had some influence and power. It went a long way.

'I think you've earned some peace, at last,' she said.

Bane smiled, 'We'll see.' He produced a slim card from his pocket. 'Here,' he said, giving it to her. 'You can contact me with this whenever you need to.'

Alicia took it. 'Thank you,' she said. 'You saved my life.'

Bane smiled, it was tinged with regret. One out of two. Alcana Ran-Lo's death still hurt, but it hurt less. 'Come on,' he said and ushered Alicia back out to the waiting speeder.

The speeder would take her back to her domicile in the Spire. They hugged again and Alicia kissed Bane on the cheek. He watched her as she got inside; one final glance at him as the door slid shut. Bane stepped back as the docking clamps disengaged and waved Alicia off as the limousine speeder arced away.

He looked into the dark for several minutes. It was cold out in the open but Bane did not feel it. He felt alive, for the first time in a long time. The nightmares had stopped, and he resolved this would be the last time he would visit this tomb. He had been given a second chance and he intended not to waste it. He had come back, against all the odds, back from the dead.

ABOUT THE AUTHOR

Nick Kyme hails from Grimsby, a small town on the east coast of England known for its fish (a food, which ironically he dislikes profusely). Nick moved to Nottingham in 2003 to work on *White Dwarf* magazine as a Layout Designer. Since then, he has made the switch to the Black Library's hallowed halls, and has had three short stories published in that time.

Back From The Dead is his first novel.